CRACKED HEARTS

CRACKED HEARTS

The Story of Ultimate Betrayal and Love

LINDA MASEMORE PIRRUNG

iUniverse, Inc.

New York Lincoln Shanghai

Cracked Hearts
The Story of Ultimate Betrayal and Love

iUniverse books may be ordered through booksellers or by contacting:

iUniverse
2021 Pine Lake Road, Suite 100
Lincoln, NE 68512
www.iuniverse.com
1-800-Authors (1-800-288-4677)

This is a work of fiction. All of the characters, names, incidents, organizations, and dialogue in this novel are either the products of the author's imagination or are used fictitiously.

ISBN-13: 978-0-595-40732-3 (pbk)
ISBN-13: 978-0-595-67828-0 (cloth)
ISBN-13: 978-0-595-85097-6 (ebk)
ISBN-10: 0-595-40732-3 (pbk)
ISBN-10: 0-595-67828-9 (cloth)
ISBN-10: 0-595-85097-9 (ebk)

Printed in the United States of America

Preface

How strong are we? Do we have the power to overcome the DARK ENTI-TIES in our lives? They threaten to steal our peace and joy with their every self-serving breath.

Every person who touches our lives leaves his or her mark to influence us one way or another. Every day we live is a mystery. We struggle with every new transition trying to find ways to cope.

"Who knows what lurks in the minds of man?"

There are so many tortured souls all around us begging for some kind of release.

The mind is the ONE private place.

INTRODUCTION

The sunlight filtered through the leaves of the huge old oak trees in Steph's plush lawn. The afternoon air was warm but there was relief in the gentle breeze that made the leaves rustle and tremble. They shimmered brilliantly in the golden glow of the sun.

"You're too big for your breeches, Little Guy!" Meg teased Tyler as she reached out to rumple his hair.

Out of Steph's house came the women chatting happily and rounding up Meg's rambunctious children to coerce them into the car.

Meg and Steph were in their twenties, both stay at home Moms and the best of friends. With a slew of children between them, they enjoyed sharing in the multitude of duties and details that went with the job.

A woman's scream suddenly alerted their attention toward Monica's house. They brought their hands up to their foreheads to shade their eyes from the sunlight and squinted against the brilliance trying to focus.

They lived in a pretty much uneventful, close knit, and safe neighborhood, ordinarily but that was about to change.

A sudden burst of fear surged through their bodies causing them to shiver involuntarily.

The immediacy of the moment didn't allow time to think. A rush of adrenalin summoned newfound courage in Steph and sent her rushing down the street toward Monica's house.

Meg stayed with the children as they all watched Steph disappear from sight inside Monica's house.

Now Steph's ear-piercing shriek caused a constricted pain in Meg's chest and left her no choice but to leave her oldest six-year-old son and concerned neighbors in charge of all the children. Her fear intensified but didn't make her hesitate for a moment.

All the hard work it took to win the track awards and medals weren't in vain. She surely broke her own record to get to Steph ahead of the collecting crowd.

The house smelled of Lily Of The Valley, reminiscent of her childhood visits to her Grandmother's house, Meg noticed right away as she followed the low unintelligible muttering sound. She sucked in her breath as it caught in her throat. She found Steph totally inconsolable, huddled in a corner in the hall, covering her face.

"Steph!" Meg called out to her. Meg hugged her trying to comfort her. "What is it?"

Steph was unable to respond coherently at first. She kept trying to tell Meg something. Finally the words came out.

"A woman flew out of here and knocked me down in the process. Did you see her?"

Meg claimed she hadn't.

"In the bedroom....," Steph cried. Her voice trailed off. She covered her face again and cried vehemently.

Meg forced herself to walk toward the bedroom door. She took in a lungful of air and stiffened her body preparing herself to see something unpleasant.

Stephanie was sobbing so loudly by then that Meg didn't hear her son walk in. Suddenly, without warning, her precocious Tyler came barreling through the door.

"Noooo!" Meg screamed. She grabbed him too late. Their eyes widened in shocking disbelief. They experienced the gruesome scene together.

Monica was dressed in a lacey black nightgown lying face up on her bed. Her mouth was wide open, terror congealed in her face, curls hanging loose on the pillow except for the ones adhered to her head and cheek with her own blood.

Meg averted her head, biting back the tears. She took hold of herself and in perfect calm, in spite of the revulsion bubbling up in her throat; she turned her son around and guided him out the door, out of the horror scene.

Steph seemed rooted to the spot but Meg got a firm grip and pulled her to her feet. Still unsteady, they managed to walk out of the house together.

A deluge of people from the neighborhood awaited them along with the beginning of the rosy sunset.

Having regained her composure, Steph couldn't help but reflect on Monica's last words to her still reverberating in her head, the image of her indelibly imprinted on her mind. She allowed herself to drift with her thoughts. Poor Monica. She was no longer alone in the world. The challenge of starting a new life without her husband was no longer an option. She's back with her husband. After all, Heaven is where we all want to be, eventually. Steph tried to find some comfort in that thought. But poor Monica was summoned home so brutally. The image of her face leapt before her eyes. She was so well preserved, not showing her years on this Earth, tell-tale lines around her eyes and mouth hardly discernible; such grace; such dignity; dignity evaporated. Steph's eyes welled with tears. She was appalled.

Meg and Steph rejoined their children trying to find the words to explain this cruel, ugly, distasteful part of life.

Meg put her arms around Tyler in an attempt to comfort him. There was no response.

"Tyler!" Meg cried out. She looked him straight in the eyes. "Tyler!" Meg grasped him by his shoulders and gave him a gentle shake, as if to jog him back into reality. *Nothing*!

Ron drove up about that time. He approached his wife.

"Steph, what's going on?"

Steph started to fill him in when Meg screamed.

"Tyler!"

For the first time in all of this horror Meg lost control. She screamed with big tears streaming down her face.

"Something's wrong with Tyler! He's not responding! He looks catatonic!"

Steph begged the Police to allow Meg to take her son to the Doctor; that she'd stay and answer the questions.

Ron offered to drive Meg and Tyler to the emergency room. Meg certainly wasn't in any shape to drive.

The hospital waiting room was filled with people who loved and cared about Tyler. Ron sat with his arm around Meg in a comforting gesture.

Hayley watched them with her usual judgmental glare, which epitomized those suspicious notions of hers.

Meg couldn't reach her husband, Dan, so Ron assumed the role of consoling husband and protective Father for the evening.

Whitney, one of the psychiatrists on staff at the hospital, finally came out to talk to Meg.

The experience was so traumatic for him that he withdrew inside himself. He would require a good bit of therapy.

CHAPTER 1

▼

Only months before, Whitney had been anxiously looking at her petite diamond and gold watch. She was running late but still took the time to park her bright red exquisitely new Jag convertible across the street to protect it from other cars.

She rushed up John and Hayley's front steps and across the porch to the open door.

John gave her a quick grin as he held the door open for her.

"Did you take the time to wax your new *Wheels* first, Whitney?"

Whitney wrinkled her nose at him and grinned without making an excuse.

"Hi, Hayley!"

Hayley took Whitney around by her tiny waist and propelled her toward Ron and Stephanie Adams.

"This is my oldest and dearest friend, Whitney Blake."

Whitney shook hands with them smiling.

"No, I'm no relation to *The Whitney Blake*, the actress."

"Ron and Stephanie have four children," Hayley continued.

"Oh! How do you manage?" Whitney mused sympathetically.

"Just barely," Stephanie replied. "I used to be a computer programmer. But Ron and I agreed that the children would be our top priority."

"Humph!" Hayley blurted repugnantly. "I sure wouldn't have quit. I started back to work when Mark was six months old. I was climbing the walls with boredom. I believe a woman gets lazy if she stays home with kids all day. Her mind wastes away to mush."

Stephanie gave her a stern glare.

"It's much nobler to postpone a career to be with and guide those precious little beings we choose to bring into this world than to go on with our lives like they don't exist. Children should be number one, *Top Priority* in the parent's lives not last on a long list of things to do. A career woman is used to getting all the attention, having an exciting social life, self-importance, money coming in, control of her own life. When she has children, all that attention needs to go to *Family First*. Bringing children into this world is a huge responsibility, the most important, the most worthwhile and the hardest job there is. There's nothing more important and testing than being responsible for molding and guiding a human being. If you're not willing to sacrifice a huge part of yourself then you shouldn't become a mother. If you don't want to be *bothered* with children then I say give them up for adoption. Give them to people who are capable of giving love and attention and who will cherish them. You think you're giving them quality time on weekends and evenings? Hah! You're with them during their sleeping time mostly. Quality time is for *Aunts* and *Uncles* and *Grandparents*. It's not for the *Mother*. If you don't have free babysitting service, it doesn't pay enough. I know too many women who have openly admitted that they pay more for a babysitter than they make working but it's a heck of a lot easier going to work than it is being with kids for twenty four hours a day. They're the women who don't deserve to have the noble and honorable role as *Mother*."

"Whew! It didn't take Hayley long to crawl under someone's skin," Whitney whispered to John.

In her late twenties, Hayley was almost as tall as her husband, enough so that she felt more comfortable wearing low-heeled shoes. She had a milky white porcelain complexion and thick, natural curly red hair that she constantly fought to keep straightened. Her beautifully defined facial features were accented perfectly by just the right touch of make-up. Hayley's lovely hourglass figure was even more voluptuous since childbirth. Her languid manner and habit of talking slowly while not looking at you deceptively hid the sting of her frequent verbal put-downs and caustic remarks. Her defensiveness sadly took away from her appeal.

Hayley's husband, John, was over six feet tall with a dark, dense, brawny body and a dark, thick head of hair. His facial features were ruggedly sculpted with a movie star quality. He seemed to wear a constant blush, like windburn and his wise smile complimented his ever freshly dressed appearance. He was always impeccably groomed and was the model of organization and efficiency and worked tirelessly at it!

Hayley and Whitney had grown up together sharing all the passions and heartbreaks of adolescence. When it came to boys Whitney was always the favored one. Hayley's long-suffering struggle with jealousy toward Whitney had gravitated toward guilt ridden loathing at times.

Whitney was small in stature but big in character. She had authority to her manner and confidence in her posture. Not only was she poised and charming, but she was kind and refreshingly compassionate. Her features were pointed and delicate and her eyes were full of quick intelligence. Her shoulder length light brown and blonde streaked hair was feathered back to reveal her tiny fragile ear lobes from which diamond earrings dangled.

Hayley served a variety of appetizers, bread, wine and cheese.

"Hayley, like I even have to ask, did you make the bread?" Whitney asked politely.

"Of course, you didn't have to ask. I spent most of the weekend kneading dough and preparing food for this shindig; but I love it! I love to cook as you can plainly see!" Hayley declared, putting both hands on her rounded tummy.

"I'm impressed. I make bread every once in a while. There's nothing more wonderful than the smell of fresh baked bread permeating through the house." Stephanie remarked.

Stephanie turned to Whitney.

"Hayley tells me that you're a psychiatrist."

"Yes, I am."

"And you're single?" Steph asked amazed.

Hayley took advantage of the moment.

"Yes, Whitney can't find anyone good enough for her," she meowed sarcastically.

The little group went silent.

John raced to Whitney's rescue.

"Whitney's worked very hard on her career. It took a lot of sacrifice and dedication. She has a fabulous townhouse of her own, a new Jag and she takes exciting vacations when she feels like it. How many women can say that? She did it all on her own. Nobody handed it to her."

"You've got my vote. I'm jealous," Stephanie sighed.

Before Steph had her first baby, Ron felt he was secondary status in relationship to his wife; a dull appendage to his successful Stephanie. He felt at the time that it was necessary to start a family to salvage their marriage. Steph wasn't aware of his feelings. She settled happily into domesticity, vastly indulging her cooking and child-rearing talents.

John and Hayley were proud of their lovely brown and white two-story home. Their dramatic entrance hall lent excitement and graciousness to entertaining. The marble floor flowed to a sweeping staircase, which led to a curved open balcony hall.

There were floor to ceiling arched windows throughout their home, luxurious bathrooms with crystal and gold faucets at the end of marbled corner tubs.

"Stephanie and Ron, I'd like you to meet Meg and Dan Lane. They have two children in the same age group as yours," John was saying.

Meg was a petite, tense girl and looked drooling sexy with her disheveled, overabundance of chestnut colored natural curls cascading about her shoulders. Her low-cut, red dress contradicted her seemingly vulnerable, defensive and aloof manner. She had beautiful warm, brown bedroom eyes and full, sensuous, relaxed lips.

Meg's husband, Dan, had a muscular, bronze build and a seeming self-cherished grin on a boyish featured handsome face. When he laughed, he revealed perfect, white teeth and along with his sandy colored hair and tan he looked like he'd just jumped off his surf board. He seemed to tower over his tiny wife and had a habit of resting his elbow on her shoulder as if leaning on her.

"It's nice to meet you," Steph said, smiling politely.

"Where do you live, Meg?"

"We live on Holland Drive in the stone colonial with white columns," Meg answered shyly.

"How long have you lived there?"

"About two years."

"How old are your children?"

"A six month old girl and a six year old boy."

"Oh? We have a six year old, Zach."

Dan intervened," We've heard our Tyler mention his name. They must be in the same class at school…I'm a mechanic. What's your game, Ron?"

Ron replied, "I'm in construction management."

With not a lot in common, so far, there was an uncomfortable pause between them.

Stephanie quickly filled the lull in the conversation, "Don't you love John and Hayley's house?"

Meg smiled in agreement, "Some day, maybe; Maybe in my dreams."

"I'm dreading having children grow up in this era," Steph said, attempting to strike some common ground. She figured that Mothers always shared strong opinions on the subject of children.

"I agree," Meg replied, "with all of the new sexual diseases, drugs, threat of war and teenage suicide, I almost wish my children would stay this age forever rather than take a chance and lose them."

Ron said, "Yes, adultery's pretty risky business these days."

Dan said abruptly, with a clever, flickering expression, trying not to miss his chance at wit.

"My God! They'll undermine the institution of marriage. A man can't get a little lovin on the side any more without worrying about disease."

Meg cleared her throat and looked apologetically at Steph.

Ron and Stephanie attempted a cathartic laugh to smooth things over.

Whitney joined the little foursome sensing they needed a little help, displaying her usual poise and proper respect.

"Have you tried Hayley's fabulous bread?" Whitney asked.

"She's quite the cook," Steph said.

Meg sliced herself a piece and spread some topping on it.

"It's delicious," Meg said, giving Dan a bite, shoving it in his mouth playfully as if trying to shut him up.

Whitney was commanding in a beautifully unassertive way.

"How's your photography coming along, Steph?" Hayley told me that you're quite the camera buff."

"I am. That's for sure. My passion is capturing my kids on film when they least expect it, their intense expressions, determined to accomplish their little tasks or the absolute joy on their little faces when they've succeeded."

"Are you planning to do something with your talent?" Meg asked.

"I'd love to but for what I'd love to do, I'd have to move to New York! I'd like to shoot for magazines, a model photographer; you know, create the perfect picture, whatever it takes. It's all in the lighting, clothes and poses, then there's the hair and make-up to bring out all the best features. It's all illusion. Lighting can make or break a person. It depends on the person's features. With the lighting alone, I have the option to make the same person look like a witch or an angel. Bring out the best and hide the rest, I always say. It's really so simple," Steph responded with excitement in her eyes.

"Steph's very adept at transforming Eliza Doolittles into glamorous Fair Ladies. She's done quite a few lay-outs for her friends and has had a few jobs shooting weddings and parties," Ron added.

Meg's eyes lit up.

"That sounds very interesting," she said shyly, pushing back her abundance of hair to reveal that indeed, she did have a mate to the other bedroom eye.

Steph laughed.

"My house ends up in such disarray, furniture out of place, piles of discarded clothes, hats, jewelry, lights, extension chords, and camera lenses everywhere. We have a lot of fun though. Of course, with all the kids, I haven't had much time to do that in a while."

Dan found Meg daydreaming into her wine glass.

"Don't get any wild ideas, Meg!" Dan frowned.

Stephanie ignored Dan and continued, "I thought at one time of being a photographer's assistant to get my foot in the door, so to speak. But an assistant spends most of his time handling his boss's camera. He loads film, switches backdrops, checks light meters, and moves tri-pods from one place to another, fiddles with strobe lights and lugs props. I'd like to create, not be a gopher."

Stephanie watched Meg focusing entirely on her husband and thought, *what an adoring, selfless, passive, creature*. She's completely subservient to Dan.

Meg's muteness passed for reserve.

Stephanie admired Whitney enormously. Her every look and gesture echoed of honesty. In her opinion, Whitney was an altogether lovely person, a creature God most certainly had to be proud to have created.

"How did anyone as beautiful and as intelligent as you are escape marriage this long?" Stephanie asked.

Whitney's absolute dignity prohibited conversation with too much personal, intimate information. In her profession, she was too used to digging information out of her clients.

"Times have changed. We're working on our degrees and our careers, instead of cultivating witty conversations and trying to *catch a man* like our grandmothers did. Besides, where is it written that we all *have* to be part of a *couple* to be happy and complete?"

Whitney had the capacity to give a person her utmost attention. She focused intently on the person with whom she was speaking, again, much due to her career choice.

"It would be wonderful to be so much your own person that you could have a truly complementary marriage; equal. So often marriages are weighted badly.

They're off balance and unfair. To have a sense of importance to each other is essential for a perfectly balanced marriage. We must value each other," Whitney said, smiling at Dan.

Dan smirked.

"Hah! We have a happy marriage because my wife follows me around like a puppy dog waiting for a pat on the head. You're my little pet, aren't you, Honey?"

Meg smiled obediently.

Whitney's speculation went right over Dan's head. He missed the whole point!

Steph rolled her eyes in disgust and whispered to Ron.

"I don't know about this guy."

This seemed to be the pattern of Meg's life and she accepted it.

Stephanie looked at her watch.

"Ron, it's getting late. We'd better be going."

Steph looked at Whitney.

"It's been so nice meeting you, Whitney."

"Please, let's get together soon," Whitney replied warmly.

"Meg, Dan, I guess we'll be seeing you at the PTA meetings," Ron said politely.

Ron and Steph hurried to their car before the rain soaked them. Stephanie jumped in while Ron held the door open for her.

They were both impressed with Whitney. Ron was saying, "What a knock-out!"

"Yes," Steph agreed. "Whitney's a doll!" She sighed, thinking how much she envied her the career. Stephanie loved her children with all her heart and wouldn't change a thing, but she did miss her job and the importance it'd given her.

"Hayley said that Whitney was her closest and dearest friend? Did you sense tension in the air, Ron?" Stephanie continued.

"I'll say one thing, if that's how she treats her dearest friends, I sure don't want the position. Hayley seemed pretty vicious towards Whitney at times. But Whitney took it very well, as if she were accustomed to Hayley's sarcasm. With all of Whitney's qualities, I'm sure Hayley's insecurity is easily overlooked and besides, she's a psychiatrist. She probably understands Hayley better than we do."

"That's the only thing that makes me slightly uncomfortable; the fact that she's a psychiatrist. She's on another plateau compared to us, but she seems so down to earth. She's very easy to talk to in spite of her knowledgeable position in life. Do you think she's reading us? I mean do you think or wonder if she knows more about us than we do by analyzing our every word and mannerism?" Steph commented.

"If it were any other psychiatrist, possibly. But Whitney makes me feel at ease. I sense that she sees the world as full of kindness and love, because she chooses to see it that way. Whitney's company is good therapy without having to pay for her services," Ron replied.

"If the world were full of Whitney's, the world would be a better place." Stephanie agreed. "What do you think of Meg and Dan Lane?" Stephanie asked, looking like a stern schoolmarm beset by incorrigibles.

"Dan's a little too arrogant for my taste. He seems to thinks he's infallible, a quality I find irritating and annoying," Ron answered without pause.

"Not to mention his infantile sense of humor and his disgusting chauvinism! What about Meg?" Steph added.

"Well, she has a beautifully dimensioned body that she obviously knows how to display; is different looking, sultry; love her hair; too quiet," Ron replied readily.

"I think she's nice. I think I'll invite her over," Steph said.

Ron and Steph pulled in their drive feeling wide-awake and very amorous. Stephanie reminded Ron that the kids were at her mother's.

Ron gave her a cunning little smile then got out of the car, walked around to Steph's door, opened it and took her hand.

"Would you care to indulge in a wild night of passion, my lovely?" Ron asked playfully in a strange unintelligible accent.

"Why Sir," Steph said in a long southern draw, "how dare you presume…"

Her words were cut off as Ron hoisted her from the car and whisked her to the house. Steph pretended to kick and resist. Ron threw her over his shoulder as he unlocked the door. He carried her through the door and kicked it shut.

Playing along as he put her down on her feet, Steph was saying, "How dare you! Who do you think you are?"

Then he grabbed her. He murmured gently, stroking her hair, pressing his body against hers.

"My first sight of you sent such yearning through my body."

Steph pretended to resist at first. She tried to hide her delight and play along to prolong the moment.

Ron tilted her head back with his knuckles to her chin and kissed her soft, sensuous mouth.

Reveling in the moment, she responded to his kiss ardently.

The rampant desire rushed through their bodies as Ron's embrace tightened perceptively and kissed her more deeply.

His lips brushed ever so gently and slowly down her neck resting them on Steph's bare shoulder as he gently sucked her skin into his mouth.

Steph's knees weakened. Her husband, even after four children, could arouse her with the art of a master.

Without destroying the magic between them, Ron slowly untied her tiny shoulder straps and slipped her dress down past her breasts, at which point her dress slithered to the floor. Being that it was summer, Steph wasn't wearing panty hose so she was standing before her pretend assailant in nothing but a fancy, lacey strapless bra and matching undies.

Ron gazed into Steph's eyes. He stroked her cheek tenderly as she trembled under his touch. Her desire swept through her and her skin tingled with anticipation. His long, slow lingering kisses produced soft moans in her throat. As he meandered slowly down her body with his lips, he expertly released her bra with two fingers, lips never leaving her body. Her bikinis were slid to the floor. Ron whisked her up in his arms and carried her to the bedroom.

*   *   *   *

Afterward, Ron dozed a few minutes but Stephanie was still aroused and longed for a longer night of love. Ron woke suddenly as Stephanie's warm lips pressed against his cheek. He felt the heat rise in her body as she nestled closer to him.

The sudden sound of glass breaking on the terrace curtailed their moment together. A stifling wave of fear came over Steph as she held herself tense and squeezed Ron's arm. She cleared her throat nervously and whispered with a hoarse voice in the startled silence, "Did you hear that?" Her arms tightened around him.

Steph glanced up at Ron as he tore himself from her clinging arms. She opened her trembling mouth to speak but nothing came out. Her throat was so tight that she thought she would surely suffocate.

Flexing his back muscles tiredly, Ron rose to his feet and ordered Steph to resume her place in bed. She raised her eyes to meet his gaze. Before she could summon up enough courage to continue, she glanced at the gun in Ron's hand. She managed to force the words from her mouth.

"Don't do anything crazy, Ron!" He nodded in acknowledgement.

Not lingering a moment longer, Ron walked purposefully toward their terrace, glass door.

Stephanie watched Ron's handsome face disappear through the door. Ron was not always a creature of logic. Steph marveled at his determination and strength of character, but worried that his fondness of projecting his protective male instinct may cause him more trouble than he anticipated.

The possible danger caused Stephanie to flash back to their beginning together. After gushing over Ron's tall, well-built athletic body to her mother, Steph remembered her asking, *well, when are you inviting this Greek God to dinner?*

Stephanie remembered assessing Ron. She remembered how taken she was with his powerful looking, very muscular body with every taut muscle in place and how well versed he was on almost any subject and how he enjoyed airing his knowledge. There was a devilishness about him that couldn't be tamed. Now looking back, wondering why we women always fall for the dangerous ones? He had high cheekbones, a slender nose and sharp, intelligent eyes. Steph was so strongly physically attracted to this virile, charming, quick-witted man who in spite of his exceptional looks seemed to have no vanity. She remembered being particularly impressed by his ability to meet and deal with people on any social level. In spite of his education Ron enjoyed working outdoors with his hands and drew pleasure and great satisfaction from watching his creations take shape.

On the other side of the coin, Stephanie and Ron were both stubborn and even though they clashed on every debatable subject, their tempestuous arguments usually led to a very exciting make-up period. If nothing else, this kept their lives together from becoming stale and too comfortable.

Ron's voice brought Stephanie abruptly back to the present.

"Come with me a minute, Steph," Ron said as he steered her in the direction of the terrace.

"Look at this."

Stephanie's eyes widened. There were nose and fingerprints on the glass of their terrace door.

"We were being watched!" Stephanie gasped.

"Oh! That makes my skin crawl!"

"From now on, we're keeping our shades drawn!" Ron ordered as he bent over to pick up the broken vase.

CHAPTER 2

▼

It was pouring rain the following Monday morning so Steph had to drive the boys to the bus stop. There was another car there with the motor running and the windshield wipers working slowly. Stephanie recognized the mass of hair.

Steph wound down her window and caught Meg Lane's attention.

"Hi!"

The bus pulled up about that time and the kids scurried out of the cars.

"Do you have anything special planned for this morning, Meg?"

"Not especially."

"How about a cup of coffee at my house?" Steph asked with a smile.

"Why not?"

"Okay! Follow me."

Meg was impressed by Steph's big split-level.

Meg wore the shortest cut-off jean shorts and a little skimpy summer top that didn't leave a whole lot to the imagination. She possessed an innate sensuality and seemed to be totally oblivious to it.

Meg commented, "What a beautiful house you have."

They walked across a gleaming slate foyer. Meg looked into a traditionally styled living room done resplendent in cool forest colors. A long blue, green and yellow flowered sofa facing two small marble pedestal cocktail tables occupied one wall. Against the opposite wall rested a small dark blue satin sofa with wooden arms; on the wall behind hung a huge original painting done in all the complimentary colors. Beside the sofa was an over-sized floor vase with dried apple blossom branches in it. On the other side was an octagonal drum table with an expensive looking brass lamp on it. The third wall was a white brick fireplace with a wood box built in. On either side of the fireplace was green velour occasional chair each with a silk tree behind it.

A cathedral ceiling presided over the living room, dining and kitchen areas.

"Is this all there is?" Meg inquired teasingly after the tour.

Steph walked toward the coffee maker.

"Sit down. What do you take in your coffee, Meg?"

"A little sugar and heavy on the cream, please."

After settling into their chairs, coffee in hand, Steph and Meg chatted casually and pleasantly, getting acquainted.

Meg confessed that she was only sixteen when she got married and then had a baby right away.

"I've never had a job and frankly I'm afraid to work. I spent my childhood, short as it was, tucked away out of my parent's way," Meg was saying unhappily.

Stephanie and Meg had basically two things in common. They were both home with kids and they both came from small towns.

"Dan is very possessive of me and he tries to control my every move. Sometimes I feel smothered, but most of the time, I think he does it because he really cares so much. I'd fly to the moon if he wanted me to," Meg said.

"You know, it's nice to have an adult to talk to during the day," Steph announced, as she poured herself another cup of coffee.

"Most of my friends are career-oriented and have one or no children so I don't have a lot in common with them. They don't want to hear about my kids and their jobs don't interest me."

Meg noticed the time.

"Oh my, it's twelve o'clock already! We should go!"

"I'd love to have you stay for lunch, if you have the time. I have tuna and egg salad made if you'd care to stay."

Meg smiled.

"If it isn't too much trouble."

Their friendship progressed to geometric proportions. They did everything together. They shopped, babysat each other's children, and helped each other paint their houses…

Steph showed Meg how to make bread and pies. They shared meals, exercised together and shared each other's tasks and problems. Stephanie loved Meg like the sister she'd never had.

One day Stephanie was entertaining one of her neighbors when Meg dropped in

"Meg, I'd like you to meet Monica Bradley. She lives a few doors down on the right. She's trying to break into computer work. Her husband died a few months ago and she needs to work."

"Oh, I'm sorry," Meg said as she poured herself a cup of coffee.

"I don't know what I'd do if anything ever happened to Dan. I shudder to think!"

Monica was a vision of elegant, mature loveliness.

She was saying, "That's the way I felt, totally lost. My whole world centered on my husband. I lived to love and be loved. I needed nothing else. I didn't want to deal with the fact that I was loosing him to cancer so I pretended that there was nothing wrong. I blocked it out. Surely by some miracle it would go away. I couldn't imagine myself without him. I kept so busy that I wasn't even there when he died. He died alone. I should have been there cradling him in my arms, telling him how much I loved him and how much I was going to miss him when he was gone. I should have given him every ounce of my love and caring and shown him how much his life mattered and that his life on this earth wasn't in vain. I felt such guilt on top of the devastation of his death. I've been so miserable, depressed, upset and angry. I laid all the facts on the table in order to analyze myself before starting my new life. I need to become self-sufficient, self-assured and strong. I wanted him to take care of me. I've always needed other people in my life to make me happy. I realize I need to make myself happy. My husband was pretty chauvinistic in a way that he didn't want me out of the house when he was home. He had to be King on his throne where he was served and pampered. If the car was in a different position in the drive when he came home I'd get the third degree. But, ya know, I didn't mind it like the girls do these days. In fact, it made me feel secure, taken care of, coddled."

"Meg can relate to that; can't you Meg?" Stephanie intervened.

"It sounds like you're talking about my husband," Meg admitted.

"I've led a very sheltered life up until my husband died. I need to overcome my fear of people and redevelop my art of conversation. My husband's always done the talking. He always had the floor and demanded to be center of attention. I've been out of touch so long that my linguistic protocol needs to be redeveloped and practiced," Monica continued.

"It sounds like you're on the right road. You're very intuitive," Stephanie said.

"My daughter is twenty years old and is majoring in business in college. She's much the liberated woman. I'm sure a lot due to watching us as she was growing up. She claims she's not about to let her life stagnate the way I had. There will be no possessive, obedient entanglements in her life! AH! It's such a different world now. I can't help but wonder, though, if it's going too far in the other direction; nobody needs anybody! It seems to me that it's turning a little too callous. It's becoming too much, *Me, Me, Me!* What's happening to the **We** in all of this *Me*ness is my question?" Monica added.

∗   ∗   ∗   ∗

Now Monica was gone.

Suddenly, Meg's eyes, startled open by Ron's gentle nudging, view the scene in the hospital with nauseous sorrow. Tears fell on Tyler's little brown-haired head as she heard Whitney say, "I'll work with him when you're ready."

Meg couldn't wait to get out of the sterile, colorless hospital with the hint of unspoken death.

CHAPTER 3

▼

The neighborhood was invited to a Gala Formal Charity Affair by an affluent couple whose magnificent home was the envy of the whole town.

Meg and Dan didn't know them but Steph and Ron convinced them to go because they needed to get their minds off Tyler and the murder.

"Come on! What's one night going to hurt? You need a break!" Steph declared.

"I don't own a gown and I certainly can't afford one with all these Doctor bills lately!" Meg complained.

"Why don't you try on some of my gowns and see if you like one. You're welcome to borrow one for this special occasion," Steph suggested.

While trying on Steph's gowns Meg's whole disposition changed. Her face lit up as she looked at herself in the mirror and Steph held her hair on top of her head. Meg had a bewildered expression, of a young girl who lived in casual cut-offs, content to cook and clean for her family and now finding herself looking like The Grand Duchess about to attend a Ball. She was living a Cinderella fantasy.

✳   ✳   ✳   ✳

Whitney joined John and Hayley at their house before the party. As John opened the door he sighed out loud. He was enchanted with this austere, fatefully beautiful creature. Not only that but he'd been in love with her; concealing his feelings ever since the first year they met. Whitney's intoxicating fragrance sent

John into a much practiced fantasy of the two of them meeting for the first time, only Hayley was non-existent, looking into each other's eyes adoringly, and their whole future ahead of them.

Back to the unpleasant reality, married to Hayley, but dreaming of Whitney...

John took Whitney's tiny, delicate hand and kissed it gallantly without a word. Whitney saw the love in his eyes as she'd noticed all too often before. She curtsied exquisitely and bowed her head. They both laughed.

"You're quite a vision, Whitney," declared John.

"Thank you, John! You look quite dashing yourself," Whitney said with her usual dazzling smile.

Whitney was wearing a low-cut, white beaded form-fitted gown with tiny shoulder straps. Her light colored shoulder length hair was winged back around her ears to reveal her stunning diamond cluster earrings. She was a sight to behold.

"Isn't Hayley ready yet?" Whitney asked, looking at her watch.

"No. She had to change her dress. There was an oil stain on the front."

Whitney had feelings for John too but she was much better at covering her feelings than he was.

Hayley finally entered the room.

"Well, Hayley, you look lovely," Whitney commented.

"Yes, you look very radiant tonight, *Dear!*" John added.

Completely impervious to the silent, passionate feelings going on in the room she'd entered, Hayley offered no return compliments to John or Whitney.

"We'd better get going. We're already late."

Hayley took John's arm and started to walk out the door in front of Whitney in her usual condescending manner.

John stood his ground stiffly and yanked Hayley back. Without a word, John made a slight nod of his head toward Whitney as if to say, *Ladies First.*

They smiled kindly at each other as Whitney preceded them out the door.

*   *   *   *

Everyone looked so elegant. This was the first time in a very long time that they'd had an occasion to don such eloquent fashions.

Stephanie, Ron, Meg and Dan walked through a long walkway toward the gargantuous house, enjoying the beautifully manicured grounds. Meg and Dan had never experienced anything like this before, not in their wildest dreams.

The massive double doors opened into a vestibule that was as big as Meg and Dan's whole house. The marble floor led to two curved staircases to the second floor. The upper hall was open to the entry hall below. They were led to the gathering room, which opened to a stone terrace. The floor was octagonal shaped earth stone and was separated by arched square brick columns and in one corner a built-in brick bar with the fanciest of bar attire. There were giant chandeliers over four massive round tables and ornate rusty orange velour chairs. Two over-stuffed corner sofas done in brown and rust chintz occupied another corner.

It was a night to behold. The room was filled with an air of opulence equal to that of royalty. The women were living their fondest fantasies that night. The men, however, could think of better things to fantasize about. The music and the atmosphere were perfect for romance.

The Crowd sat at one table. The room was buzzing about the murder, entertaining all sorts of solutions and devising plans of attack as if the police weren't already on the job or were totally inept.

The hostess asked how Tyler was fairing out of all of this.

"His speech hasn't yet returned. Thank you for asking," Meg answered.

The hostess went on dutifully to the next table, making her rounds.

Meg and Stephanie were enjoying analyzing the other guests, when Ron meandered over with a new round of drinks in his hands. He sat down next to Meg. It was always Steph, Meg and Ron, *The Three Musketeers…*

Dan never heard any of the teasing that went on between Meg and Ron and Meg never mentioned the long visits Ron paid her when Dan wasn't home. Everyone in the neighborhood was afraid to ruffle Dan's feathers where Meg was concerned. His reputation for unreasonable jealousy preceded him.

Stephanie didn't mind the teasing. It was all in good fun and besides, she wasn't blind; she knew Meg had power over men.

Dan asked Stephanie to dance to a slow song with.

"How about wrapping you body around this perfect bronze love-machine?"

Steph laughed.

"When did your mirror break, Dan?"

Dan was a little too arrogant for Stephanie's taste, but she managed to hold her tongue most of the time.

Ron asked Meg to dance to the same song. There was usually a rush for Meg as soon as Dan was occupied dancing with someone else.

When Dan caught sight of Meg and Ron wrapped around each other on the dance floor, he glared at them throughout the rest of the dance.

Well! That was the end of their dancing for the evening! Meg and Dan sat sullenly in a corner after that without a lot of words between them.

Stephanie teased Ron.

"Well, how did you like dancing with Meg?"

Ron growled like a tiger.

"She molded her body to mine and it felt as if we were one."

Feeling a bit insecure and curiosity eating her alive, she couldn't help asking.

"You like dancing with her better than me?"

"She's soft and cuddly and just the right height," Ron replied.

Not quite sure how she felt about those statements and the strange sparkle in Ron's eyes, Steph said, "Humph!"

Saying to herself, *I trust Meg! I don't always trust Ron but I DO trust Meg!*

Steph was sure Meg adored her husband Dan; Steph couldn't understand why, but that's why there's chocolate and vanilla and strawberry. There's always something or someone for everybody. Never-the-less, Steph gave it no further thought.

John and Whitney were sitting at the bar enjoying each other's company when Hayley waltzed over to them.

"Well, John, if Whitney's so irresistible, why is she still single?" She spit out with a bitter, spiteful tone.

Whitney started to respond but her training taught her restraint and understanding so she abandoned any further thought on the matter.

Without giving anyone a chance to retort, Hayley continued.

"Did you see Ron dancing with Meg? Oh! That Stephanie's such a fool! I can't believe how she allows all that disgusting teasing to go on between Ron and Meg! I'll bet they're having an affair right under all our noses! She's wide open to letting that little spitfire into her marriage."

Getting no response from Whitney or John, she continued, "...and the way the whole mood changes the minute Dan walks on the scene makes me sick! Anybody can see that there's more to Ron and Meg than they're letting on!"

John finally interrupted.

"Okay, Sherlock, it'll be our little secret."

Ignoring John's sarcasm Hayley continued.

"That Ron! He's only good for chronic bachelorhood!"

A handsome, distinguished looking gentleman approached Whitney. He introduced himself and asked her to dance.

Hayley leaned over to John and over enunciated her words.

"Well, maybe she'll soon have a man of her own."

John squinted his eyes in disgust having heard quite enough of Hayley's cattiness. He left her stranded at the bar.

John couldn't understand why Whitney put up with Hayley's insatiable thirst for stirring up antagonism.

John asked Stephanie to dance, leaving Ron sitting by himself.

Seeing that everyone else was dancing except Hayley, Ron decided he'd be better off by himself so he pretended not to notice her.

Later the room was filled with laughter as everyone was loosening up after a few drinks and getting acquainted with new people.

Stephanie and Meg's jaws hung in amazement and disbelief as they listened to a new acquaintance telling a story about a couple who'd been in an auto accident.

"When the police arrived on the scene, they thought he was dead and began attending to his girlfriend, who was understandably quite hysterical. The driver looked up and asked if they'd mind turning off the motor that the vibration was hurting his chest. This guy had a four-foot long fence post speared through his chest. The post had him speared through the seat so they had to cut the seat to remove him from the car so they could get him to the hospital, post and all. The impact of the collision had rammed the post through the windshield of the car, through his body then through the seat."

With that Stephanie's face turned a shade of green and the bridge of her nose turned white. Feeling ill, she made her way to the bathroom to recover.

Seeming to get pleasure out of Stephanie's reaction, the man continued.

"Miraculously, this guy survived and only three months later he and his girlfriend got married. After all that, he was killed in a hit and run on his honeymoon!"

Whitney needed some air after that story and slowly walked out to the terrace with her drink in her hand. She was vulnerable anyway, because she'd just lost a boyfriend to his ex-wife.

Making sure Hayley was totally engrossed in some juicy gossip, John followed Whitney to the terrace.

"What a perfect night for a party," John commented. A little over-wrought, Whitney turned to John. He raised her chin with his fingers to see a tear in her eye.

"Look on the bright side, losing someone gives you the opportunity to find someone new," John said softly, trying to comfort her.

Loving her so dearly from afar was getting exceedingly more difficult. At least, staying with Hayley much to his growing distaste, assured him of a way to be close and be a part of Whitney's life.

"Oh, John," she managed to say, "it's not just that, but I'm getting tired of being alone and having to share other people's families. If I could just find the right man…"

In her heart she was saying that no other man measured up to John and she couldn't seem to get him out of her heart. Of course, she would never take him away from her friend for anything in the world even though she suspected he cared for her.

Whitney started to cry. John took her into his comforting arms. How right that felt to both of them. She felt so lost and discouraged. She knew she could never have John and John felt such disgust that she was hurting this way because of another fool of a man!

John asked, in his usual joking manner in an attempt to lighten her spirits, "Why don't you marry me?"

She managed to smile obligingly.

"I don't care much for bigamy."

Hayley stood in the doorway watching this touching scene. She was speechless. For once she couldn't come up with a single appropriate slam or caustic remark. She turned and made haste back to the party.

A bit later, John and Whitney were sitting quietly on a sofa, observing people's mannerisms and habits. Hayley approached them with a glass of champagne in her hand. She wore an unusually benign expression on her face and swayed a little from the hips due to her unstable equilibrium.

"I have an intolerable thirst for champagne tonight," Hayley announced.

John gave her a cold, speculative glare. Fully alerted to her condition, John asked her to dance. He managed to inconspicuously dance her out to the terrace where she broke down into uncontrollable sobs.

"I'll get our coats," John said in an unsympathetic tone.

John left Hayley sitting alone in her extreme discomfort.

Ten minutes later, Whitney and the hostess approached Hayley.

Hayley stood up to meet them head on. Handling the situation quite well under the circumstances, Hayley commented how much she enjoyed the party and threw her arms up in a flamboyant gesture, marveling at the vastness of her magnificent house. The three of them expressed their regrets for leaving so early as they walked toward the front door.

Ron tapped his glass with his knife demanding everyone's attention.

"I have an announcement to make."

Ron stood up proudly.

"Steph and I are expecting our fifth baby," Ron announced, beaming at Steph.

Everyone started clapping and smiling.

"Good for you, Ole Buddy!"

"Congratulations!" Dan said in a serious tone, shaking Ron's hand and patting him on the back.

The women at the table started making plans for a shower right away and smiled at Steph sympathetically.

"Well, Steph! At least you have a house big enough to equip five kids," someone said.

Meg leaned over and whispered in Steph's ear.

"Yes, but do you have the stamina to handle five kids?"

"I guess we'll find out," Steph said, shrugging her shoulders helplessly.

All in all, the evening went rather well. Everyone left wearily but the experience would remain in their memories forever.

*   *   *   *

The next day, Steph was washing dishes after dinner when the doorbell rang. Zach called out.

"Mom it's for you."

Drying her hands on a towel, she entered the living room to greet an investigator concerning Monica's murder.

"I've already told you everything I can remember," Steph said.

"Sometimes people can remember more details later after the initial shock has worn off or they may have forgotten a seemingly unimportant detail to them but one that may make all the difference and be an important key in the case," The Investigator said.

Steph let out a loud sigh.

"Okay, won't you sit down?"

"Thank you. Do you know if Mrs. Bradley was seeing anyone special, male or female?"

Steph thought for a short moment.

"Not that I know of. She was very distraught over her husband's death and was trying desperately to get her life back in order. Honestly, in my opinion, after talking to her, I don't think she was interested in any other man. She didn't hit me as the type to have an affair, if that's what you're hinting at."

"Are you aware of any conflicts in either her or her husband's life? Anything at all, even gossip you may have heard in passing, any here-say, anything, whether you believe it or not?"

"As I told you, I didn't know her that well and as far as gossip, no, not that I can remember, off hand. I will give it some thought and question some of our neighbors. I'll call you if I latch on to anything."

"Do you remember anything else about the woman you saw running out of the house?"

"Nothing more, really but those eyes just seem so familiar. I see them over and over in my dreams or I guess you might call them nightmares."

"We're working with a new artist. Since you weren't satisfied with the other composite, would you mind very much coming back to the station and try this woman out?"

"Maybe tomorrow, if I can get my neighbor to sit for me."

"That would be fine. I thank you very much for all your trouble to help us. Have a nice evening."

With poor Monica heavy on her mind, Steph went back to her dishes.

✳   ✳   ✳   ✳

A few days later, Stephanie and Hayley were chatting on the phone. Steph was listening to Hayley ramble on about Whitney and all her women friends as she schemed to get revenge. According to her, everyone she knew was after her John.

The neighborhood didn't care much for Hayley but they tolerated her for John's sake because everyone thought a lot of John.

Hayley was the original Doom and Gloom, always looking for trouble and if there wasn't any she'd find a way to stir it up.

Stephanie had given Meg one of her dresses. When Hayley saw Meg in it, she said to Stephanie, "My! It doesn't look like the same dress! Meg sure has everything in the right place, doesn't she?"

Already feeling inadequate next to Meg, not needing to be reminded of it, Stephanie's comment was, "Meow! Did you enjoy that, Hayley?"

Every time she'd call she'd inquire if Ron was over at Meg's again, in her ever-so-typical annoying, whiney voice.

"Yes! He's over there fixing her stove again," Steph slipped up and dared to reply.

Hayley complained.

"That Dan is a poor excuse for a husband!"

Steph made the ultimate mistake of complaining.

"Quite frankly, I'm getting sick of it too! Nothing ever gets fixed around here but just let Meg call and he's over there like a shot!"

Steph certainly opened a can of worms with that statement! Good ole Hayley couldn't wait to jump on the attack…

"I'd be raving if it were me…"

✳   ✳   ✳   ✳

Ron and Stephanie decided to join John, Hayley, Meg and Dan on a ski trip before Stephanie was too cumbersome with child.

Everyone had his own skis except Meg and Dan. After renting their rooms, the group waited for Meg and Dan to rent their skis.

"You know, you really should invest in some skis." Ron suggested.

"Why?" Dan retorted. "How important can having your own skis be?"

Meg would attest that Dan was the squeakiest tightwad around.

"Just as important as your mechanics tools are to fix your engine! Unless you're still in the habit of wiring your car door shut so it won't fall open when you turn the corners, instead of buying a new one," Ron answered.

Meg tried to stifle a giggle.

The moment the skis were fitted, the impatient little group hit the slopes.

After crossing a series of moguls, Ron felt warmed up enough to attempt showing off his expertise.

"Look at Ron!" Hayley shouted. "He's doing the Hannes jump."

"Show Off!" Steph yelled.

In trying to watch Ron, Meg lost her footing. She fell face down in the snow with her skis going in two different directions.

John and Dan kept going but Ron stopped dead with the art of an expert and rushed to Meg's rescue.

Steph and Hayley were out of hearing range.

"I lost my ski pole!" Meg whimpered unhappily.

"I'll get it for you," Ron said without pause, always ready to help Meg.

Ron pulled Meg to her feet and put his arm around her waist in an effort to steer her. Meg pushed her hair from her face and reached for her ski pole.

"You need some mogul training. I'll show you a few hints," Ron offered.

"Okay Hotshot!" Meg replied.

"First you need a sense of humor when you ski! Half the fun is falling down and getting a face full of snow. Laugh at yourself. You'll be better off!"

Meg let out a loud sigh.

"Frankly, skiing is the most uncomfortable, cumbersome thing I've ever done! What do you people see in it?"

Steph and Hayley skied over to them.

"My muscles are so tight," Meg moaned.

Ron wasted no time.

"I'll be glad to give you a rub-down. Anytime you need a *good* massage, I'm ready, willing and able."

"I'm the *best!*" Ron whispered in her ear as he leaned over.

Stephanie ignored Hayley's *I told you so* glare and pretended that she couldn't fathom its meaning.

"The best is only brought on by patience and tolerance."

Ron stuck to Meg like glue on the pretense of giving her guidance.

Meg hit an icy spot and somehow landed on her back in a snowdrift where Ron fell flat on top of her.

Meg was entirely aware of Ron's applause and she inadvertently gave him the opportunity to express it.

Steph and Hayley came around the corner and witnessed the aftermath of this cozy, hilarious scene. Steph joined in the laughter.

"Just remember, Ron! Meg's *my* friend!" Stephanie warned with a controlled smile.

Ron jumped up and Steph and Hayley helped Meg up, one on each arm.

"There are too many icy spots out here for me," admitted Steph. "I found myself bouncing out of control and picking up speed I didn't plan on. It's too hazardous out here for me. Meg, I think Hayley and I'd better take you inside. This is no place for a beginner. What do you say we head back for some hot drinks, girls?"

"Sounds good to us!" Meg and Hayley agreed.

Hayley and Steph, still holding onto Meg's arms, started down the slope.

Stephanie looked over her shoulder.

"See ya, Love," she said, smiling with tense lips.

*   *   *   *

There was nothing more peaceful after a long day of navigating the snow in the bracing cold, still air, than lounging by the fire after unloading the cumbersome ski garb. The fire crackling, the snowflakes delicate fluttering against the windows and the warmth of the flames on the girl's faces provided such peaceful-ness that was lacking in their every day grind.

An hour later, Ron dropped his heavy boots on the bench beside the girls and pulled off one of his gloves with his teeth.

Dan and John followed him in.

"Are you girls thawed yet?" Ron asked.

The guys interrupted the girl's discussion of the trials and tribulations of child rearing.

"Mommy, get this and Mommy, get that; Mommy, this, Mommy, that; Mommy! He hit me; Mommy, she won't give me my what-cha-ma-call it; Mommy! Mommy! Wahhhhhh!" She paused. "Ya know, you can learn to hate that word!" Steph was saying.

Meg and Hayley laughed in agreement.

"Now, on the subject of husbands, since they decided to grace us with their presence," Stephanie continued with a smile.

Dan excused himself from the group to head for the bathroom and to buy some hot coffee.

"Well, first you have to take great care in choosing a husband," Meg offered.

Stephanie added, "Of course you really don't know the guy till you marry him and live with his temper and all of his idiosyncrasies." Stephanie grinned in Ron's direction.

"Amen!" Hayley said.

"Men should express their appreciation of their wive's effort to dress becom-ingly for them." Meg said.

Ron's eyes brightened as he took full advantage of Meg's comment. He turned toward Meg and took her hand as he dropped to the floor on one knee before her.

"Meg, I appreciate it so much when you wear your little shorts and halter tops in the summer!"

He fixed an incandescent gaze on her.

"You left an impression on me that, I assure you, will never fade."

"Ron!" Meg exclaimed, her face turning red with embarrassment. She scolded, "Please, get up!"

"Appreciation and devotion mean everything to a wife," Meg continued.

"You should be gracious to people who fall at your feet, Meg!" Ron scolded with a look so private and impenetrable.

Stephanie flashed Ron a reproachful look.

"Looks like we're in the same boat," Hayley whispered to Steph, quite pleased with herself.

Stephanie smiled, not warmly.

"Surely, you don't mean the Titanic!"

She refused to allow Hayley's vicious remarks get to her because she loved Meg. Steph trusted Meg. Meg was always uncommonly kind and generous in their relationship. She always had a sunny disposition and a cheerful personality, quite unlike Hayley.

John overheard.

"Hayley!" John reprimanded. "You're such a comfort! Please, keep your nose out of it!"

Meg blushed. "Oh, Ron, you're so charming."

"Be careful, Meg! It's hereditary. *His dad's a snake,*" Stephanie said, trying to keep her sense of humor.

Ron smiled with gritted teeth, annoyed with Steph's attempt at sarcasm.

"You're so original, Darling! You just keep 'em flying!"

Everyone tried to lighten up when Dan approached Meg with two cups of Irish coffee.

"French men are trained to express their admiration of women all the time. They make it a habit. American men should take lessons," Steph was saying.

"Not just to women in general, but to their own wives," Hayley said sternly. "God knows, we wives need a pat every once in a while for having to put up with our husbands."

Hayley looked straight at Ron and lingered a moment.

While handing Meg her coffee, Dan announced that there was a band playing up stairs.

Ron's eyes lit up.

"How about we get a little body warmth from these ladies on the dance floor?"

Stephanie looked at Ron. She nodded solemnly as she contemplated the evening ahead.

Meg saw the sadness in Steph's heart-shaped face.

"What's wrong, Steph?" Meg asked, concerned.

"Nothing, Meg; Nothing at all. Really!"

After all, it wasn't Meg's fault that Ron was an unmitigated *Jackass*! Steph camouflaged her feelings.

"I think I'll change my clothes," Meg announced.

Steph agreed.

"Good idea! I can't stand these wet, uncomfortable pants much longer."

Meg led the way while Hayley and Steph followed behind.

"Keep a stiff upper lip, Steph. I think we're headed for some icy moguls that all the fresh snow in the world won't smooth out," Hayley whispered.

*　　*　　*　　*

The gals walked toward their husbands after having transformed themselves back into real women.

Meg pivoted in front of the full-length mirror she came upon for a quick check.

Meg asked the guys.

"How do you like my new outfit?"

Ron couldn't resist.

"You merely put a frame on the Mona Lisa."

Meg quickly checked out Dan's expression. She tried to avoid setting off his jealous rages at all costs. She observed that he was quite pleased with himself much to her relief. Dan had been drinking pretty heavily so he seemed to be in a jolly mood in spite of Ron's attentiveness toward his wife.

In an attempt to conceal her melancholy and depression, Steph joked and laughed along with everyone else and continued to keep that *stiff upper lip*!

Meg pulled Dan onto the dance floor in spite of his display of unwillingness. Meg was a very capable dancer and after a few drinks, her provocative moves could reduce any man to a whimpering fool.

Hayley tapped Steph's shoulder to get her attention. Without a word, she pointed to Ron.

Ron was obviously entranced, as if no one else was in the room but him and Meg.

"Ron! Where were you just now?" Steph insisted. "Ron! Please, don't stare! You're embarrassing me!"

"Meg's like poetry in motion. Mmmmmmmmmm," Ron commented as if in a daze.

Meg had a subtle, unconscious way of flattering Ron's vanity and making him feel superior.

Ron ignored Steph's plea and still blatantly enjoyed Meg's moves.

"I have a sudden hunger to exercise my primal instincts," Ron said with a growl.

With that, Ron jumped out of his seat and made his way through the other dancers. He politely tapped Dan on the shoulder as if to cut in. As Dan turned his back to walk back to his seat, Ron grabbed Meg and threw her over his shoulder. Her kicking and screaming resistance only served to get her rear smacked. A primate like expression came over his face as he walked swiftly out the door in ape-like strides attempting to imitate a Neanderthal man. His long torso caused his shirttail to untuck in the process.

Wave after wave of laughter swept over the room.

Having missed the drama, when Dan reached his seat he couldn't understand what everyone was laughing about.

Stephanie sank into her chair in embarrassment. She hid her face in her hand, her misery intensifying.

John thoughtfully poured a ginger ale and gave it to Steph.

"In honor of the occasion."

Steph straightened up, smothering a sigh; she thanked him and raised her glass to meet his.

"His feeblemindedness seems to pass for humor," Steph uttered, aggravated by the thought of Ron's ineptitude.

John thought it best to leave Steph alone for a moment so he walked toward the restroom for the lack of knowing what else to do.

Hayley slid into the seat beside Stephanie.

"Meg's nothing but a clod-hopping slut. Ron doesn't deserve you," she snarled.

"Hayley, I don't care to hear it!" Steph sighed.

In spite of Steph's fierce protestation, Hayley continued her annoying aspersions on Meg's character.

"Meg has only a ten minute attention span. He'd be bored with her after a week! Ron's an intelligent man, even if he doesn't care to show it at the moment! After he gets over his insatiable itch for her body and the novelty wears off, what would they have together?"

"Is it asking too much," Steph demanded in a fierce tone of voice, "if you stop talking? Has Meg ever done anything unkind or cruel to you?"

"Don't be afraid of the enemies who attack you; be afraid of the friends who flatter you," Steph continued with quivering lips

"She's not as delicate a creature as you believe her to be! Are you retracting the statement that Ron's an unmitigated jackass?" Hayley retorted.

Steph defended Ron.

"Ron never has been a creature of logic. He just likes to impress people."

"Well! He sure is a genius at making a fool out of *you*!" Hayley insisted.

John spotted Hayley talking to Steph. He knew he'd better make quick steps over there before Hayley did too much irreparable damage. He made it just in time to hear Stephanie say, "There are only two things I dislike about you, Hayley!"

"I shudder to think; what?" Hayley asked.

"*Your face!*" Steph exploded.

With that Steph snatched up her coat and belongings. Her sinking heart and feelings of despair wouldn't allow her to listen to any more of Hayley's snide remarks.

John sat down beside Hayley without a word, feeling quite pleased with the outcome he'd over heard.

"Hell hath no fury like a woman scorned! Gee! You'd think I was selling military secrets to the enemy!" Hayley grumbled.

✳   ✳   ✳   ✳

Ron carried Meg to a spacious balcony where they were alone.

"I'm not sure I find this amusing. Dan's going to be searching for us with a vengeance," Meg said.

A sudden rush of heat came over Ron. Desire for Meg swept through him, as his heartbeat quickened and his skin tingled with anticipation of stroking her lovely skin. He wanted to wrap his body around hers.

"You're so beautiful," Ron breathed, his gaze filled with passion.

"I suggest you change the subject, Ron! You're scaring me!" Meg said, offering him a nervous smile.

"We're very much alike down deep, aren't we?" Ron asked.

Meg threw Ron a startled glance, afraid to look him in the eyes. Her soft doe-like bedroom eyes were so lovely. She had a well-defined face and a stubborn mouth. Her abundance of chestnut colored hair glazed with sun streaked golden highlights was a constant source of irritation for her.

Ron took a deep breath after a brief silence.

"You know, at first I thought you to be stuck up and unapproachable but it wasn't long before I realized you were just shy."

A strange expression crossed Meg's face, as Ron held her hand tenderly and moved his thumb slowly, gently back and forth sensing the soft skin of her hand. One thing about Ron, he didn't need to cultivate his charm.

"There comes a time when each of us must search for what he needs. Fears, hunger, and needs rule us all."

Trying to change the subject, Meg declared, "You're not being very kind to Steph or to Dan! You should never neglect to show human kindness or respect."

Out of urgency, Ron grabbed Meg and kissed her passionately. Momentarily thrown off balance and out of spontaneous impulse she kissed him back.

Within seconds, Meg was sorry and pulled away. A stifling wave of remorse swept over her. What was once a momentously wonderful idea now seemed risky and unsavory. A sickening fear came over her.

"How could I have done that?" Meg lifted her eyes. "Please, don't ever do that again!" Meg insisted.

Not wanting to prolong the moment, Meg turned and started walking. Ron followed her; they walked along at a steady pace, uncomfortable in the silence between them.

Meg broke her stride and came to an abrupt halt.

Steph was standing in the doorway. Their eyes met.

Speechless, Meg shot through the doorway and deliberately disappeared into the crowd.

Ron cleared his throat loudly, flashing Steph his winning smile.

"Now remember Steph, it takes character and self-control to be understanding and forgiving."

The sight of them caused Steph's heart to leap in an unexpected manner and was indelibly imprinted on her mind. She was conscious of only the yearning she felt to be loved again, to be understood, to be needed.

"You know, Ron, no one will ever love you as much as I do," Steph murmured, leaning her head against the door jam as if she no longer had the strength to hold it up.

"A great man shows his greatness by the way he treats his wife," Steph said aghast at his audacity.

Squeezing her eyes shut to suppress the sudden sting of tears, her voice cracked. "What ever happened to loyalty?"

Ron half-heartedly strived to justify himself.

"Understanding is more profitable than criticism."

Steph was drained of her boundless energy and enthusiasm.

"Why are you always so gallant and considerate of every woman but me?" Steph asked slowly, softly.

"Why must you agonize over everything?" Ron snarled, losing his patience.

"Why can't you overlook my faults and pay attention to my qualities?" Steph implored.

"What qualities?" Ron shot back at her.

Always the assaults on the spirit to antagonize and demean Stephanie.

Still trying to remain calm, her mouth tightened with resentment, Steph uttered,

"You're shallow, selfish, arrogant, self-righteous, and most assuredly heartless!"

"*I am not!*" Ron insisted, half sarcastically.

"No! You only lie when you open your mouth. You're so used to lying; you believe your own lies and build them up from there. Your words are hollow!" Steph finally exploded, blinking back tears. "You have as much sense as a half-witted jackass!"

"AH, AH, AH, thoughtlessly uttered in the heat of anger...," Ron sang, mocking Steph.

Steph gave Ron a penetrating look. She shivered with anger and hurt. Her face was wet with tears.

"You love Meg! Don't you, Ron?"

"Meg's married!" he offered as his only defense.

"A brilliant defense, I must say!" Steph snapped.

Steph drooped in dejection. Her heart throbbed painfully. Emotion welled up in her and hardened into momentary hatred.

No, she confessed to herself, she couldn't hate Meg. Steph couldn't help liking her. She still enjoyed being with her more than anyone else.

In this wrenching moment, Steph shook her head vehemently.

"You bastard!" Stephanie cried.

Steph turned away from Ron. She had no particular destination in mind, but it didn't matter; she knew she couldn't stick around there any longer.

✶   ✶   ✶   ✶

After a good, long, cleansing cry in the sanctity of her bathroom, Stephanie managed to pull herself together, at least long enough to freshen up and change clothes.

To her surprise, she found a single red rose on her pillow. She picked it up and held it to her chest with both hands.

About that time, Steph heard the key in the lock. When Ron walked through the door Steph was waiting for him with open arms.

"Ron!" Steph cried.

"I accept your apology."

Ron held her at arms length and looked into her eyes.

"What apology?"

Steph held up the rose.

"Isn't that why you put this on my pillow?"

"I didn't put the rose there but if it put that smile back on your face, I'll claim having done it!"

They kissed.

"I'm sorry, Honey; I guess I had too much to drink," Ron said.

As always, they made up between the sheets.

Afterward, they walked hand in hand to the dining room.

Meg wasn't there.

"Where's Meg?" Steph asked Dan.

"She's not feeling well. She's not used to drinking," Dan answered, believing every word.

*   *   *   *

Stephanie knocked on Meg's door. When she answered, Steph put her arms around Meg and gave her a long, forgiving hug.

"Aren't you hungry?" Steph asked.

"Yes! I am now," Meg replied, wiping a tear out of her eye.

"Come on! Let's eat!"

*   *   *   *

Two weeks later, Steph was preparing to entertain her brother's wife, Bianca, and of course, Meg and all the kiddies. She was unmolding a jell-o concoction when the doorbell rang.

It was Bianca, a strange girl and two children.

"Hi, Steph! I hope you don't mind. I'd like you to meet Rick's secretary, Danielle.

Steph's heart jumped straight to her throat at the sight of the two redheads. She couldn't take her eyes off of them. The little girl looked exactly like Steph did when she was that age and the boy was the spitting image of Rick! Steph was so upset she started stammering.

Steph managed to repossess control of her tongue.

"It's nice to meet you. I've heard your name mentioned quite a bit through the years. Come. Sit down."

"Do you mind if I show Danielle through your house, Steph?" Bianca asked.

They seemed to be so chummy. Some brother she had! Steph felt ill. How could her brother do such a thing?

Steph was so glad when Meg finally got there to help keep up appearances. Steph had such difficulty acting normally. What would she talk about? All she could think about was *how **could** he*? And he has multiple sclerosis yet! What could he be thinking? Or is he incapable of thinking? Maybe MS has affected his brain! Bianca's such a nice person, so classy, so nice, and so pretty! She's a terrific cook and her house is always immaculate…. *Why*?

In talking to Danielle, it was uncanny how much she reminded Steph of Bianca, her mannerisms, her speech, her hair, and even her tastes. Maybe Danielle admired Bianca so much that she tried to emulate her….*Even down to her husband*!

Steph took Meg into another room and filled her in on her suspicions. Now Meg understood why Steph had been acting so strangely. She agreed to help Steph with her uneasiness and fill in the lulls in the conversation.

This situation was incredible but there was no doubt that these kids were her brother's.

Bianca was talking about the party she and Rick were giving Saturday night.

"Steph, you're always so good with parties. Would you share some recipes with me?" Bianca asked.

While Steph was standing on a chair in order to reach her cookbooks, Bianca explained the marvelous molds and nut rolls that Steph had made for her last party.

How unbelievable! Bianca and the *other woman* were best friends!

Meg and Steph stole an occasional glance at each other in total disbelief. It was crazy! Knowing what she knew in her heart, Steph struggled to dislike Danielle, but she seemed like such a nice person!

When Bianca and Danielle left, Meg and Steph let out a sigh of relief. Steph tried to fill Meg in on Rick's life.

"My brother found out he had Multiple Sclerosis when Bianca was pregnant with their daughter. He used to black out and fall off scaffolds and crush his numb fingers. He'd temporarily lose his vision and occasionally drag his feet. This was devastating to Rick because he's such an ambitious guy; a hard physical worker and he'd just started his construction business. He vowed he was going to fight it every step of the way and make his fortune in spite of it. The doctors warned him that he wouldn't live a full lifetime. We watched him work day and night, putting healthy men to shame, to make his business a success. He and Bianca are leading a more than comfortable life, in need of nothing. Rick is a very kind-hearted guy. He's done many unselfish, kind things for people anonymously, expecting nothing in return. On the other hand, he has a violent temper and is capable of doing childish, sometimes cruel things. He insults Bianca in public and schemes unrealistically and childishly to *get even* with people. He seems to have a duel personality, which may be attributed to his condition. One thing about Rick; you don't know whether to kiss him or slap him! Being a very mild-mannered, easy-going person, Bianca has managed to tolerate his mood swings, or at least I've never heard her complain. Rick doesn't smoke or drink; he goes to bed very early every night in order to have the strength to carry on. Naturally, Bianca refused to have more children for fear that Rick's condition may be hereditary. Rick loves children and has always talked about having a house full of them."

Meg and Steph had a lot on their minds.

"What can I do?" Steph asked Meg.

CHAPTER 4

▼

Stephanie and Meg shared their most private, intimate thoughts with each other. Through talking with Steph and hearing her troubles expressed through her eyes, Meg sensed a dangerous deterioration of Stephanie's self-esteem. She seemed to be developing all the symptoms of depression.

Meg had punched Steph's release button.

"Ron thinks I live in a fantasy world. He claims I close my eyes to the real world. Men don't seem to think of marriage as sacred and irrevocable," Steph was complaining.

Meg poured herself a cup of coffee and placed a plate of cheese and crackers on the table.

"May I freshen your coffee, Steph?"

"Yes. Thanks, Meg."

Meg sat down in order to give Steph her full attention.

"I can't understand men, or at least, I can't understand Ron," Steph claimed.

"Who can?" Meg chimed in.

"How can they go to bed with absolutely anyone? It sickens me," Steph continued. When Ron and I were married, I thought we were the only two people in love and the only ones who could make love so beautifully and skillfully, for the lack of a more appropriate word. Then when I found out he could be this intimate with a total stranger, I was so heart-broken. He may as well have ripped my heart right out of my chest, literally. I'm sure the pain couldn't have been any more excruciating! I thought we were special. I was so wrong. Soooo wrong! The sex act that I prefer to call *love making* that I used to feel was so essential in my life, now seems to be cheap and even an act of sickness. It's the old story, I make love and he screws. Look at all the sex crimes. I'm beginning to think that, in fact I'm sure of it, men are driven by sex. They blame everything on their sex drive. They couldn't be held accountable because their sex drive made them do it. *Well, she gave me the come-on! Or, she was asking for it! Or, you don't realize that a man can't go too long without it!*...IT! What is the big IT? Is it a fix? Is it a drug? Is it a disease? What ever happened to *I want to make love to you because I love you so much?* Men are raping their daughters, little boys, and old women...My God! No one's safe. Doesn't it scare you, Meg?"

"Yes. But I don't let it into my bedroom. I love Dan and lovemaking is still lovemaking to me. He's been true to me so far," Meg replied with a sigh.

It bothers me that the human race is only one step away from animal, and lately, I doubt that step! Love used to be the number one priority in my life, but now I'm so confused. Sometimes I feel that Ron doesn't really love me. I *know* he doesn't respect me! *God knows, I'm **only** a woman!* As far as he's concerned a woman doesn't deserve respect. Didn't you know, Meg, that you're a third class citizen?"

Stephanie took a bite of cheese, her mind still racing.

"I don't want a hundred men. I just want one good one! Why is that asking too much, these days? Sometimes I feel so alone! I wonder, what am I doing on this earth? Who'd miss me if I were gone? I don't seem to do anything right or to please anyone! I'm so tired of trying to please everyone and trying to be what everyone wants me to be. What's wrong with me just the way I am? Why can't people accept me the way I am? Granted, I'm not perfect, but who is? I feel like I'm wearing a disguise and the real me is surrendering away...The mask is tightening around my face; sometimes I feel like I'm suffocating!"

Meg poured Steph another cup of coffee.

"Gee, Meg, you'll have me bouncing off the walls soon."

Meg admitted, "You're already bouncing! I guarantee another cup won't make any difference."

After a brief pause, she let out a long sigh.

"I wonder if it's true, you have to lose your life to save your life?" Steph said in a long, pondering voice, "I'm waiting for that moment in life that will make it worthwhile. I can't seem to find a refuge from my thoughts. I want so badly to feel indispensable in *somebody's life*! I seem to be a failure at enriching other people's lives. I find myself exploding over absolutely nothing. I meet my obligations and my responsibilities but that doesn't seem to be enough. I feel empty. Sometimes I feel so intimidated by people that I can't even think clearly. I lose my train of thought and can't carry on a decent conversation. I desire grandeur and picture myself socializing in grand style but in my heart I know I can't handle it.

Meg let out another deep sigh.

"You don't like yourself much, do you, Steph?"

After a reckoning moment, Steph cried.

"No; not much, I guess. Did you ever feel that life just wasn't worth the trouble, or effort? Sometimes I feel so hopeless, such desperation. I feel that Ron is my enemy. It seems that he's working against me every step of the way."

Steph stared off into space for a moment.

"I've had devotion before. I've had love, kindness and friendship before. This isn't it!"

A sickening fear came over Meg. Stephanie's situation seemed hopeless.

"It sounds to me like he has a real problem. Maybe he should see a psychiatrist or a counselor."

Stephanie shrugged her shoulders.

"He won't go. I've tried before. If he's so displeased with me, why does he insist we stay together? He's thrown me out of the house before in my nightgown over a lie I caught him in. He screamed at me claiming that I looked like a dog compared to his girlfriends. I was so miserable and fed up by then that I just started to walk off into the night. I just didn't care. Ron ran after me and grabbed me. He threw me over his shoulder. I fell limp and lifeless, total dead weight over his shoulder, as if I just didn't care. He carried me back into the house and wouldn't let me go. Sometimes I'm so scared! If I stay or if I leave, I'm scared. One minute he pours his heart out to me and the next he's telling me I'm not worth loving. He sounds like a monster, doesn't he? It's hard for even me to believe and I'm living it! When everyone else is telling me he's the nicest person they've ever met here I am thinking like this. Dr. Jekyll is the man I fell in love with. The marriage vows brought out Mr. Hyde."

CHAPTER 5

▼

A voice called out in the darkened room. Meg's eyes opened suddenly from a deep sleep. Groaning and thrashing sounds broke the late night silence. Meg rose in concern and turned her attention toward her husband beside her.

Dan was handsome in a conventionally masculine sense but the dim street light coming in the window revealed the twisted, disturbed expression on his face.

Meg reached for the table lamp to switch the light on. She cleared her throat as she shook Dan's arm in an attempt to waken him.

"Honey! Honey! It's all right! It's just a dream! Dan!"

Meg planted a kiss on his forehead. Dan opened his eyes in panic. He looked pale and drawn around the eyes. His rich bass voice was now gruff from sleep.

"Meg."

Meg's heart went out to him. She eased herself next to Dan and cradled him in her arms.

"It must have been a whopper of a nightmare!" Meg whispered.

Dan's face contorted.

"It was!"

Meg's eyes remained on Dan's face as if searching for clues to this mysterious dream that seemed to muddle Dan's mind.

Meg refastened a few hairpins while waiting for Dan to recover enough to talk.

Dan narrowed his eyes in concentration.

"Sex organs," he began slowly. "Somebody was cutting off men's sex organs and he was standing over me. I was next!"

Their gazes locked in mutual need. Meg shuddered at the thought and cleared her throat nervously. She was expected to comment but no words came.

"There's no immediate cause for alarm," Meg finally said after a long sigh and in a soothing voice.

She pulled back the blanket to reveal his love muscle still in tact and at full attention.

They both laughed with relief.

*   *   *   *

Stephanie was seated in Meg's kitchen resting an elbow on her table with her fingers wrapped around a coffee cup.

Dan was in his garage working secretly, restoring an old motorbike for their son's birthday.

Meg picked up the phone after the second ring. Her "Hello" started with a pleasant smile but the "How are you?" turned into a scowl when she found out it was her mother-in-law.

"Daddy's trying to fix the hot water heater and the water leaked out all over the floor," Meg's mother-in-law was saying, in her premeditated, helpless voice. "Could Dan possibly come over and help him clean it up?"

Her endless whining turned on Meg's wrath.

"Yes, Mom! I'll send him over right away."

Meg hung up the phone with an angry slam. Steph was surprised the phone didn't fall off the wall!

"That woman! I felt like telling her to get off her lazy ass and help him herself! The next thing, she'll be having him run over to wipe her ass for her," Meg declared with a vengeance. "I'm so tired of biting my tongue!"

"Meg! I've never seen you so angry," Stephanie said.

After Meg gave Dan the message, he dropped everything as he's always done and rushed right over there.

Meg settled into her kitchen chair across from Steph, coffee in hand, preparing to let Stephanie in on the reason for all this anger.

Meg pursed her lips in disgust. She wiped excess mascara out of the corner of her eye with her fingernail.

"I swear! I don't understand it!" Meg said, her eyes communicating daggers.

"Such loyalty to people who clearly don't deserve it; Why? There's a baffling undercurrent in that family. Something isn't right. I can't figure it out.…*yet*!

"Oh?" Stephanie mused.

Meg's reflections on them were tinged with resentment.

"There's always this strange willingness to do for them. Dan and his brothers and sister seem powerless in their command and yet strangely defensive of them. It's far from the conventional, normal family. It's such a repressive atmosphere. They're almost like robots when their parents are around; affixed, dutiful smiles of agreement with them even if they disagree; their sudden *drop everything and rush to their aid* attitude; their neglect of their own families in order to serve their self-centered parents' every whim. They all say what they think the other person wants to hear. They know it's a lie and the other person knows it's a lie. What's the point? But everyone's happy! Very strange. As a matter of fact Dan's sister's first husband left her because of it. Dan's sister is a contract attorney; her IQ is in the genius range; she hires people to clean for her and take care of the lawn and such but she'll be over there doing her parent's menial, little tasks for them herself. Their parents are over weight. Maybe they're afraid they'll have heart attacks if they work too hard physically. I don't know."

Stephanie commiserated with Meg.

"Ron's parents are selfish like that too. I think it's the generation. It's almost as if their kids weren't asked for but since they're here they may as well make use of them. Remember, they didn't have much in the way of birth control back then."

"I've had to compromise myself throughout my marriage," Meg continued. "The family resents me for not making an effort to blend into the landscape gracefully and keep my unruly instincts to myself. I refuse to suppress my feelings and my opinions! I have to do it with Dan but I refuse to do it for the family! I refuse to live a facade! They trigger my *foot in the mouth* syndrome. When his mother calls and whines how dirty her house is; instead of saying the expected, I suggest that she hire a maid. I say under my breath, *why don't you clean it up yourself if it's soooo dirty*! Nobody's ever cleaned **my** house for **me**! I refuse to make my children my slaves. I've always taken care of my own responsibility without bothering everyone else to death with it. I just can't understand how people have the nerve to even suggest to someone or ask someone to do their dirty work for them. Don't they realize that they're announcing to the world that they're lazy or presumptuous or selfish? I had my children because I wanted them. I say allow children to be children. It's such a very short amount of time. I want my children to look back on their childhoods with fondness, not rebellion, not resentment, certainly not hatred. I'm hoping that some day they'll look back and think that we parents weren't so bad after all! I just couldn't bare it if my children were some how damaged because of something I did in raising them. Anyway, I refuse to give in to them and say *What Is Expected*. I refuse to be brainwashed! I rebel *for* Dan!"

Meg didn't reign quite as complacently under her in-law's observant and uncompromising eye as she did her own husband.

"They have no trouble dropping not so subtle hints that I'm not especially talented or brilliant," Meg continued. "I'm haunted by the fear that they might be right! They see me as the embodiment of the quote *air-headed blonde*. They manage to stoke bonfires in me. I'm surface and no depth. My palms go damp and my throat runs dry when they're around. Dan's father foils any criticism of himself by criticizing me first. He's armed with deadly wit. It's been a conscious effort on my part to keep my sense of perspective."

Steph commented, trying to console Meg.

"Are you sure these aren't just a few wrinkles and not major issues? Maybe it's a touch of paranoia you're suffering from. It's pretty common not to be fond of the in-laws. Most of the time resentment like this is more due to your feelings of not measuring up, whether it's true or not, we all feel insecure around our in-laws."

Meg sucked in her breath and paused.

"Paranoia? No, it's more than that. I'm always trying to adjust their perception of me. I take solace in the fact that others seem to like me for whom and what I am and I receive many compliments in the areas they criticize. I've learned to accept my limitations but resent being accused of something that just isn't so."

"It's a delicate family situation alright. I've never seen you so worked up over anything before. You're usually so middle-of-the-road on most subjects," Steph announced."

Meg sighed.

"My, what pressure our guys were under. They weren't valued. I wasn't valued as a child either, though. But somehow I think I turned out all right in spite of it. Of course, I had to grow up fast. It's very sad. They demanded and expected but never appreciated. I guess Dan and his brothers and sister will always be searching for love and acceptance."

Steph took a sip of her coffee and put the cup down heavily on the saucer as if her thoughts needed to be aired right away.

"I've decided I'm determined to teach Ron how to love. If I don't give up, I'll show him that he's worth loving. One thing though, there's no way to replace that parent-child love, acceptance, and nurturing."

"Why the willingness to take it? Meg asked. "I'd say because it's the only way they know; the only way they receive anything that resembles love; they have to earn it. How sad! That's one thing you don't earn. You're loved because you *are*."

"We know so little about the workings of the mind. It's always easy to be a back seat driver," Stephanie commented.

Meg paused a moment.

"I expected stimulation and excitement in my marriage but not this kind."

Steph agreed.

"Ron and I are forever wrestling each other for supremacy. I'm a woman. You're a man. *I'm not a **mere** woman.* Stop messing with my head. *I don't need you permission*! Then my hunk of male virility will kiss me on the neck and I crumble. Do with me what you will. Take care of me. Love me. Protect me, my Knight in *dull* armor. That's what I have to look out for. I should let him have it with a right cross!

Then there's the mutual need to answer the primitive call. Sometimes primitive is *good*. Anyway, I want to put the competitive battles for supremacy aside and surrender myself to him. It just feels so good after a long battle, feeling unloved, to make up and make love. I think it makes you appreciate each other more and then lovemaking is more special. I guess, because it's kind of a relief that the ugly feelings are over. It's almost like starting over with a clean slate."

Meg made the observation.

"Well, at least you two have a great sex life. Ours is good too and so far as I know, I haven't had any trouble with Dan running around on me, but then, the wife is always the last to know. That's another thing that annoys me about Dan's parents. The sexist comments, his father's immeasurable vulgarity and the way he takes adultery a little too for granted. When his son-in-law left his daughter and started dating another woman, Dan's father almost applauded him. He made comments about that woman like, *a gorgeous woman with legs that stretch into next week,* and, *I wouldn't mind getting a piece of that myself.* We all sat in stunned silence. Dan's mother just sat there under that fake dutiful smile of hers as if totally oblivious to the insensitive comments. I wanted to punch him in the mouth!" Meg said with a bitter edge in her voice. "Dan's mother annoys me as much as Dan's father, maybe more with her remote, pitiful uninvolvement! You should have heard him the time his granddaughter walked in the house wearing a hot pink, spandex halter dress. Our little niece is quite the looker and she has such a casual attitude about having a bod comparable to a thin Marilyn Monroe. Her own grandfather asked, *Are you the class vamp? You look like a slut! You make me want to feel you up.* Can you imagine a grandfather using such language talking to his granddaughter? It only typifies his callousness. No thinking person could say a thing like that! Well! That comment sent Dan's sister out of the room in tears. I guess they can't always hide their feelings. He must enjoy the thrill of combat. He's always trying to provoke the people around him. He has a razor sharp wit and he elicits strong opinions in everyone and anyone. There's always verbal sparring when he's around. Negotiation isn't generally a strong point with him. He's too used to getting his own way. He's the most spoiled human being I've ever met! I said to him before I left the room to console Dan's sister, *you'd better make sure your last will and testament is in order. Somebody's going to be pushed too far one of these days.*"

"He's quite a lightening rod for controversy, ya might say," Stephanie remarked. "It's almost hard to fathom when we find out that not everyone can be trusted or even liked. There's so much in life we're forced to accept whether we like it or not."

"I know it's supposed to be give and take but I have a fear that someone's going to take me," Meg added anxiously.

✳   ✳   ✳   ✳

Meg groped for the switch on the lamp, her eyes still swollen from sleep. The sudden brightness of the light made her eyes squint in discomfort.

Dan's sobbing sounds in his sleep woke Meg. This was becoming a habit that caused her great concern and puzzlement.

The early morning sunlight filtered through the fabric of the curtains, softening the light in the bedroom.

Dan groaned.

"Meg!" His eyes glistening near to tears marked Dan's obvious discomfort. He uttered a deep, forlorn sigh; his face bathed in sweat.

"What is torturing you so?" Meg insisted.

Dan's eyes glazed over as if he didn't hear a thing.

"Dan! What's torturing you so?" Meg repeated.

"Nothing!" Dan said with an acquired manner of hiding his irritation.

Meg had learned to respect Dan's moods but she knew that there was more to this than he was saying and she felt compelled to find out why the image of these nightmares was magnified and empowered. She sensed that Dan was dangerously on the verge of a breakdown.

"Dan, I'm not leaving this room today before I find out what's going on!" Meg insisted, her voice rather aggressive. She prepared her face with a calm, patient expression.

Dan found all his exits closed so he had to open up to her, at least partly.

Dan's expression was marked by a forlorn sadness.

"I heard the familiar scratching on the door and a shadowed figure came at me with a knife."

Dan paused.

"Again, the knife! Well?" Meg asked, groping reluctantly toward the truth.

"That's all! It was just another nightmare," Dan insisted.

There was an eerie gloom in their bedroom as it filled up with ghosts.

"What do you mean by *a familiar scratching at the door*?" Meg asked, after thinking a moment.

There was a dead silence.

Meg's tone became playfully mysterious.

"Somehow that sounds like something your father would do to keep you from having any fun!"

Dan went into a frenzy of self-hatred, torturous indecision eating him alive. He broke down and cried like a baby.

Meg's eyes were round with shock. What has she done, she wondered? Her naiveté came to the fore. Unspoken words hovered between them.

This emotional swing was enlightening. It was refreshing to catch a glimpse of vulnerability in this man she'd married, who as a rule was a hard nut to crack.

A slow flush crept over Meg's face. She didn't know what else to do but hold him and try to comfort him.

The message clearly implied trouble. A faint ripple of fear swept over her as she began to analyze the events. She came to the unpleasant realization that maybe she didn't want to know after all.

Dan finally recovered himself and blew his nose.

Meg needed to summon up courage in order to support Dan in whatever he had to say.

"I'm sorry, Meg. I guess these nightmares are getting to me worse than I thought."

Meg raised an eyebrow.

"You can't use that as an excuse." She leaned over and kissed Dan's forehead lovingly.

"I love you. What ever it is, I can take it," Meg said, hoping upon hope that she meant it.

Dan lowered his head demurely in reply.

"My sister tried to commit suicide when she was sixteen."

Half relieved and half confused, Meg hesitated a moment.

"What does that have to do with these nightmares and besides, that was so long ago."

"She was pregnant and after a few months had a miscarriage and that's when and why she tried to end her life," Dan continued.

"I'm confused," Meg stated honestly. "So your nightmares are of you wanting to cut off her boyfriend's privates?" She paused. As if a light bulb suddenly illuminated in her head, she cried out, "It wasn't you! *Incest*!"

The mere thought of it was so alarming to her that it sent her into a tailspin. She jumped up in tears.

"That's why the knife is always about to cut *your* privates off?" Meg gasped.

Dan wasted no time in trying to set her straight.

"*No!*" Dan insisted in all sincerity, trying to put his arms around her and pull her back down to the bed to comfort her.

This unfortunate train of thought had led her to the wrong conclusion. Dan wiped her tears away and kissed her back to reality.

With a shadow of sadness still on her face and the knot of tension still in her chest, Meg uttered a deep shuddering sigh.

She wanted to believe him. She *had* to believe him. She loved him so much!

Pulling their satin comforter up past their shoulders, the subject was postponed, an unspoken mutual agreement.

*   *   *   *

Meg was on her way home from dropping the kids off at school when she spotted Dan's sister's car in their parent's driveway.

Meg wondered what the old goats had connived to coerce the poor girl to be there so early.

"Good morning!" Meg called out, letting herself in the door.

She spotted Dan's sister in the kitchen on her hands and knees, scrubbing the kitchen floor.

"How demeaning for a woman with your IQ to be scrubbing floors!" Meg said.

"HI, Meg! Well, Mother's running errands because she's having company for dinner tonight and Dad has a dental appointment this morning."

Meg shook her head and rolled her eyes in her usual disapproval of this situation.

"Even the lowliest potato-peeling private gets a weekend pass once in a while!"

Meg walked over to the coffee pot. She took out the drip pan and filled it with coffee granules. After she poured the water in the coffee maker, she rolled up her sleeves and grabbed a sponge to help relieve Dan's sister of the burden of these never ending menial tasks. She wasn't doing it to help their parents. She was doing it to help Dan's sister!

Dan's sister had a radiant scrubbed cleanliness about her but her carelessly worn clothes gave her an appearance of dowdiness that begged for adornment. Clothes had no value to her. She was a restless person with lots of energy. Being a very open minded person, she didn't indulge in gossip nor did she judge people. Meg thought her to be closest to what God wants us to strive to be.

Quite unlike Dan's sister, Meg, her face contoured, blushed, and highlighted; her eyes lined with eyeliner and shadows, ambles in the door in her pelvis-first stride, her ankles wavering in the three-inch heels she always wore. She was wearing a bright turquoise satiny blouse that brought out the gold highlights in her hair. She had an unerring sense of what made her look glamorous and striking. Meg had center stage wherever she was.

"You're right, *Meg.* I do need a vacation. I feel so run down lately what with juggling my career and six kids," Dan's sister admitted freely.

"I don't doubt it!" Meg said. She was thinking *and being your parent's personal slave to use and abuse...*

While on their knees, scrubbing, Dan's sister paused for a moment, dreamy eyed. "I have this enduring image of unearthly paradise, turquoise water, and white sandy beaches. I dream of myself living in a sprawling three story house hanging on the side of a cliff overlooking the beach. I'd sit for hours watching the soothing, hypnotic waves. Ah, the resistless waves. That's what I need. I've always wanted to write a book. I'm afraid that would be the only way I could do it, though. I sure couldn't do it leading the life-style I'm living now. Maybe someday, when all my responsibility is done."

"You're so dramatic!" Meg announced. A faint ripple of pleasure swept over her. "Yes. That's what you need all right. But I bet you won't see that until you're on the *Other* Side. I'm sure of one thing, though, you've certainly earned your way to heaven. If you don't go, I'd bet none of us make it."

"Now that we're finished this wretched floor, how about breaking for coffee? Meg implored.

Without giving her a chance to back down, Meg poured two cups of coffee and fixed the kids a snack to tide them over till lunch.

The children took their snack outside so they wouldn't mess up the clean floor.

Meg sat twirling her gold hoop earring, while Dan's sister nervously stacked newspapers and straightened the table.

"Can't you sit still for two minutes?" Meg insisted in a stern tone of voice.

This perfectionist streak in Meg's sister-in-law and the whole family was like an exposed nerve to her. As far as she was concerned, they wasted so much valuable time doing nothing of any importance; busy, busy, but accomplishing nothing worthy of their time. They were very busy being busy.

Meg spotted some old photo albums on the hearth. She jumped up and crossed the room never taking her eyes off of them.

"Do you mind if I look at these albums? I love pictures, especially vintage ones." Meg's natural inquisitive nature wouldn't allow her to pass these up! This driving force of hers has gotten her into trouble in the past.

"*Oh*, look at Dan in his cowboy outfit. Ahhh! He's so cute! Look how much he looks like Tyler. Or, rather, how much Tyler looks like him. I love to take trips down Nostalgia Lane!"

Meg turned the page and was taken aback by a picture of Dan's sister in the tub with her father bathing her.

"How old are you here?" Meg asked.

"Oh, about eight, I guess. This was when Dan sneaked in and snapped the picture. See how surprised we were?"

She provided Meg with the perfect opening.

"You were **eight years old**? God! Mozart wrote his first symphony when he was eight! Hah! No offense, but I'd have thought you, of all people, would have been bathing yourself at two....and doing your own laundry and waxing floors."

Meg wasn't trying to be haughty or hostile. Her super critical streak flared a bit out of control. Meg noticed a suspicious glimmer in Dan's sister's eyes as if she'd been briefed not to divulge. *I have to pry this oyster open,* Meg thought to herself......*Oh! For pity sake.* The idea was ludicrous. *What's wrong with me?* Meg struggled to get her mind out of the gutter.

Changing the subject promptly, Meg announced that she hadn't eaten breakfast.

"Do you think your parents have a couple of cans of tuna here somewhere?" Meg asked, while searching through their pantry closet.

"Here we go. Are you hungry?"

"Sure."

"Do you like tuna salad?"

"Love it!"

Dan's sister was a mere wisp of a thing, very delicate looking and frail. She was usually a whirlwind of activity but she seemed to be dragging today as if she were forcing herself. Weariness was etched on her face.

Meg pulled out the toaster.

"Would you mind getting started on the toast while I make the salad?"

"Have you worked on any interesting cases lately?" Meg asked in an attempt to get the conversation back into gear.

"Being a contract attorney isn't exciting like a court room attorney, I'm afraid," Dan's sister replied. "My biggest challenge is the men I have to deal with. Men don't like being outflanked by women in areas that have been traditionally pursued by men. There's constant pressure. I have to be sober and dignified at all times. I don't dare let my guard down for a moment."

Meg laughed.

"Have you considered wearing leather and chains to work one day?"

There was that warm, winning smile back again. Meg was usually pretty good at getting a rise out of her one way or another.

"When I get home the first thing I do is get out of my heels and suits and don comfortable jeans or sweats. My poor hubby never sees me look dolled up! I'm just too tired at night."

Meg listened intently while she chopped celery and onions. The toast popped up. She walked across the kitchen to the refrigerator and got out the pickle relish for the tuna salad. Dan's sister continued to peel the hard-boiled eggs that she'd borrowed from the appetizer fixings.

"It's amazing how flexible and adaptable we human beings can be in the face of adverse and stressful situations."

"I always say if you can dream it you can do it," Meg said adamantly. Her black heavily mascaraed lashes looked like tarantula legs. She obviously hadn't washed it off the night before. There were bags under her eyes, obviously over tired.

Meg returned to the sink to wash her hands again. Opening the lower cabinet door, she used the bottom shelf as a step stool for her foot so she could reach the top shelf where the plates were stored.

Dan's sister refueled her coffee cup and sat down at the kitchen table.

"Men are afraid of my wit. I guess I present a *don't mess with me* attitude and stimulate their sense of competition.

Meg presented her with a sandwich before she took sandwiches out to the children sitting at their little picnic table.

Meg came inside and sat down at the table in front of her sandwich. Chewing with exquisite concentration, Meg admired Dan's sister with wide-eyed wonder. She had an overwhelming instinct for conquest and wasn't meant to be possessed, except by her parents.

"The social world has lost its allure for me. I guess I've become too serious," Dan's sister said, finishing her last bite.

"I crumble in the face of confrontation. I wish I could be regarded as a force to be reckoned with. I hate being patronized as being *nothing but a pretty woman*. People use a certain tone with me that I find humiliating. Right away, if you work hard at looking good, they're trying to prove you're an idiot," Meg declared.

"It would be a shame not to capitalize on your looks, though. Most of us would give up our mothers to have looks like yours. There's nothing wrong with using the cards you were dealt. People patronize you out of jealousy. You get your foot in the door with your looks then, sock it to them! Nobody needs people looking down on him or her. Looking down on other people gives a person a false temporary sense of security. It's human nature, unfortunately. We somehow have to learn not to worry about what the other person thinks because nothing is accomplished by it and nine times out of ten it may not be true anyway. Besides, you'll find out eventually that they're less secure than you are," Dan's sister offered.

"I love my family more than my own life, but every now and then when there's a project I'd like to work on or something I'd like to do, I feel that my whole family resents it. How dare I do anything or have anything that doesn't include them. What ever it is, I always take care of their needs first," Meg added.

Dan's sister acknowledged.

"It's in a child's nature to be selfish where their mother is concerned. Remember, a child's biggest fear is to be abandoned. So if they think for one minute that you're interested in anything or anybody else they lose a little piece of their security blanket. As far as husbands, frankly, it's pretty much the same thing. It may be selfishness in a way, but doesn't it make you feel loved and needed? Imagine how horrible it would be if they didn't care!"

Meg shook her head.

"Yes, I guess so. I like the way you look at it."

"Times are changing. It's hard for them to change along with someone else's rules. I guess we'll live our lives in transition. Our generation will do the suffering, I think. At least, we're preparing our children for equality. Our daughters will have a better chance. Maybe their generation will wipe out the myth that women are only here to forfeit. I guess the reason I resent this treatment so much is because Dad spoiled me when I was growing up. Dad indulged me in just about anything I wanted. If I wanted a real feather bed, he'd have found a way to get it for me," Meg's wise sister-in-law continued.

This statement surprised Meg. She didn't see any of this.

Meg gave her a challenging gaze.

"I could have sworn that he was the one who was spoiled."

Meg changed the subject before her sharp tongue offended her.

"Poor Dan! He's been having horrible nightmares lately. He wakes up in a cold sweat and sobbing his heart out."

"That's funny!" Dan's sister commented, "A while back, an acquaintance recommended a psychic to help me figure out a recurring dream I'd had since childhood. I was bitter about my divorce. My career was suffering. My kids were driving me mad. I had babysitting problems. Every man I met disgusted me. What was I losing by going to a fortuneteller? Well! She was a psychic who came highly recommended. After all, the police departments use them. My skepticism started to melt away as soon as I met her. I liked her right away. She was not at all what I'd expected. There was no crystal ball or black veil! She really did have an aura about her. She not only described my family with startling accuracy but she also spoke of my recurring dream in precise detail. In my dream, my parents were walking at a fast pace ahead of me. I was a little girl trying desperately to catch up. I watched them being swallowed up by the clouds. The woman looked me straight into my teary, shocked eyes. She told me, *you had no one to go to. This is the source of desperation and it's all behind you now. The unhappiest part of your life is over.* Things started getting better after that and I haven't had that dream since. The next thing I knew, I was in love and married again. My career took off and I found a trustworthy sitter that I'd like to adopt."

Meg shifted in her seat. Her intuition became acute. She thought, *the ravages that a sense of insecurity causes when there's nothing that can be done about it, the absence of moral support, working without a net.*

"You, the queen of positive thinking?" Meg began, endlessly trying to dig out the truth. "Everyone needs to be cherished and loved. If we don't get it in childhood, then we tend to search for it endlessly throughout our lives and are never satisfied. I believe that that's why a lot of people run from one person to another, never committing, only using their bodies for a temporary fix. It's very sad what parents do to a child."

Meg noticed tears welling in her sister-in-law's eyes. She knew it! There's more to this story.

Meg's sister-in-law looked into her coffee cup trying to hide her tears.

"I just needed a little reassurance at my peek of uncertainty."

This only supplied Meg with more ammunition to confirm the definite possibility of a deep-rooted family problem.

"My parents have always tried to give us every luxury possible."

Meg was thrown by the enormity of that statement. *Oh! We're back defending them again!*

"Have you watched any good movies lately?" Meg asked, trying to change the subject.

"No, I try to stay away from TV as much as I can. It depresses me. We don't go to the theatre much either. We attend a dinner theatre every now and then. If we didn't have TV we wouldn't know all the horrors in the world, all of the ineptness, perverseness and greediness. Other countries are jealous of our rich, free America of great opportunity. Our air and water are poisoned. People are playing musical families, musical houses; who belongs to whom? There's the constant threat of power-hungry insanity trying to torture our country out of jealousy. We can't trust our leaders anymore. No one does their job with pride anymore; no one seems to care enough. I look at my children and wonder why I brought them into this world. My precious children, their sweetness, their innocence brought into a world that's about to be gobbled up by demons. It's unfair! They haven't done anything to deserve this. I remember Mom saying how sorry she was for people who didn't have children."

"Yes, I remember that. Then she followed with, *who's going to take care of them when they're old?*" *Meg concluded with a sneer.*

"Need a refuel?" Meg asked in the tense silence. Meg walked across the kitchen straight to the coffee pot, turning toward Dan's sister.

"No, thanks. I have to start the chicken."

"You're cooking the meal too? Are you going to stay and serve in a maid's uniform too?" Meg asked with a sharp look. Meg's mind was racing with confusion and questions. With a sudden decisiveness, her nostrils flared, Meg accused crossly, "It's the guilt! Isn't it? It's the guilt that makes you cluck over your parents like a mother hen."

Meg's sister-in-law pivoted around towards her, expectantly, encouraging her to go on, unnerved by all of this sudden attention she was receiving.

Meg concluded triumphantly and confided in a tense voice.

"I'm sorry! Dan told me about your harrowing ordeal when you were sixteen." Her plight gave her center stage in Meg's heart.

Dan's sister, looking rather grim, and her shoulders drooping in dejection, didn't have to reach very far. Her ill fortune was embalmed in her memory. She lowered her eyes away from Meg's challenging gaze. Feeling put on the spot, Meg's overbearing enthusiasm was sometimes hard to take.

"It's painful for me to dig up all that unpleasant adolescence again No, I'm not serving my parents out of guilt. I don't want to end up a zombie like my mother!" She all but blurted out a little prematurely before her thought process had a chance to correct the hasty ill-chosen words. Her eyes were sad with barely restrained tears.

Meg had never heard her sister-in-law speak ill of her parents in any way before.

"I got pregnant. In my third month, I was setting the table for dinner when I got an excruciating pain in my side. By the time I managed to get to the bathroom, it was too late. In the flow of blood in my panties was a perfectly formed little being, so minuscule, but so real. I washed off the blood and held it in my hands and marveled at what my body had created. I grieved and cried half out of relief of not having to deal with my problem and the other half because I already loved my creation. The baby would have been my very own to love and cherish; someone to love and someone to love me."

"Oh! GOD!" Meg cried out, a little too loudly. She put her comforting and forgiving arms around her sister-in-law as she shivered with the reality of the memory.

"You won't tell *anyone* about this. Will you?" Dan's sister begged.

"Of course not!" Meg said slightly indignant. Her cheeks flushed at the thought that she would think she'd blab such a thing.

Alert to her discomfort, Meg made an attempt to move the conversation on.

"If we jump to conclusions to fuel our desire for excitement, well, haste makes waste, as the saying goes. Yes, the story of my life." Meg found it difficult to talk to her sister-in-law sometimes. Her super intelligence intimidated Meg a little. Her clandestine behavior was arousing suspicion in her as if there were more to her than she was letting on.

"My hubby and I are in an arguing mode lately. Usually, I get panicky if I think I'm losing him, but I'm just too tired to put the energy into worrying about it. I try to keep the four F's in mind, forgive, forget, fulfill and flourish," Dan's sister announced, changing the subject.

Meg offered her a cunning, little half-grin.

"I can think of one more *F* to add to your list!"

"Oh, Meg! Is that all you can think of?"

After she received her playful reprimand, Meg added with great interest.

"I recently read an article that some experts say it's stress, not boredom that kills passion. A love affair begins when two people are *willing* to fall in love. My opinion is, the way to a man's soul is a good blowjob at least once a day! He'll wear a smile all day and come home for more. That's all they seem to care about anyway. I think they think that's all we women are good for! Why do you think that is, when we expect so much more between a man and a woman? I'll answer my own question. For the same reason a tomcat licks himself, because he *can!*"

"On a serious note, what you get back is a reflection of what you give," Dan's sister interrupted.

Meg begged to differ.

"Are you sure you're living in the right century? I don't find that true at all. My friend, Stephanie, gives, and forgives, but her husband treats her like a dog! I think that some men just don't know how to love, period. This guy has a problem. Everything has to revolve around him."

A car door slammed. Meg disappeared into the dining room in search of trays and platters.

Meg's sister-in-law was standing over the sink when her father walked through the door. Without a wasted step, he approached her from behind and with a peck on the back of the neck, he reached around her and cupped her breasts with his hands, then gave them a quick squeeze. He had an unhealthy glimmer in his eyes and an excited flush in his face. Dan's sister flinched with an expression of horror and disgust which turned into a sheepish, helpless, dutiful half-smile. He breathed with an unrepentant gratified sigh, "How about a little something to grace my declining years with?"

He plucked up a cherry from the fruit bowl and popped it into his mouth on his way out of the room.

Breathing deeply, in the tense silence, to counter the unpleasant truth that lodged painfully in her chest, she turned suddenly to see Meg's mortified expression, who'd obviously witnessed what'd just happened.

Meg could hardly suppress a gasp. This unanticipated act shook her to her very core. She raised her eyebrows, her eyes widened inquiringly, and thinking that *they're going to need an awful big hat to keep this under!*

Dan's sister sucked in her breath, momentarily thrown off balance and stood tall, in spite of the burden of concealment expanding in her chest. Discomfort tinged with shame swept over her. Her light blue eyes dulled.

"He protected me from so much. If I wanted anything, he'd find a way to get it for me. He put me through college, not the others." She rambled on in her defense.

That incomparable Lane smokescreen! Meg was thinking. Meg rolled her eyes upward in bemusement.

"How convenient!" She said with a touch too much emphasis on the word. With a simple tone of voice she could reveal her disapproval.

With a sudden decisiveness, she threw her head back, her nostrils flared. Meg recoiled, her face taut with anticipation. She spouted in an uncomfortable rush of words before she managed to stop herself, "I mean, I don't think I could ever…." She couldn't bring herself to finish.

Feeling a glimmer of fear, Dan's sister flushed and grew uncomfortable under the probing scrutiny. She went into a tirade of self-hatred and cut in indignantly, all her defenses going up.

"What do you want me to say?" Her reluctance to relinquish her true feelings was obvious. She needed time to think.

Meg could have bitten off her tongue, with sudden diminished confidence. Sadness crept into her eyes as she choked up but Meg's natural inquisitive nature wouldn't allow her to back down.

"I'm beginning to feel like a super-sleuth. I'm sorry!" Meg eyed her curiously and slipped her arm around her waist in a gesture of sympathy. Dan's sister snuggled against her as she hid her face in her hands to hide her painful tears.

"Sorry", came her muffled voice. "It's like lesions in the skin that won't heal! How do you explain a human heart?"

"Why no hostility? Why didn't you tell your mother? There must have been *some* protection for you," Meg asked.

"Feelings of guilt and humiliation kept me quiet. See how people act? What was your reaction? Everybody thinks they could have handled the situation better. Nobody knows what he or she'd do in a given situation unless it happened to him or her. Outside looking in, it always looks so simple. ***Nothing is simple!*** Just try living it once! I didn't want to be the cause of Mom and Dad getting a divorce and worse, I was afraid Mom wouldn't have done anything about it. As it turned out, I was right!" Dan's sister confessed sadly, the words choked in her throat, and then came painful tears.

"Mom walked in on us once. She turned a blind eye and backed out of the room. To this day she's never said one word about it."

Meg shook her head in disbelief, further confirming her dislike and disrespect for Dan's mother! Meg tightened her comforting hold as she cried.

Meg urged her to get it all out as she spoke of the sad, gritty details of her harrowing tale of her ordeal.

Reconnecting the painful memory circuits she began cautiously at first but with increasing fervor.

"You're the only person I've ever confided in. No one knows any of this. It started with his whispering obscene remarks, always waiting for the vulnerable moment in which to pounce. He can't stand ineptness in people. His super critical remarks and his perfectionism are hard to live with. It's natural to love your father and to want acceptance so it's easy to confuse this with sex. When we were kids we couldn't do enough to please him. Even if we knew in our hearts he was unfair or wrong, we still tried desperately to please him. It's so important for a child to feel accepted and loved. You know that! Even though we knew he wasn't capable of being pleased we still kept trying anyway. Sex seemed to be the only thing I did to please him. It was the only thing I've ever done that actually made him smile. Dad had a way of wearing you down; of eating away at your self-esteem and making every day you woke up a living hell. It's no wonder Mom's the way she is. I think she just exists until her final peace comes. He always felt the need to malign our sensibility and our sensitivity. He always has and still does accuse me of flaunting my bod."

Meg thought to herself in her special talent for analyzing everyone and every situation, how what her sister-in-law was saying explained so much about her character. This must be the reason she dresses down and her guilt probably forces her to wait on her parents in that never-ending quest for love and acceptance.

"May I borrow your strength?" Dan's sister continued.

"*You're* much stronger than I am! I never would have survived incest. I can't even imagine it," Meg declared.

Dan's sister moved quickly.

"His tone of voice always carried a note of warning."

A guilty smile flitted across her face.

"He cheapened and shamed me. As long as I was amenable to what he wanted my life went along very well, not only that it insured less pressure and pain for the rest of the family."

Meg raised her eyebrows and smiled understandingly.

"You certainly don't lack a sense of purpose. I guess this is where your protective instinct got started."

There was a dignity about her in spite of her demeaned life. It goes to show you that this incest thing can happen to anybody.

Meg could picture her father-in-law prowling the room. He certainly did fit the part. He was such a sleazebag! She flashed back to that morning with her Dan, to her moaning and pulling him down to her, limbs entwined, their hair plastered against their heads in wet curls. So much love and now to hear this. Meg just couldn't imagine making love to her father. Why! She couldn't even picture her parents *doing IT*! Parents were like a whole different sex, a whole different entity, and whole special, untouchable, unique beings.

"It's worse on the soul than it is on the body," Dan's sister divulged, during this crisis of conscience.

Meg collared her.

"Has your soul healed any since then?"

"I'm tough as nails! I can't and won't regress into dependency. No one will ever walk on me again! We're all a product of our past," Dan's sister declared.

"Good for you!" Meg blurted. "Men like that should have their penises cut off and pickled in alcohol! You can't always blame wickedness on a traumatic childhood. He'll have his come-upance sooner or later. The sins of parents; does any child escape?

"It was hard to maintain a semblance of balance, mother, wife, daughter, servant, care-giver, peace-maker...," Meg's sister-in-law added.

"All people are fascinated by the dark side of humanity. I hope you don't hate me for asking, but, was the baby you lost your father's?" Meg asked, mournfully.

Dan's sister paused a moment, expecting the question sooner or later, then confessed with tear-filled eyes.

"Yes! You have no idea what that was like. There was no sense of safety, nowhere to run, nowhere to go, and no one to go to........ .I'm sure my parents thought they were doing the right thing at the time."

Meg thought angrily, *there she goes again!*

CHAPTER 6

▼

Stephanie was spending entirely too much time worrying about her brother, Rick and his wife, Bianca and their *mutual friend, Danielle*, not to mention that she noticed a change in Ron. Everything was getting on Steph's nerves. STRESS< STRESS<STRESS

*   *   *   *

Ron and Stephanie met Dan and Meg at a new restaurant that had just opened.

"You're only fifteen minutes late. Don't tell me that your car is actually running?" Ron announced, looking at his watch. He couldn't wait to give Meg a hard time the minute she and Dan were within hearing range.

Meg apologized.

"Sorry! Our sitter was late."

Ron rushed to Meg's chair before Dan got a chance. As he pulled her chair out for her, he whispered in her ear.

"You look good enough to eat!"

Ron saw Steph still trying to get her sweater off so he helped her. Then as a second thought actually pulled her chair out for her to sit down.

"If I were married to you, I wouldn't have time to eat. How do you find the strength to pull yourself away from this bod every morning, Dan?" were the first words out of Ron's mouth.

Steph interrupted before Ron embarrassed her any further.

"The menu looks wonderful! Look at all the seafood dishes they have."

The waitress approached them.

"Are you ready to order?"

"We'll start with drinks. My wife will have a pina colada without alcohol and I'll have a glass of your Merlot. I'll bet my girlfriend will have a Margarita, on the rocks with salt, right?" Ron announced taking control as always.

"That's right!" Meg replied.

Ron looked at the waitress with an over confident grin.

"See? What did I tell you? I know my women."

Ron's eyes went to Dan.

"White Russian for you?"

"That will work."

After a moment to gather his thoughts, not quite sure how to take Ron's teasing, Dan announced.

"Our sitter is a hot looking little thing."

With a swift kick under the table, Meg scolded.

"You just keep those peepers in their sockets, if you know what's good for you!"

"Yeah, Dan, get back on your leash!" Ron said, sarcastically.

Fixing a stern eye on Ron, Steph then turned her attention to Meg quickly. Steph recognized with such clarity that the subject was cold and closed.

"How's Tyler getting along with his new teacher?"

Meg answered with wide eyes, as if expecting something to come of Ron's last comment.

"He's doing much better with this one. He seems to like her a lot. She's younger too. I guess he feels he can relate to her."

Steph complained, trying to camouflage her embarrassment and to keep the conversation going without the men.

"I'm having trouble with the boys lately handing me a lot of back-talk. I can't believe these are the same precious little babies whose diapers I changed and rocked to sleep. They can be so nasty and belligerent."

Ron growled in a fierce voice.

"You don't discipline them right! You let them walk all over you! It's your own fault!"

Steph's face turned red with the stinging criticism. She sighed heavily and her mouth tightened in aggravation as she lashed back.

"Don't *complain about the snow on your neighbor's sidewalk when your own doorstep is so* slippery. What gives you the Lordly right to criticize me?"

Ron retorted in a disgruntled and hateful tone of voice.

"Because as long as you're my wife, **I am** your **Lord** and **Master**! You do as you're told and keep that fat mouth of yours shut! Don't you dare talk back to me!" Ron commanded.

Stephanie stiffened in her chair. She was dumbstruck! Her embarrassment and humiliation from the unwarranted remarks brought a lump to her chest that caused a sudden shortness of breath. She dare not say another word for fear of what was to be next.

Discomfort swept over Meg and Dan in the awkward silence. After a three minute embarrassed loss for words, the foursome was relieved when the waitress brought their drinks.

Dan started to explain an x-rated movie he'd just watched.

".....and they showed everything. These guys were gang-banging this poor girl and the things they did to her made me cringe."

Steph confided, finally swallowing her pride and getting up enough nerve to open her mouth again for the sake of salvaging the evening.

"I used to have fantasies when I was young, before I ever even kissed a guy, that I'd been captured by a handsome, hot stud. He had me tied up and my blouse was ripped, exposing most of one breast but I couldn't cover myself because I was tied to a tree. You can tell how young I must have been from how innocent the fantasy was."

Before anyone had a chance to comment, Ron objected loudly.

"Why would **you** have a fantasy? As if you're so hot-to-trot! You never want it any more! Do you know how many times we've done it in the last two weeks? Once! I've kept track. That's all right. You're a turn-off anyway. I can't handle *fat*, pregnant or not." His voice was angry and he made sure the whole restaurant heard him! He turned to Meg and Dan and bragged.

"I never tell her I love her anymore."

Painful tears welled in Steph's eyes and her mouth tightened with resentment. In her coldest tone, she replied, trying to salvage some semblance of dignity.

"Any fool can condemn and complain and **most fools do**! Your mouth is always open just waiting for the inevitable big, fat foot of yours to fly straight into it!"

Her heart took a dive straight to her feet. Trying desperately to hold back the tears, her defiance fully in tact, Steph protested shrilly.

"Maybe if you pursued *me* once in a while instead of lying flat on your back, with your eyes closed, enjoying the luxury of my complete attention, you'd have sex more often. Maybe I get tired of playing the initiator. Maybe I get tired of you playing hard-to-get. Maybe I get tired of you pretending I'm someone else. Maybe I'd like a little love and kindness once in a while. There's more to love than sex. Love is as love does!"

The dam could no longer hold back the painful tears. She tried so hard to tough it out and be strong and witty in front of her friends.

The tears started to trickle down her cheeks before she managed to get her last words out. She was so choked up she could barely be heard.

"As my luck would have it, I'll be paying for the rest of my life because your sperm has such a good sense of direction!"

Stephanie sprang up from the table, her anger spiraling, and managed to make her way through tear filled eyes to the lady's lounge, where she no longer had to bother to suppress her tears.

The door opened. Feeling an overwhelming pang of sympathy, Meg put her arms around Stephanie's shoulders in a comforting gesture.

"You were set up. That was obvious. I wonder how long it took him to plan that scene." Meg said in absolution.

There was weariness in Steph's face as she sobbed, heart-brokenly.

"Why does he always choose to humiliate me in front of people like that? I never know we have a problem until we're with other people, then he attacks." Steph paused a few moments contemplating the embarrassment of returning to her table.

"I'm too ashamed to go back in there. Please! Go ahead. Eat without me. Then leave."

"No!" We'll wait for you. No one noticed."

Stephanie confided in a soft, despairing voice.

"Ron knows sex inside and out but he knows nothing of intimacy. He leaves the most important things in life to chance. I'm always the last on his list of priorities, when he's first on my list. In fact he insists on it! He's so adroit at handling people, controlling everything around him, which in most ways that's a plus. I don't know what I'd do without him because he makes me feel safe. I know that what ever comes up good or bad, I know he'll handle it. He's a man who can speak knowledgably on almost any subject. And argue either side and win. In fact, he's given credit for an ability out of proportion to what he really possesses, out of the power of persuasion." She paused a moment to blow her sniffles away.

"He's full of courage and confidence and he bristles with pride, all of which I admire in him. It annoys me that he's such a social animal. He lives to impress people with scads of abilities and talents and he seems to need the praise he receives from people that he helps. He'll do anything anyone asks of him. Frankly, I think he loves the reflection of himself in their eyes. I guess I'm jealous because no matter what I need or want, it's put on the back burner and maybe if I'm a good little girl I might get it in ten years, when I no longer need it. He's superficial and he craves superficial. He loves anything that looks good on the surface but down to feelings, he knows nothing about. See how he thinks he needs a mediator? How he chooses public places to display his disappointment in me? Maybe he's afraid of *me*. Hah! Wouldn't that be a laugh?"

A tremor snaked its way up Steph's body.

"I hate it that I think so poorly of him. I love him! But I can't stand him!

This deafening contrast unnerved Meg.

Meg reprimanded shrilly.

"I can't believe you! You remind me of Dan's sister; your never ending forgiveness and understanding of louses!"

Steph took a tissue from her purse to dry her tears with.

"I know Ron can't help it. I know Ron's a good person underneath that chauvinistic façade of his. He's confused and afraid of his true feelings, that is to say, *if* he *has* true feelings! There's always something boiling and stewing inside him."

Steph took a moment and regained her composure.

"Well, I guess we'd better get back to our meals before our guys leave us," Steph announced.

"Good girl!" Meg said with relief.

Steph smiled through her swollen red eyes and sat down beside Ron.

Ron leaned over and whispered in Steph's ear, without possessing the slightest notion of having caused any hostility or pain.

"Are you happy now? You made a fool out of yourself again!

❋   ❋   ❋   ❋

Stephanie made an appointment with Whitney to see if there was something she could do to pull herself out of her slump that she'd managed to slip into.

"Hello, Whitney."

"Come in and sit down, Stephanie. How may I help you?" Whitney asked in her professional tone of voice.

"To get to the point, I never feel well. I mean, physically, I'm fine but I feel miserable all the time. I can't explain it exactly. Sometimes I feel like my nerve endings are exposed to the air, as if I just can't make myself comfortable. I can sit down and cry over nothing and everything and feel totally lost. I feel sorry for myself and I *really* hate that! It isn't fair to the kids. I have to force myself to carry on my duties but I feel totally drained emotionally. You know how on television drug addicts look when they're coming off drugs? They look like they're going to lose their minds? Well that's kind of the way I feel. I keep waiting for it to go away but time doesn't seem to be working its magic. I've got to feel better soon. I have another baby coming. I keep telling myself I have so much to be thankful for but why can't I appreciate it? There seems to be no joy in my life. I feel that I'm capable of being a better person, but I don't know how. I can't seem to talk myself into self-approval, no matter what I do.

Steph paused for a moment and sighed heavily.

"Sometimes, I'm sure Ron hates me!"

Tears filled Steph's eyes. A moment passed without a word.

"He seems to resent me as if he's sorry he married me. I can't bear it! I find myself constantly defending myself and trying to convince him I'm not that horrible creature he describes."

Whitney tried to fill in with a word of encouragement.

"Of course, one suggestion may be that you're pregnant. Feeling depressed is quite normal and it may pass when the baby comes."

Steph shook her head.

"Yes, Ron especially hates me when I'm pregnant. I turn him off. I'm glad *something* turns him off! It's just a shame it has to be that. It's his whole attitude towards women in general that really scares me. At first I thought he was kidding. He enjoys shocking people and getting a rise out of them. I realize now that he's not kidding; he's dead serious! He makes derogatory remarks and comments about women in general then looks at me with such hatred in his eyes. He treats me as if he owns me not as his partner in life. He's so critical of me. I never do anything to please him and anything that goes wrong in his life he points his finger at me and blames me. He not only insults me privately but also rips me to shreds in front of our friends. I'm afraid to go anywhere with him any more. Then he accuses me of being an anti-social bitch. I don't dare open my mouth or I'll be in big trouble for that!"

Whitney took out a piece of paper and wrote as she spoke.

"I'm making you a list to follow. Your problem, I'm afraid, may take years to correct. Here's a list of your entitlements: I deserve the right, #1—to be respected.

> #2—to make mistakes and not be forever hounded for them.
> #3—to say NO.
> #4—to have my own opinions and my own feelings.
> #5—to protest unfair treatment, criticism and judgment.
> #6—not to have to take responsibility for anyone else's problems or unreasonable behavior.
> #7—not to allow him to humiliate me, nor control me, nor raise his voice to me."

Whitney folded the paper and handed it to Steph.

"I suggest you keep this in a safe place and refer to it often until it's ingrained in your mind enough to become your natural habit."

"Be prepared for the inevitable next confrontation with comments like, *I refuse to hear you when you raise your voice to me, or I'll discuss it with you when you've calmed down, or If you can't talk to me with love and respect, please don't talk to me at all, I will NOT accept your aspersions on my character, or People who care about me don't speak to me that way.*"

Stephanie continued.

"I feel so guilty talking about him this way. I feel so disloyal, but at the same time I feel like I'm going to explode if I don't get it out! Sometimes he can be so sweet and thoughtful, so loving, then without warning, completely out of the blue; he goes into a rage if *anything* gets in his way, which always results in aspersions on my character and the fact that he's miserable in our marriage. During his vicious outbursts, kicking in doors, running his fist through walls, trying to emulate *The Hulk,* he has actually grabbed a door and ripped it off its hinges with his bare hands! I learned a long time ago that I can't get away from him, that nothing stops him when he's after me and, for heaven's sake, don't ever close a door on him to shut out his painful words! During the fight I actually believe his ugly words and cruel, heartless remarks. Then afterward, in retrospect I realize not a word was true so in that knowledge and realization, I chalk it up to one more hurdle that was jumped over and somehow survived. It's like living with a time bomb. We creep around and walk softly so as not to dare disturb the air currant for fear that bomb will explode. I just need some sort of validation, something to make me feel that I'm worth something in this life."

Whitney sat back, brought her hands together and steepled her fingers, contemplating her next maneuver to guide Stephanie back onto a safe and healthy road to recovery.

Whitney advised.

"You can't accept the responsibility for his ugly behavior and you shouldn't try to justify it," Whitney advised. "You have to stand strong. You must not allow him to know how he affects you. You mustn't allow him to get away with believing that you are to forfeit yourself and be compliant to his demands. You shouldn't let him think you're dependent on him for your emotional security. That's his ultimate goal, *control*."

Stephanie's eyes started to tear.

"I'm embarrassed to tell you about this but I don't know who else to confide in, lately. I've been shut down sexually. I find it hard to make love after being ripped to shreds being told how ugly I am and worthless I am. Feeling unloved, only *used*, I feel that making love is so hypocritical. Now, he's telling everyone I'm a cold BITCH! He pressures me with, *well, if I can't get IT here, I'll just GET IT elsewhere!* Such ugly threats! I used to be aggressive in bed and even insatiable at times. It's a vicious cycle. The more pressure and the more he makes me feel inadequate, the less aggressive I am which in turn invites more brutal hostilities from him. *I play the part! I perform! I go through the motions!* I feel like a prostitute any more! I'm servicing him, only I don't have the advantage of his departure after an hour. *I just want to disappear.*"

"Has he ever hurt you in bed?" Whitney asked cautiously.

There was a moment's pause before Stephanie answered shyly, "Yes. He deliberately hurts me, then when I object or show discomfort, he has the audacity to roll over and let out an annoyed sigh as if I'm to blame!"

Whitney reached out and patted Stephanie's hand.

"He's taking out his hostilities on you by inflicting physical pain through sex. It's normal for you to feel this way. If you allow yourself to be pushed into sexual sacrifice in which Ron's needs take precedence over yours, certainly, your going to be shut-down sexually."

Stephanie continued.

"I asked Ron to tell me how I could be better so he would be happier with me. Naturally, he was more than happy to oblige, but the more I give the more he wants. No matter how I adjust or what I do, or don't do, he's never satisfied. If something pleases him on Friday, that very same thing turns him into a rage on Saturday!

Every time I don't jump at his command, he screams at me that I'm selfish and that I'm to be subservient to him. He's screamed at me, believing every word, so many times, *your soul purpose on this earth is to see to it that I'm happy! It doesn't matter what you have to do or what you have to give up!* **You see to it that I'm happy!**"

Whitney intervened quickly, before Stephanie moved on.

"Once you allow him to attack your self-worth and allow yourself to be demeaned, you're leaving yourself wide open for more. Once you accept the routine from rage to apology, you're setting yourself up for more pain and it could get progressively worse! Your emotions have been on an emotional roller coaster. You *have* to get off."

"Yes! You're right! I know!" Stephanie replied, "he's just like Dr. Jekyll and Mr. Hyde. After his violent rages and abuse, he'll come to me and apologize. He acts like nothing ever happened. He's happy as a clam and I'm still feeling the pain of all those stinging, ugly words. They ring in my ears forever after. He'll tell me how much he loves me and he can't live without me. He needs me so much and I'm the most important person in the world to him. I'm the best in bed he's ever had like it's a sport or a marathon. He sometimes even sends me flowers with the most beautifully written love letter and so heart rendering, I just shake my head in total disbelief that this is the same man who was just destroying me a few hours ago."

Whitney interrupted again, sounding a little agitated.

"May I interrupt a moment? Just because you need another person for your survival doesn't mean you love him or her. You love each other when you are capable of living apart. Then you may *choose* to live together. It's a matter of necessity, not love. You choose to love."

Stephanie frowned. She didn't want to hear the last comment. Those apologies were all she had to hang on to.

"He'll buy me expensive presents, things I wouldn't spend the money on, as long as it was *his* idea. Asking for them wouldn't do the trick. He'll hand a thousand dollars to anyone who asks for it and gives them the impression that he didn't care if they never paid him back. Yet with me, he resents me touching anything of his. If I use his copy machine, it's *what do **you** need to copy? How much paper did you waste? You can't use anything of mine without asking!* If I buy anything, no matter how trivial or inexpensive, it's, *what do you need that for? Did you get my permission? Take it back! You don't need it!* Yet, he'll go out on a whim and buy anything he wants no matter how much it costs. He'll drop $5,000.00 on a toy for himself. But I'm not allowed to open my mouth because it's *his* money and he'll do anything he wants with it. Of course, before I exchanged my paying job for my twenty four hour a day unpaid job full of exhausting hours of unappreciated, thankless, endless chores, I made more money than Ron did! This is so demeaning.

"You're describing misogynistic behavior. A misogynist is a man who hates women. He acts as if he hates the very woman he claims to love. He causes this woman tremendous pain. Unable to recognize how he orchestrates his own problems, he sees you as the enemy. His fear of losing you, his possessiveness, his need to control, his whole distorted reality all make him dependent on you. No matter how powerful he appears, he's only powerful when he's controlling you."

"How is Ron's relationship with his parents? What kind of parents were they to him? Has he ever confided in you about his childhood?" Whitney asked.

Stephanie grew tense.

"I blame a lot of problems Ron has on his parents. That's why I tend to forgive him so easily and let things go. He comes from a nineteenth century style family, run by the typical tyrannical father figurehead, with the typical subservient wife. Women are to live their lives suffering and sacrificing or they're worthless. His mom actually controlled the whole family in the way that she needed to *keep the peace* by seeing to it that no one rocked the boat. Everyone had to bow to the *Master*."

Whitney flashed Stephanie a knowing, understanding smile, as if what Steph had said was expected.

"You're right, Steph. It's *very* sad. His mother has given Ron this enormous sense of entitlement, that he shouldn't have to endure any undue aggravation, frustration, or irritation that the wife is to run interference for him. He fully expects to get what he wants, when he wants it. After all, that's the way his father lived. He expects the same treatment. When a mother over controls her son and is constantly rescuing him, she sets him up to believe that he can't survive without a woman."

Stephanie exclaimed, "It must be a pretty good life when you think you're GOD! What really gets to me is that everyone *allows* him to believe it. Why doesn't someone put him in his place? Why do they **let him do it**?"

Whitney smiled at Stephanie, a little stunned by her quick retort, and continued, "Yes, this creates an unreasonable sense of dependency, which causes him to see you as having the same power to annoy him, frustrate him, and make him feel weak. Ron's lack of confidence is a result of his mother's dominance over him.

He was ruled by his mother all his life and he isn't about to take anything off of *you*."

Pausing a moment to collect her thoughts, Stephanie shifted her weight in her chair and crossed her legs.

"He makes me feel guilty if I visit my parents or if I help someone do something or even if I leave the house to do errands. He acts as if I'm neglecting him. When he knows I've made plans he'll find some excuse or deliberately make an appointment for me so I can't do it! I'm *not* his *Mommy*. He doesn't need me to hold his hand."

Whitney tried to explain.

"He thinks he does. The *good wife* is someone who focuses all her attention on him. Anything less than total attentiveness to him brings back all the old feelings of neediness. He actually feels you are depriving him. Because of Ron's unfair neediness during his childhood, as an adult he cannot be bothered with even the most minor annoyances, which result in his rage. It sounds like his mother probably neglected him to do for his father. He's punishing his mother through you. All of the controlling behaviors he uses on you come from his out of proportion fear of abandonment. He's trying to keep control of you by destroying your self-esteem and self-confidence, so that you can never leave him and he'll be safe. Age-wise, he's an adult, but psychologically he's still a frightened child in need."

"I know he is. I really do! I've always known that those parents of his had to cause damage! Now, I have to pay for their mistakes for the rest of my life. Life just isn't fair! I wonder if after they finally relieve this earth of their presence, maybe Ron would change."

Whitney admitted.

"That's hard to say." Pausing a moment to make a note, she continued, "There are many men suffering from this disorder and many women like you who love them. It takes a *very special* kind of person to be willing to put so much effort into trying to salvage a relationship like this, Stephanie. This disorder is the cause of a lot of divorces."

After a long reflective moment, Steph sighed.

"Sometimes, I think Ron's a lock that has no key."

Whitney gave Steph a list of things to do.

"I'm also giving you a number of a good support group. I strongly suggest that you check this group out. This problem is more common than you think and these women may be able to give you some pointers and just having someone else to share it with can do so much to help you cope. Remember, you must start your sentences with, *I really appreciate it when you...,I love it when you...,It was nice of you..., Thank you for...,*Do you see how this could work? Try never to accuse like, *why can't you...or you did this or that...*If he sees he's not able to push your buttons any more, maybe things will settle down to a little more of an equal relationship. However, if your efforts don't improve your marriage, for your sake and even the children's you might consider getting out of the relationship. Start every morning with the thought, *I'm expecting good things to happen today.* Write it down. Post it on your bathroom mirror. It's not the problem that steals our joy; it's *how* we handle the problem. Aggressively *see positive*, not negative. Trust me. Negative never helps. In fact it can become a habit. So, it's better to get in the habit of being positive than negative. Negativity only serves to keep you in turmoil. Don't relive the problem or bad experience in your mind. Change your thought process *on purpose. Expect* good things. Don't accept anything else. Form a habit of *expecting* good things in life. Have a *glad heart* not a *sad heart.*

OPERABLE
WORD
E X P E C T

Keep in mind that it's he who has the problem, not you.

DIGNITY, INTEGRITY, RESPECT

✳   ✳   ✳   ✳

Holding her head high, heeding Whitney's words, Steph decided to put her foot down and demand respect. Ron's self-serving attitude was unbearable, unfair and **unacceptable**! Comments like, *I don't go over there to visit Dan! I can't stand Dan! I go over to see Meg!* needed to stop!

Stephanie decided to have a heart-to-heart with Meg. She made an anguished plea for help to salvage her marriage to Ron.

Steph confided.

"Meg, my intuition tells me that Ron is falling in love with you."

Meg assured her.

"You're way out of line! You're imagining things! We're just friends, like you and I are."

Steph tensed up feeling that Meg was taking offense.

"I just don't think it looks right that Ron's over here all the time when Dan isn't here! I'd appreciate it if you would ask him not to come over any more when Dan isn't here."

Meg's expression turned into a scowl. She insisted.

"What do you think we're doing over here with the kids running in and out? How can you think such a thing?"

Meg put her fists on her hips, indignantly as she recoiled.

"I enjoy our little talks."

Steph was stunned at Meg's reaction. She had to wonder just whose friend she was! Steph was growing exceedingly more resentful.

In an attempt to co-exist without any further confrontation between them, Steph dropped the subject, hoping that Meg would eventually feel remorseful after giving it a little more thought. As jealous as Meg and Dan were of each other, Steph couldn't comprehend Meg's reasoning, especially after all the things Steph had turned her head on! If the tables were turned, *well,* there's no way that would ever have gotten started!

＊　　　＊　　　＊　　　＊

Ron continued to *drop in* on Meg when Dan wasn't home. When Steph confronted him about it and asked him sweetly and kindly to please save his visits for when Dan was at home, his reaction was, "no woman tells me what to do! It's a free country!" He slammed out the door and that was that.

When Meg would visit Steph, Ron blatantly sat between them and quite uninvited, included himself in their conversation. He'd make a point of pouring Meg's coffee for her, lingering over her longer than need be.

When Meg walked through the door, Ron's whole attitude would change and the expression on his face told the whole story. There was no doubt in Steph's mind it was the look of love, or at the very least, *lust*!

Stephanie's pregnancy caused her to make frequent trips to the bathroom. Upon reentering the kitchen where Meg and Ron were sitting, Steph overheard Ron.

"If you weren't married, I'd be chasing you all over Washington!"

＊　　　＊　　　＊　　　＊

Steph couldn't handle it any longer. She couldn't imagine that Meg didn't realize that Ron's flirting had gone way beyond a casual, *for fun,* pastime!

Losing another night's sleep fuming over the injustice of this ridiculous situation, Stephanie decided to confront Meg head-on!

Stephanie stormed in Meg's drive, raising a huge dust cloud under her tires. She made hard, fast steps down her walkway and opened the front door with a vengeance, not bothering to knock. She walked through the door calling Meg's name.

"Meg!" Stephanie accused, having lost every ounce of her composure. "It's more than obvious that you care more about Ron's attention than you do about my friendship! I'm tired of being made a fool of! I'm tired of people snickering behind my back! I'm sick of Ron treating me like dirt and you like a *Queen Bee*! If you can't have enough compassion for me to abide by my wishes and *stop* seeing *my* husband, then we have nothing more to say to each other!"

"I wouldn't accept a date with Ron even if we were all single! He's **not my type**!" Meg announced loudly, without a doubt and in a patronizing manner. She was stunned and insulted by Steph's attack.

"Well! You **are his**! That's the *problem*!" Stephanie cried out in a shrill voice.

Stephanie was on her way out the door while Meg was still trying to defend herself.

Steph's heart was breaking. Not only was she losing her husband, but also she just lost what she thought was her best pal.

Steph withdrew further. Never again! There's no such thing as F R I E N D! As long as Ron was her husband she could no longer have friends. The grass was always greener elsewhere for Ron.

Steph knew in her heart that she'd never have Ron's heart completely because she was sure by now that he wasn't capable of giving it.

*   *   *   *

John and Hayley decided to have the next bash at their house. The usual crowd showed up and more, some knowing of Steph and Meg's fight and feeling rather uncomfortable.

Steph spotted Meg rambling on with her usual senseless drivel as she proceeded haltingly into the party with Ron by her side. After making the rounds, Steph and Meg temporarily reconciled, for the sake of appearances. Attempting enthusiasm, Steph was listening to a friend talking ecstatically about her new career, operable word, *new*. Steph was conversing rather well for the first time in quite a while and she found herself much to her surprise, actually having a good time. She was totally engrossed and genuinely interested in everything everyone had to say. She was listening to a friend of hers, Steve, who was a confirmed bachelor, boasting.

"Single girls are looking for husbands and married girls are running away from husbands. Quite frankly, I'd rather be with the one running away!"

Everyone laughed except Whitney. Steve was teasing and flirting with Whitney all night.

Steve turned to Whitney and smiled his disreputable smile, much like a tomcat ready to pounce on a poor defenseless bird.

"How about allowing me to see you home, Whitney? A gorgeous little trick like you shouldn't be alone at night. You'd surely entice every pervert to come out from behind his tree and follow you home."

Whitney replied in a cool tone.

"Oh! I wouldn't want to put you to any bother!"

Steve's eyes brightened with encouragement.

"Oh! It's no bother. I assure you."

With a self-satisfied grin on her face, Whitney said, in a soft, low, self-assured tone of voice, "It is to me."

Stephanie overheard. She let out an uncontrollable cough and laugh, then turned to Whitney and winked at her with approval.

Whitney asked Steph.

"Does he have a problem?"

"He falls in lust with every girl he meets," Steph answered.

"That's what I thought," Whitney said with a knowing grin.

Stephanie and Hayley were discussing the upcoming PTA meeting. Hayley turned to John and asked if he'd go with her.

"Sorry, Honey! That's the night we're settling on the big merger I was telling you about. Remember?"

Hayley bristled and countered in her coldest tone.

"Marriage is a merger too, you know!"

Taken off guard, John insisted.

"Hayley! Calm yourself! I never begrudge you time to take care of your responsibility."

Stephanie disassociated herself from the situation. She'd had enough of marital battles lately.

After making the rounds to his guests, John approached Whitney, his eyes dancing mischievously. He teased.

"Why don't you marry me and make me a dependant? That will help you with your taxes."

As John had intended, Whitney reacted in her usual playful indignant manner, trying to hide her delight when he teased her.

"Frankly, John, I'm getting a little tired of turning you down," Whitney giggled, actually enjoying every minute of his teasing. "I'm beginning to think that people may have formed an exaggerated estimate of my financial resources, which, may I say are by no means inexhaustible. I happen to be a hard working industrious working girl."

Having overheard Whitney and John's banter, Hayley meandered over to them.

"Well, Whitney, are you flaunting your professionalism again?" she said in her usual sarcastic manner.

Whitney composed her limbs and sat primly.

Agitated by Hayley's remark, John suddenly felt a small shivering tremor and dryness of the mouth. Hayley could arouse such turbulent emotions in John that he wondered why he bothered to carry on with this terrible bondage of marriage. His adrenalin flowing, he coiled like a tiger ready to spring. His faced darkened.

Whitney caught his arm.

"Don't be harsh with her. Her comments don't bother me. We need to forgive people for their faults and shortcomings if we want to keep peace in our hearts."

Steph joined Whitney and John.

"How's it going?" Steph asked.

"Pretty well, considering!" John and Whitney looked at each other knowing full well what he meant.

"How's that house coming along that Ron's been working on?" John asked.

"He's having trouble with one of his subs but other than that it's coming along quite well. Whitney, you should see this house. If you'd like to see it before it's completely finished, I can get the key. It has five bedrooms, a library, a clubroom, a maid's quarters, a professional office, and a three-car garage. It has a brick terrace all along the back and a deck off the master suite. The master suite has French doors leading to the deck and another set leading to a dressing room full of cedar-lined closets. The bathroom has an over-sized sunken tub with a two-foot step all around it. One and one half walls are built in vanity, sink, and makeup area with extravagant mirrors and strip lights. A bath fit for a queen."

Whitney asked, "What does a house like that go for?"

"Nine hundred thousand dollars," Steph answered with a despairing expression.

"Whew, that's definitely out of my league, I'm afraid," Whitney sighed.

Steph added, "As for most of us."

"How are your brother and sister-in-law?" Whitney asked.

Steph let out a long, deep sigh.

"Awwww! I don't know where to begin. Bianca found out that Rick has been having an affair with his secretary for years, not only that she had two children for him. Bianca and Danielle, his secretary were great friends and Bianca loves those kids like they're her own. She's babysat for her ever since they were born. She feels like such a fool! It's just a *mess*! Bianca kicked him out of the house and Danielle kicked out her patsy husband. Rick moved in with her and the kids, so Rick is supporting two households with no mention of a divorce that I've heard. Rick and Danielle seem ecstatic. As far as they're concerned they ended up getting what they'd always wanted. Rick seems happy to be living with Danielle and of course, he adores the kids. He did confide in me the other day that he sure missed Bianca's cooking. Bianca and their daughter were very quiet and they respected the fact that Rick needed a lot of rest but Danielle's children are the typical noisy children. The house is never quiet enough for to take his much needed naps. So his temper flares quite often which of course is pretty distressing for Danielle. She's never seen this side of Rick before or at least never directed it at her and the children. I can see it's wearing both of them down. I see tears in Danielle's eyes and such weariness in Rick. It's quite an adjustment for both of them. Danielle's good to him. She paints the house herself and does all the yard work because Rick's in no condition to do it. Now, aren't you sorry you asked?"

"How are the kids?" Whitney asked.

Steph let out another sigh.

"They all just got over the flu. I'm sure glad that's over. I'm beat! Waiting on four miserable, sick kids is no picnic. Packy's getting all A's and B's and is in the sixth grade. Zach is learning to read this year and is so proud of himself. They're both on baseball teams which naturally run Ron and me ragged, trying to see them all and getting them both to all of their practices all at different times, of course! Mandy's cutting teeth and is cranky most of the time these days because of it and Myra's still wetting the bed. That's about it for the moment."

"Whew! I'm exhausted just listening to your life! My nice cozy townhouse full of peace and quiet is waiting for me with open arms. I can't help but feel like counting my blessings. How's the murder investigation coming along?"

"They haven't much to go on; no fingerprints; no one's ever seen the woman the artist sketched from my description; there seems to be no motive, not even burglary. There was nothing missing. Of course, she lived alone so there was really no one to ask if anything was missing, but all the expensive items were still there. Even though I see that woman's face in my nightmares, I'm afraid I didn't do a very good job explaining her face to the artist. This woman may not have murdered her. She may have just been at the wrong place at the wrong time. Oh well! Who knows?"

"You say you didn't know Monica well?" Whitney asked.

Steph replied with a sorrowful expression on her face.

"No, not well! The only time I talked to her at any length was not long before she was killed. I learned quite a bit from that visit though. Her husband died of cancer. He wasn't murdered. So there was no connection there. I really liked her though. She seemed very nice."

"The poor woman; such a shame," Whitney said.

Stephanie excused herself and picked up her purse. She headed for the bathroom to freshen up. In the bathroom, she stood in front of the mirror and opened her purse to look for her compact. There was a rose just inside her purse. She shuddered. This was the second rose someone had given her all of which Ron swore he had nothing to do with. If Ron isn't giving them to her then who is? The person must be here at the party, she thought! On the ski trip, who'd have access to her motel room? She shuddered. Maybe Ron's lying. Maybe she had an admirer.

Steph returned to the party and sat down in front of Meg and Dan. Ron came over and arrogantly settled into the seat next to Meg instead of next to Stephanie. Obviously, Meg had Dan believing that she was the victim in all of this! Yes! Poor, innocent puritanical Meg!

Stephanie got up and approached Ron. She leaned over and asked Ron if he was kidding about the rose incident on their ski trip.

"I told you, Steph, I had nothing to do with it! It was probably the custom of the motel." Ron insisted as if Steph was annoying him.

Ron immediately turned to Meg and asked her to dance. They jumped up and walked hand and hand to the dance floor, leaving Steph standing there feeling humiliated and embarrassed. She wasn't about to tell Ron that she might have a secret admirer...As if he'd care!

Feeling perilously close to losing him *and* her, Stephanie watched Ron and Meg dance to one of her favorite slow songs. Ron's eyes never left Meg's face, as Meg flashed Steph a triumphant smile. Ron had a real aptitude for provoking a scene. He was trying to prove to everyone that he wasn't about to allow Steph to get away with trying to keep him away from Meg. And Meg let him do it!

Her heart sinking, Steph watched uncomprehendingly through tears of disappointment and inner rage. Inordinately pleased with himself, Ron danced every dance with every other woman at the party, mostly Meg, of course!

Steph approached Ron between dances and asked if he'd dance the next one with her. Puffing out his chest proudly, Ron announced loud and clear.

"I don't come to these parties to dance with you; I come to dance with all the other men's wives. I can dance with you anytime."

This stab of dismay was so unnerving. A sense of loss gripping her with yet another daunting setback, she felt her vulnerability creeping over her again. Ron's blatant self-involvement was causing Steph enormous distress. She hoped that this phase would soon be over. Once she had the baby and she was thin and shapely again, maybe it would be over.

Steph's natural optimism surfaced. Grabbing the opportunity, Steph decided to put her own conniving talents to good use. She made the decision to attack her dilemma with renewed vigor. She motored over to Dan and asked him to dance to a slow song so they could talk. Knowing how jealous he was Steph started a conversation that was sure to head straight to his nerve endings.

"Are you enjoying the spectacle Meg and Ron are making of themselves?"

"They're just trying to have a good time. You're worried about nothing. It's all in your mind. After you have the baby you'll feel so much better about all of this," Dan said.

That did it! Stephanie was tired of hearing that it's all in her mind!

"Ron says he enjoys his intimate discussions with Meg so much when you're not home. I find out quite a bit about you too. It seems you and I have quite a bit in common according to your wife and my husband. The other day Ron spent three hours over there discussing us. Aren't we lucky to have all our problems solved for us?"

Dan tried to hide his discomfort but his angry stance gave him away.

"Meg would tell me if Ron tried to put the make on her."

The dance was over so Steph gave Dan a lingering body hug and ended it with a quick kiss. She took on the male role for comedy sake, escorting Dan back to his seat.

There was a radical change in her disposition as she reveled in her triumph. She put on a convincing performance. She danced with all the men pretending not to notice Meg's scowl and Ron didn't even notice that Steph was enjoying herself without him. Ron never cared what Steph was doing at a party as long as he was enjoying himself.

Meg's face was dark with rage, an expression Steph recognized all too well. Her bristling anger showed in her tight-lipped smile. Steph knew her plan had worked. She smiled impishly back at Meg as she and Dan sat solemnly in the cor-ner. *Well*, Steph thought, if having an intelligent heart to heart with Meg didn't work to keep Ron away from her, maybe Meg's husband can manage it. It was only fair. Her plan solved the problem with expediency.

Later, Stephanie courageously sashayed up to Ron while he was entertaining some of their friends with one of his many stories, and announced, "With your kind indulgence, I'm leaving."

"Go ahead! I'm staying!" Ron replied.

Bubonic plague couldn't have made Steph feel more shunned. Her sense of isolation convinced her to continue her façade, making her regrets to the host and hostess for leaving so early, deceptively smiling all the while. Stephanie went over to Dan and deliberately kissed his mouth in front of Meg. She turned and made a hasty exit before the tears were noticed.

Steph sobbed all the way home. She needed more time to get her thoughts together and figure out a way to combat her ridiculous situation.

$$*\qquad*\qquad*\qquad*$$

Stephanie sat in front of her house, trying to compose herself before facing the sitter. She decided that she needed more time alone, so she drove endlessly, with no particular destination in mind.

Finally arriving home again, she took the time to freshen her makeup and reflect a little more objectively on this heart-breaking evening and this whole Meg and Ron business.

After another fifteen minutes behind her, Steph finally got up enough courage to get out of her car and make her way to the back door. She was fumbling in her purse trying to see through new tears welling in her eyes as she flashed back to see Ron and Meg in each other's arms on the dance floor. Steph's chest was so tight she thought it would surely explode. She couldn't shake the picture of them out of her mind. They may as well have been making love on the dance floor. What's the difference? Ron obviously wants to bad enough. If he's pictured it in his mind, he may as well have done it, not only *sins* of the *heart* but also the *sins* of the *mind!*

With still shaking hands, she managed to find her keys only to drop them in the grass. There wasn't a sufficient amount of light to even begin to search for them. Her knees weakened suddenly, allowing her to drop to the ground in such desperation and helplessness. Her life seemed revoltingly unfair.

A rustling sound gave her a start as she jumped straight upright with a snap. Her stunned, swollen eyes were wide with shock as she stared face to face into hostile big, brown eyes.

My God! It was the woman Steph saw running out of Monica's house! She was an imposing looking woman with an eerie air about her. She had a diabolical expression on her hard looking face. Stephanie stood breathlessly and immobile as if in a trance.

"Why do you let him do it?" the woman whispered.

Steph's door suddenly flew open. She let out an inaudible sigh of relief as the woman took off.

"Thank God!" Steph said in a grainy, courtly voice. She dashed through the door and crashed on the sofa.

"Did you see the woman?" Steph asked her sitter.

"What woman?"

"No, I guess you didn't."

"I was asleep on the sofa when I heard curious sounds outside in the yard," her sitter was saying.

Steph was so shaken by the trauma she asked if her sitter would please spend the night and she would explain in the morning.

All Steph could do in her exhausted state was not move off the spot.

Steph's sitter could see the condition she was in so she threw a blanket over her so she could sleep where she was.

Only a half hour passed, when Steph started awake by the sound of a key turning in the lock. She jumped up and beckoned the sitter.

Her sitter rushed to her side. Stephanie grabbed a pair of scissors she found on the coffee table.

"Call the police!" Steph whispered to her sitter.

She was sure it had to be that woman with the menacing face. There was something very baffling about the woman. Somehow, she seemed so familiar, not that she saw her at Monica's house but something else. Those haunting eyes were burned into her memory. With such an excruciatingly lurid account of her chronically sad life penetrating her mind, a pregnant Stephanie stood in devastating fear. She stood wrapped in a blanket, hovering in her darkened hallway, praying for the police to get there in a hurry.

Monica's poor mutilated body, those wretched haunting eyes and the revelation of her husband and her best friend seemingly devouring each other emotionally and indulging each other in Stephanie's demise were racing each other in her mind.

What seemed like hours, which turned out to be about ten minutes later, the back door opened.

It was Ron. Putting Ron's disconcerting, unsolicitous actions on a back burner for a moment, Stephanie raced to him. She broke down in uncontrollable sobs.

"That woman I saw running out of Monica's house was waiting for me tonight. Did you try to come in the door a while ago?"

"No, I just got here and wondered why the door was unlocked," Ron answered.

"Do you think you can stop thinking through your underwear long enough to help me face the police when they get here?" Steph asked still crying.

About that time the police arrived.

Stephanie informed the police that the woman spoke to her, that she asked her why she let him do it. She glared at Ron asking herself the same question. This woman seemed so familiar somehow but she still didn't get a good look at her face because it was so dark.

Ron announced bluntly.

"She probably intends to murder you. You're the only one who can identify her."

The police said they'd keep an eye on Steph's house and insisted she not be left alone.

Stephanie grabbed her stomach. A new expression of fear was now on her face.

"Ron! Call the doctor. I'm having a contraction." Stephanie demanded.

The doctor called back after his answering service notified him. He advised her to stay off her feet for a while. *Go to bed!* If they continue and become regular, call him back. Also he advised her to calm her life down a little!

"It's no wonder that baby wants to get out of there!" the doctor said.

Stephanie thought to herself, if he only knew.

*   *   *   *

Stephanie made another appointment with Whitney. She needed to tell some-one about her many confusions and fears that were eating at her

"Hello, Whitney!" Steph began. "I hope you can help me sort out my feelings and tell me I'm not losing my mind."

"Sit down, Steph, what's on your mind?" Whitney asked.

Whitney noticed that Steph was trembling and her voice was an octave lower than her normal tone.

"Don't be nervous, Steph. Start anywhere you like," Whitney insisted.

Stephanie admired Whitney's aristocratic self-possession and she knew that under that gorgeous face there lurked a ferocious intelligence.

Stephanie dropped heavily into the chair, wishing that there would be some magic words that would make her tormenting thoughts disappear. Hundreds of questions tumbled about in her mind.

Whitney's poise was straight-backed and attentive.

Stephanie could feel her strong obsessive drive taking over.

"It's a riveting story," she breathed fervently.

"There's a bond between my husband and Meg that far exceeds casual friendship. They seem to cherish the excitement of non-possession of each other that keeps anticipation ever stimulated. I can't stand it!" Steph said, tears beginning to flood her eyes. "I never balked in the beginning at casual teasing and flirting. I love Meg. I've always found her someone special in my life. I could talk to her and confide in her and not feel intimidated by her. I thought we were so close! I actually preferred spending time with her to Ron. Ron's a hard person to talk to without ending in a fight. So there's always tension trying to talk to him because I have to be ever so careful what I say and how I say it. Anyway, that's the whole story. At least Meg and I were compatible. We could talk about anything for hours and as it turned out we found that we had quite a bit in common! Apparently I was wrong! It's obvious now that she prefers Ron's company to mine! She really doesn't care about me at all! She was using me all along to feed her ego. She's acting like a proud little tease and she enjoys turning my husband into a whimpering idiot at my expense.

The ugly pictures flooded her mind of the flaunting, the excitement in their eyes, the flirting, and Ron's expressions.

Stephanie uttered a moan of pain and continued.

"While dancing at parties Ron holds her so close you'd think they were making love on the dance floor." Tears flooded her eyes. "It hurts me so badly! They've both changed. I don't recognize either of them anymore. He resents my existence. I'm in his way! He never tells me he loves me anymore. According to Ron Meg's perfection and I'm the last resort. He visits her for hours when her husband's at work and I think he's out on a job. They both claim they're discussing me. Is she so blind that she can't see that that is Ron's rouse to get her attention? He's as cold as ice to me, privately and in a crowd, even in front of my family. I'm so embarrassed! He's had flirtations before but this is different. He acts like he's in love. I can't tell you what this is doing to me inside. Even if they fell in love and ran off together it would be better. At least it would be *over*! And this anticipation would finally *end*. He makes love to me and I know he's pretending it's her. When I confront him, do you know what his defense is? He says simply, *she's married!* Can you believe his nerve? He hates me! Meg hates me! All the neighbors hate me…I hate *myself!*" Her heartbreak brought on the tears again!

Stephanie entered a new dimension of senses. Her voice withdrew and acquired a judging dispassion.

"I decided to have a heart to heart with Meg pleading with her for her help in salvaging my marriage. I confided in her that I was sure Ron was falling in love with her. She turned her back on me and told me I was imagining things and she refused to stop seeing him! She claimed that she enjoyed their talks. *I guess she did! What's not to enjoy; watching a man pant over your every move and having him hang onto your every word!* I was so hurt! She didn't care about my feelings at all! She was so indignant as if I were asking her to commit murder or something!

Feeling the rancidness of failure, Stephanie reflected.

"It seemed that our confrontation only encouraged Meg and Ron. Ron was encouraged by Meg's refusal to stop seeing him. He thinks he has a chance at winning her heart away from Dan."

In her professional capacity, Whitney was supposed to remain unemotional dealing only with facts but the intense flow of conversation aroused her feminine perceptive instinct, causing her to shift her weight uncomfortably in her chair.

Stephanie's incredulously bewildered expression continued as she spoke.

"Once, we made the mistake of going to Ocean City together. Ron and I were sitting by the pool after dark. Meg, moving precisely as if in a preordained pattern, strode boldly across her balcony in a nearly transparent nightgown, with the light of her room behind her, baring all!"

Mere words about the incident couldn't express Steph's fury, even now just thinking about it! Her face darkened, her mouth tightened around her teeth. She cried frantically. "*Why? Why?* How could she be so insensitive to my misery? What have I ever done to her?" Stephanie groaned, burying her head in her hands.

Whitney said softly.

"We, the human race, are related to animals, you know. Our animal perceptions feel desire and we sense when we are wanted and desired. Obviously, Meg's absorption in herself is such that she has little feelings or caring of feelings of other people. Maybe she needs the attention more than you think. Maybe her marriage isn't as wonderful as she claims."

Stephanie grabbed hold of herself so she could continue.

"I decided I would no longer give her an inch of my territory! I wrote *Miss hot pants* a note: We've reached a point in our friendship that before we hurt each other further, I think we should see each other only in a crowd, if you know what I mean."

Steph paused a few moments before she continued.

"The prospect of living in close association with a superior being or at least what Ron considers superior…" Steph's voice trailed off. "The trouble is I think he's right. I think Meg is a special person and I'm not blind. She's everything any man could ask for.

. If I were a man I'd want her too. I guess this is why this situation is getting to me so badly.

.

Steph sighed long and hard. She shook her head as if there were no hope to be had.

"Now I feel out of synch with the world. I'm convinced behind each smiling face there's scorn. I'm sure everybody thinks, *why shouldn't Ron want Meg? Every other man does!* Behind each comment, there's condescension. I'm a joke!"

Stephanie paused for a moment then continued with a puzzled expression on her face.

"Ron's popularity is so immense, our friends usually seem impervious to his display of sarcasm to me. Either that or they choose to ignore it. I seem to be his biggest critic. Everyone loves him. He keeps an arsenal of jokes on hand and has impeccable timing with a ready quip on his lips. He's a master of the game. Everybody treats me like I'm just a jealous witch!"

Whitney intervened.

"Your aloofness provokes indifference which in turn validates your suspicions." She watched Steph's eyes to gauge her reaction.

Steph continued.

"I can't help it. I feel I'm amid vicious rumors and constant scrutiny. I don't want to show my face!"

"Friendships change because people change and sometimes the changes are hard to deal with. We have to learn to handle petty annoyances lightly rather than grumble and allow them to build out of proportion."

Stephanie felt a quiver of apprehension. In an emotional meltdown Steph continued in a flat voice.

"Meg feels and has everyone else convinced that the incident isn't her fault but for which, nevertheless, she's held to account."

There was a brief silence Stephanie held her breath through.

Whitney broke the silence.

"I think any hardship is good for the character. Feelings are hurt too easily in a too close relationship. Friendship is love in a sense only without the passion. Close friends make an emotional investment in each other. The feelings they have for each other are caring and concern. A ritual of togetherness can be claustrophobic and boring. It's hard to allow a friendship to fizzle out but once you're getting no more pleasure from it you may as well move on so you can continue to grow. You both need a fresh start. Feeling unique is important. Be good to yourself."

Whitney rose from her chair and walked to her window to give Steph a chance to absorb what she'd said thus far. She adjusted the blind then walked back to her desk where she rested one hip, leaving the other foot on the floor.

"As for men," Whitney continued, "they have more *turn-on* buttons than *Air Force One*." The pupils in her eyes adjusted to the light change like a shutter in a camera. For men fidelity isn't natural, only culturally attained. The visual sense causes the arousal initially. All it takes is a well-put together body to cause lust to stir in his loins. For a man it feels perfectly natural to *want* an attractive woman, or women, plural."

"Just thinking about Meg triggers an annoying groan in him," Stephanie announced in despair.

"Infidelity enables him to keep you at emotional arms length. He's incapable of having an honest, mature relationship. He's punishing you for knowing his shortcomings. He's probably short changed on self-esteem even though he seems quite the opposite. New conquests help reassure him he's still a hot commodity and they're easier to win over because all they know about him is what he tells them. A clean slate is a lot easier to play with," Whitney continued.

"He's never hidden the fact that he's a devout lover of women. His bittersweet, sensitive heart is well protected from any woman," Stephanie added.

"Men are a different breed of animal. It's a different dance to a whole different tune," Whitney claimed.

"Ron is so warmly available to other people. I think he keeps himself hidden from himself. He's never been introspective. Self-analysis and psychiatry are ludicrous to him," Steph said honestly.

Stephanie's brain struggled to make any logic out of her feelings.

"I've spent most of my marriage trying to figure Ron out."

Whitney pointed out.

"Men think of women as one big playground to play in. He makes himself inaccessible to the woman he's supposed to be committed to by allowing himself to be available to all women."

"Yes, Ron told me once that he'd never turn any woman down. I was naïve enough to think he was kidding!" Stephanie agreed.

After a long moment to collect her thoughts, Stephanie admitted wearily.

"It's all so sad. Women will always want what they can never have. All I've ever wanted was to be indispensable in Ron's life. You know, that he'd love me no matter how beautiful and perfect other women might be; that love conquers all. Foolish, I suppose." She was filled with a tremulous quaking feeling.

"Stephanie!" Whitney scolded. "You're addicted to your husband. You need to emancipate yourself." Trying not to destroy all of Steph's dreams, Whitney added, "Not all men feel this way. There are some special men out there, just as *special* as you are. *That* special man could turn your world upside down for the better. Your life would have a whole different meaning. You're a beautiful, intelligent, talented, vital woman with so much love to give. You wouldn't have any trouble at all attracting any man out there."

The protocol for such a statement wasn't readily available as Steph sat looking disarmingly disheveled.

"I've never felt anywhere close to beautiful," Steph admitted honestly. "Beauty is in the eye of the beholder, I guess, as they say."

"There's another of your qualities, you're humble too. Based on the premise that true beauty exists, all beauty has to be nourished and worked at," announced Whitney. "You know what Eva Gabor always said, *there's no such thing as an ugly woman, only a lazy one!*"

"We can't depend on someone else to love us," Whitney continued with a smile. "We must love and respect ourselves first, and then everything else will fall into place. The Noah's Ark mentality is guiding us to think we can't live without a man. A relationship that does us harm certainly isn't worth having. Perseverance doesn't always pay off," Whitney tried to explain.

"Ron has an inner emptiness that can't be filled. These symptoms of seeming to be uncaring and unloving, doing as he pleases and flaunting his nastiness, display his feelings of inadequacy of himself, not you. He's so busy looking for love and acceptance that he has little time to love."

Whitney paused.

"Would you like a cup of coffee, Stephanie?"

"I'd love one. Thank you, Whitney."

Whitney poured two cups of coffee.

"Children growing up in an atmosphere in which love and care are lacking go through their lives in search of inner security," Whitney continued. "They feel they never *have enough*, no matter what or how much they have or have achieved and that no one can be trusted, and never being worthy of someone's love. It's no wonder these people need to struggle for attention and love or at least acceptance wherever they can find it. It's a sad, vicious cycle because they find the person who gives them this love that they feel they don't deserve then in a desperate attempt to hang onto it they'll throw it away with their manipulative and hateful behavior. They lack self-discipline. They're not able to deny themselves instant gratification. Honesty becomes less and less important to them. The more dishonesty they get away with the more dishonest they're going to be. They won't take responsibility for their actions. In the end they're endlessly angry, because they endlessly feel let down and disappointed by others because they depend sourly on others making them happy, which in reality will never happen because they're so unhappy with themselves. If you depend on someone else to make you happy, you'll be endlessly disappointed."

"Life isn't easy," Whitney continued. "Once we truly realize and accept that, we're able to put it behind us and go on from there. Once accepted, it's no longer something to worry about because it will be expected. Life is one problem after another, one hurdle after another. It's all in the way we solve those problems, how we jump those hurdles. Whitney said, *those things that hurt, instruct.* The need to face our problems head-on and to experience the pain involved are necessary suffering. Mental health is a never ending battle with accepting reality."

"The words *I love you* confuse me. How can Ron tell me he loves me and then treat me this way? Stephanie confessed."

"As do most people," Whitney stated. "This is a very common area of heartbreak and confusion. The words are said too easily and too often. The experience of *falling in love* is confused with the excitement and rapture of a new person and new body, newness, the experience of feeling good. Feeling this good must be love. This experience, naturally is temporary because once the novelty has worn off the excitement seems to be gone, at which point some feel that the love is over. This is why there are so many divorces and break ups. It's at this point the real love sets in. The ecstatic feelings and the forever and always fairy tale that characterize the experience of falling in love always passes. As they say, *the romance is over.* Love is something we'll never truly understand until we're on the other side. We don't have to love. We *choose* to love, not grab at what's there. Real love is permanent. Real love allows the person to grow within himself or herself, not lose himself or herself. We'd all love to live the romantic fantasy, *live happily ever after*, but this is just that, *a fantasy*. This illusion causes more harm and misery than just about anything else. I see it every day in my profession. There's so much suffering. Once we realize that once the ecstasy is over, and that real *love* sets in *after* the *romance* is over, we'll be able to concentrate on loving each other instead of committing adultery to get the old excitement back. Real love is seeing the warts and loving in spite of them."

"Ron will never be satisfied with me as long as I live but there is a chance that once he accepts my faults that he may love me and stop searching for his perfect love?"

"It's an analogy but you have to accept yourself first, the way you are," Whitney replied. "It'll be easier for him to accept you and love you. You can't hide out forever. Be your old, independent self again. You can't dwell on Ron's problems forever. Conquer your own problems first. Do what makes *you* happy and *fulfill yourself.* The trick is to live every day as if you're dying, then, not dying. Learn to appreciate each day, one at a time. After all, we're all dying from the moment we're born. No living being is going to satisfy Ron completely. Once you accept that, you'll be free to change. You can't live your life; give up your life for him. It would be nice to convey this to Ron and have him understand but it's highly unlikely. You first, then him."

"Sometimes I feel like I'm living with the Devil himself. There seems to be no conscience, no remorse," Stephanie said abruptly.

Steph drooped in dejection. The memories were so vivid in her mind as she struggled with her feelings. Riddled with guilt for thinking such ugly thoughts of her husband, she reflected, her lips tense.

"What kind of person can deliberately hurt another human being and seem to get pleasure from it?" Tears welled in her eyes again. Distinctly uneasy, she drew in her breath in anger and pain. Such unbearable sadness invaded her heart.

"A person who is suffering," she reminded Steph. "You first, then him."

*   *   *   *

After a month passed, Hayley picked Steph up to go to a bridal shower.

Quite out of character, Hayley seemed very sympathetic toward Stephanie's dilemma and offered her usual bits of advice. Hayley was more than happy to commiserate with Stephanie.

Steph broke down into tears.

"How dare Ron and Meg treat me this way! I hate feeling this way! But how dare Meg flaunt her body at Ron! And how dare Ron not resist! I love Meg! I hate what this stupid situation has done to Ron and me and Meg and me! I want it to be the way it used to be, on one hand, yet, on the other, I don't want to ever be placed in a situation like that again to allow another woman to invade my marriage."

Hayley couldn't wait to jump on that one.

"Well! It's not like I didn't try to warn you. But you refused to listen to me."

Steph continued.

"It looks like the only way to prevent it is to disassociate, stay to ourselves, away from temptation, since Ron can't seem to handle himself with *eye candy* being dangled in his face! How can Meg do this to me? She knows what Ron is like but she still opens herself up to his line of *bull*. I'm sure they're not having an affair but I can't stand *my husband loving someone else*! Meg doesn't want Ron but she refuses to give his heart back. Our house is always full of tension.

*   *   *   *

After months of this treatment, Stephanie consented to attend a function where she knew Meg was going to be, just to please Ron. Besides, he was showing signs of recovery so Steph thought she'd swallow her pride, *once again* and see what happened.

Everything seemed to be going fine. Steph and Meg were civil to each other and even had a sizable conversation between them. Meg said with tears in her eyes, "We used to be *best friends*! How could you do this to me? I'd never do this to you!"

This really touched Steph's heart. She wanted to hug Meg and vow this whole messy situation would be over, but she couldn't. She knew that Meg was too much of a temptation and the feelings were still fresh in their minds.

"Hayley told me all about the conversation that you two had about me when you two went to the shower together," Meg continued.

Steph let out a sigh.

"Good ole Hayley! When will I ever learn *not* to *trust* Hayley?" Knowing Hayley as she did, Steph was sure that Hayley had added her special touch of spice and told Meg certain statements out of context.

"Did she manage to include that I felt rotten about this whole mess and that I love *you* and *hate* hurting *you* like this?" Steph asked.

Meg was teary eyed.

"*No*! That's not what she said. She said you didn't want Ron anywhere near me and that you didn't want to go anywhere where I was."

"Well, yes, I did say that too," Steph admitted. "It's not the way I want it. It's the way it has to be. Can't you see that? It's like putting candy in front of a child and telling him not to eat it!"

Meg just shook her head like she still thought Steph was out of line.

Meg said, wiping a tear from her cheek.

"Hayley has been doing a lot of un-asked-for spy work! She even went so far as to call my sister-in-law to tell her that you and a friend were plotting against me and that you were saying horrible things about me! The only reason Hayley picked you up was so she could get more dope to feed me!"

Stephanie knew she'd hurt Meg severely. Tears smarted Steph's eyes feeling such remorse and wanting so badly to make it up to her.

Steph finally pulled herself together.

"That ruthless, scheming witch! She's been playing both ends against the middle! I should have known! She says terrible things about you too to keep me stirred up! She's always been jealous of our relationship.

Steph reached over and grabbed Meg. She gave her a long, forgiving hug as they both cried.

Suddenly, Steph had an overwhelming compulsion to put her hands around Hayley's throat!

Steph purposely joined the group where Hayley was laughing in her adolescently shrill voice. Hayley had no personality so to compensate, she giggled incessantly like a silly little schoolgirl at everything. Stephanie was sure she giggled to cover her feelings of inadequacy but there was no sympathy in the glare Steph gave Hayley. Hayley knew Meg must have told her something. She backed off. She tried to avoid Stephanie by pretending to be preoccupied with tipsiness from over drinking. From then on, Stephanie offered Hayley only utterly cold snobbishness never equaled among women! Stephanie believed that too much closeness with people only caused her pain.

CHAPTER 7

▼

Stephanie's due date was fast approaching. Leading a pretty much secluded life, not partying or seeing Meg on a daily basis anymore, Ron and Steph had a chance to put their lives back into perspective. Ron still harbored a slight resentment but he was trying hard to restore the feelings he and Steph once had for each other.

Stephanie realized that Ron was a very virile man. She didn't think that he'd intended to hurt her with his demeaning actions but Ron was a very precarious guy. In Steph's precognitive manner where Ron was concerned, she was aware that he could easily be led astray. He was impulsive and impetuous. Ron was under the disillusionment that he had to impress his friends by playing the chauvinistic role. Sometimes he would get his priorities mixed up as most men often do.

One night in bed, Steph tried to get into Ron's head to attempt to understand him a little better.

"Why do you do these things to me? Are you looking for support for your ego? Aren't I good enough? What am I doing wrong?"

Ron looked into Steph's eyes seriously.

"Steph, it isn't you. It's me! I've learned from home that the only way I can maintain control is through my rage. Before the nineteen hundreds women were considered a man's property and husbands were allowed to beat their wives and murdering them was almost accepted as if the wife must have done something to deserve it. Unfortunately, I was gifted with an acid tongue. After I'm so hard on you I really get upset with myself. I'm sorry, Steph! I hate hurting you! I really *do* love you! I know I don't always show it. As a matter of fact, sometimes I actually forget that I love you so much! I need you more that I need anything else in my life."

Ron's eyes filled with tears, a sight Steph had never seen.

"Sometimes I just lose it," Ron admitted. "I can't control my temper. There's something inside me that comes out that I can't always control. I really am afraid of losing you but I have a hard time coming clean with you. I guess because I don't want to appear to be a wimp! As for women, I really love you, but I don't mind admitting that I *could* go to bed with *any* woman. Sex is sex. It's mechanical and has nothing to do with feelings. All men think that way, whether they admit it or not. *You* mean *everything* to me! Please don't leave me! They kissed. Life was looking up.

*   *   *   *

Danielle, Steph's brother's mistress, called Stephanie. In a strained tone of voice she cried.

"Steph, I think Rick's losing his mind! He yells at the kids and me all the time and nothing I do seems to please him!"

Steph tried to explain.

"Rick needs his rest. You know he's in pain most of the time and at the very least uncomfortable all the time. He's frustrated because his strength is failing him and that his life is rapidly coming to an end. Put yourself in his position. I know I wouldn't be as accepting as he is. He realizes he's no longer capable of exercising his manhood and that he'll never recover. You know how important that is to him"

"But I'm willing to stand by him," Danielle cried.

Steph said, "I know that. But even so, he feels guilty where you're concerned and angry that life has dealt him such an unfair hand."

Danielle added, still crying.

"But he keeps yelling at us to get out of the house. You know he can't take care of himself."

"Danielle, I don't know what to tell you except that if you're unhappy, then do as he's demanding and move out. He always manages."

The evening of that same day, Bianca called Steph.

"You won't believe this but Rick has been calling me. He wants to come home. He claims that he misses me. What do you think, Steph? Should I take him back?"

Steph let out a deep confused sigh, wondering how she managed to get herself in the middle of all of this.

"Well, I'll let you in on a little secret. Danielle called me earlier crying that Rick hasn't been treating her and the kids right and he's trying to kick them out of the house. So the decision is yours. He's obviously unhappy and realized he's made a mistake. Are you willing to forgive and forget? Down the road, will this situation fester?"

"I'm thinking seriously about taking him back," Bianca said, after a moment of silence.

Steph thought to herself that that brother of hers sure has the luck of the Irish! Bianca hung up sounding happy for the first time this mess broke out.

*   *   *   *

A week later, Ron, Steph and all the kids came home from a movie.

"What's Bianca's car doing here?" Steph asked.

"I don't know. Maybe there's something wrong with Rick!"

Things were back as usual as far as Rick and Bianca were concerned. Rick allowed Danielle and the kids to stay in the house so he was still supporting two households. At least he paid for both houses.

"Oh no! I hope Rick hasn't done something stupid again. That guy! Nothing stops him. I think Mom was right that something happened to him at birth, not enough oxygen."

Stephanie walked through the door fully expecting she'd have another problem to worry about.

"*S U R P R I S E!*" There was a room full of people waiting for her. Steph turned around to Ron and flashed him a look of relief. He returned it with a mischievous grin.

It was a baby shower. Everyone was there, even Meg. There was a table full of food that Ron and the kids immediately pounced on. All sizes and shapes of beautifully wrapped presents were piled up to one side of the green occasional chair waiting to be torn open.

Steph smiled delightedly and put her hands to her cheeks, shaking her head in disbelief. It was obvious to everyone that the surprise had worked and that no one had slipped up and let that slippery cat out of the bag.

"Ah, come on, guys! This is my fifth baby! You didn't have to do this!…. But I'm sure glad you did!" Steph said.

Steph walked excitedly to *The Guest of Honor's Chair* and sat down heavily and with great relief. Bianca handed Steph a plate of food. Steph marveled at the fancy presentation.

"What's this?"

"Pate de foie gras and smoked salmon! You're recipe!" Bianca answered with pride.

"Wow! I'm impressed! Thank you, Bianca! You're so thoughtful to do all of this for me. I'm starving!" Steph laughed.

Steph stood up and gave Bianca a long tight hug of appreciation.

Stephanie devoured the plate of food, chatting happily with everyone. Her brother, Rick, was sitting on the sofa propped up with pillows. His feet rested on a stool. He looked rested for the first time since he'd moved out of Danielle's house, but he still looked weak and fragile. It broke Stephanie's heart to see her big, strong brother being reduced to an invalid. She had to give him credit. It's never stopped him from trying and living. He was sitting beside one of her playful neighbors, exchanging dirty jokes and laughing with her. Steph smiled, delighted to see Rick having a good time. She was so proud of her brother for being so stubborn and not allowing multiple sclerosis to conquer him. He was fighting it every step of the way and never felt sorry for himself.

Steph's food was gone. She put her hands together to her chin and said, wide-eyed with excitement

"Now! Let's dig into all these gorgeous presents!" Steph wrapped her arms around her swollen mid-section as if cradling the baby inside her. She looked down at her stomach lovingly and said to her unborn child.

"Look at all these presents for you, little Garret or little Brittany. Aren't you excited?"

At that point Steph looked up in surprise and smiled. She announced with great satisfaction, "He or she just answered me with a kick!"

Everyone laughed and clapped their hands.

Steph tore into her presents like a little child would do, overwhelmed by all the presents under the Christmas tree.

She looked at Meg and smiled.

"Thank you for your gift!" Meg smiled back with big sad puppy dog eyes. Steph couldn't control herself. She jumped up and ran across the room to give Meg a big hug! Steph was so glad to see her!

Stephanie was so happy and excited to see everyone she loved happy for a change!

LIFE *CAN* BE GOOD!

∗   ∗   ∗   ∗

A few weeks later, Steph, Ron, and the kids were watching the snow come down. It was a winter wonderland. Everybody was trapped at home thanks to these big, beautiful, white wonders piling up in a hurry to form glistening clouds of heaven. The kids were so excited.

"I want to go outside and play in the snow!" The boys pleaded. "Please, we'll come in when we get cold and wet. We promise!"

Steph looked at Ron.

"What do you think?"

Ron cocked his head.

"I guess it wouldn't hurt for a half hour or so. Okay, boys, get your snowsuits, boots, gloves and make sure you wear your hoods."

They hustled excitedly to put on their entire garb. After a quick inspection from Dad, they rustled out the door.

Ron and Steph watched the children out the window for a while, so proud of their creations.

"Aren't they darling?" Steph said full of pride. "They're all so perfect and so wonderful. How lucky can we be? Looking at them like this I'm so overwhelmed with love for them," Steph confided.

"I know what you mean."

They took a moment and made it special by looking into each other's eyes. There was a long pensive pause.

"I love you, Steph, more than I can ever put into words, more than I could ever love anyone. You mean everything to me. I appreciate your understanding, your tenderness, and your forgiving nature. You love unconditionally and you never give up. They don't come any better than you, Steph. I mean that with all my heart. Please don't let me push you away. It isn't me when I act like a fool. I swear!"

Ron's lips barely touched Steph's lips as he ever so gently nibbled on her lower lip, then slowly his lips took her upper lip between his lips as if appreciating the taste of her.

"I know it isn't you when you act like a demon," Stephanie admitted. "This is the man I love; the one who's before me now. This is the one I wait for and know will come back to me eventually."

Ron kissed her sweetly, tenderly, protectively and appreciatively, as they fell into a loving embrace, while watching their babies romp in the snow.

Myra's fussing broke the wondrous moment.

"I guess Myra's finished her nap," Steph sighed and gave Ron a quick hug before she left his side to attend to Myra's needs.

Steph greeted Myra in her room.

"Oh, what a good little girl you are. You didn't wet the bed."

Ron walked back in his office, smiling as he overheard Steph's sweet, tender, loving words to their daughter.

"Are you going to help Mommy fix dinner?"

Myra shook her head yes, and immediately pulled a chair up to the sink, then climbed on it so she could reach the sink.

"Here, help Mommy pound the meat."

Steph wrapped a towel around Myra's tiny body so the meat juice didn't splatter her clothes. Steph rolled a saucer edge with pressure over the meat to tenderize it, while Myra pounded the meat happily with the meat hammer. Steph coated the meat with flour mixture and placed it in the pan to brown.

Suddenly, Steph grabbed her stomach.

"Uh oh!" A contraction seized her. "This is no time to go into labor!"

Thinking to herself, should she say anything to Ron or should she wait? Maybe the snow will stop soon. Her labor usually lasts for hours. *But* this is her fifth baby! Oh! Dear! But why get Ron upset? He'll just go crazy and insist on running her to the hospital himself and wreck the car! She'd better warn someone though. She'd need someone to watch the children.

Steph took Myra with her to the bedroom so she wouldn't burn herself on the hot burners. She dialed her neighbor's number.

"Hi, Ann! Are you enjoying the snow? I'd like to ask a favor of you. Would you be on call in case Ron and I have to make a run to the hospital?"

"You're in labor?" Ann's voice screamed over the phone.

Steph tried to calm her down.

"Yes! But don't worry! It just started."

"Only *you* would choose weather like this to have a baby, Steph!" Ann said.

"Yes, Ann. I know! Just look at it this way, you don't ever have to worry about getting bored!"

Ann admitted, "Frankly, I could use a little *boredom*!"

"Thanks, Ann!"

Steph and Myra walked calmly back to the kitchen to finish preparing the swiss steak. Myra was pounding away while Steph was browning the meat and cutting up the vegetables.

The boys ran past her, covered with snow, leaving a trail of melting snow behind them.

"Oh! My!" Steph said as she grabbed Myra and took her off the counter. She chased the boys into the bathroom where she helped them pull off their wet clothes.

Back to the kitchen, "Oops!" Another contraction! Steph thought to herself, if she tells Ron now he's liable to try to rush them to the hospital and kill all three of them!

After Steph put the swiss steak in the oven, she went to her room to lie down and take the weight off her feet and relieve the pressure. The kids were running through the house, wrestling and making a lot of noise. They ran into Stephanie's room and jumped on her bed.

"Mommy, Zach won't give me any candy!" Packy whined.

"He's lying, Mommy! He's just trying to get me into trouble!" Zach cried.

Ron stormed into the room.

"What's going on in here?" Ron demanded. "It sounds like a herd of elephants up here! Now, get out of here and leave your mother alone!"

Ron looked at Steph.

"Are you okay, Honey?"

"I'm just a little tired. It isn't easy carrying around all of this extra weight! You aught to try it sometime!" Steph tried to hide her discomfort when another contraction attacked her.

"Steph! Are you sure you're all right? You look drained."

"I'm fine," Steph assured him. Go back to work. Maybe I'll take a nap before dinner."

"Good idea! I'll close the door and try to keep our hoodlums quiet."

There was no way Steph was going to sleep through contractions!

An excruciating hour passed so slowly.

"Ron!" Stephanie screamed.

Myra peeked through the crack in the door.

"Myra! Run and get Daddy!"

"Okay, Mommy!" Myra obeyed.

Ron ran upstairs.

"I knew it! You're having contractions, aren't you?" Ron insisted.

Steph said in a panic, "I can't stand up! Call an ambulance! Call the doctor!

Ron said sharply, "It's as good as done."

It took the ambulance a half hour to get there because of the snow. Ron had already taken the kiddies next door.

"Bring the stretcher!" Ron demanded.

"Did you give the swiss steak to Ann, Ron? Do you have my bag?" Steph asked as she was being carried out of the house on a stretcher.

"Everything's been taken care of, Stephanie," Ron said.

As Ron was closing the door behind them, Steph asked, "How about the oven? Did you turn off the oven?"

"*Yes! Stephanie! Yes!*" Ron answered in a firm voice.

Through all the delay of traffic tie-ups and cautious driving through the snow, the ambulance finally made it to the hospital. Ron got out carrying their fresh new baby boy and poor Stephanie was carried into the hospital on a stretcher.

*   *   *   *

While recuperating in the hospital the next day, Steph was looking out the window, watching the snowplows push the snow off the roads and the hospital parking lot.

"Hi, Mommy!" Steph's head turned toward the wonderfully familiar little voice to see her sweet little Myra's face peering at her from the door.

"Myra! Come give Mommy a big hug"

Myra ran into Steph's open arms. Packy, Zach and Mandy soon followed.

"Did you see your baby brother yet?" Steph asked.

"We're waiting for you, Mommy," Packy said.

Then Ron walked in.

"Hi, Hon! How are you feeling?"

"Not too bad. This morning," Stephanie said, excited to see her family.

"Come on, Mommy! We want to see Baby Garret," Zach said impatiently.

"Okay! Let's go!" Steph said.

"Are you sure you're up to it? You had such a rough time of it," Ron asked.

"Sure I am!" Steph insisted.

Ron helped Stephanie out of the hospital bed.

"Walk slowly, Kids. Mommy has to take it easy. Please don't make noise. Remember! This is a hospital."

The kids were so excited.

Packy announced, a little too loudly.

"There he is!"

The nurse was holding a pretty big baby, for a newborn.

"He looks like he's three months old already," Ron said.

"How do you like that dark curly hair, Ron?" Steph asked.

"He's beautiful! Job well done! A stroke of genius!" Ron kissed Steph on the forehead.

"Thank you, Honey for giving me five such beautiful kids! I'm so proud of you, Steph," Ron said, glowing.

Steph felt a hand on her shoulder from behind.

"Bianca!" Steph said. She was so glad to see her.

"How are you feeling, Steph?" Bianca asked out of concern.

"Well! Certain parts of me have felt better days, I assure you!" Steph admitted with a giggle.

"Oh! Stephanie! He's beautiful," Bianca said enthusiastically as she peered through the glass of the nursery.

Ron laughed.

"Steph *almost* made it to the hospital in time, but she just couldn't wait to see him any longer. She thought she may as well have the baby in the ambulance so she'd have something to do while we were held up in the traffic."

Bianca laughed and gave Stephanie a big hug.

"Bless your heart!"

Shortly after that, the hall was full of people to see Steph and little Garret.

CHAPTER 8

▼

Whitney dropped in to see John and Hayley with exciting news.

Whitney was beaming.

"Guess what I just did. I just booked myself on a relaxing cruise to Mexico. I'm so excited! I've never been on a cruise before and I thought what better place to organize my thoughts and get a much needed rest?"

"Well, maybe you'll stumble onto love while you're basking in the sun," commented Hayley.

"I don't want to *stumble* onto love! I want to *fall* right *in* it!" Whitney said.

John smiled in agreement.

"That sounds smart to me. When are you leaving?"

"Next week," Whitney answered

"That's wonderful, Whitney. You're long overdue for a vacation," John said.

"I agree," Hayley said.

Whitney's eyes sparkled with exhilaration.

"I plan to shop for a whole new wardrobe. A whole new me will board the ship."

"But I kind of like the *old* you!" John said matter of factly.

Whitney smiled sweetly.

"Thank you, John. You're the sweetest guy I know."

Whitney gave him a quick playful peck on the cheek.

Hayley glared resentfully. She descended into new depths of depravity.

"Little Miss Sanctimonious and Mr. Wonderful!" Hayley hissed. "Wouldn't you two make a splendid couple? Why don't you pitch me to the wolves, then you two can live together, *happily ever after!* Ah! Wouldn't it be sickening, though?"

A frown sped across John's face.

Such disastrous advice. Hayley realized immediately that she'd blundered drastically. She'd dreadfully bombed out.

Hayley apologized.

"I'm sorry. That was nasty of me. I didn't mean it."

"You'll hear no recriminations from me!" John said.

John was blunt and had animosity in his voice. In order to maintain this farce of a marriage John had been forced to swallow his pride much too often. He refused to compromise any longer.

Nodding brusquely to John, Hayley launched a barrage of sentences, leaping nimbly from one sentence to another. Determined to undermine his plan, Hayley tried to offer a plausible excuse.

"I've had a headache all day and I haven't been feeling my best." She smiled nervously, not generously but with tight lips.

"In that case, you must never feel your best! You must try to rise above your limits," John added.

The note of sarcasm induced an even more defiant mood. Hayley fumbled for the right words.

"Don't over estimate yourself, My Darling!"

John continued.

"Only due to Whitney's infinite sophistication and class would she not lower herself to your level and slap your face for all the indignation she's surely suffered from your ruthless accusations!"

Her lips trembling, her eyes moist, Hayley cried.

"Well! You expect me to sit back and watch your obvious desire for Whitney and not be hurt or resentful?

"Why can't you exercise a little self-discipline?" John yelled back growing more agitated by the conversation.

There was something fond and protective in the way John treated Whitney; that was obvious.

Whitney didn't want to interfere even though she was the main subject. She tensed up, resisted, then looked at the floor, and laughed nervously.

"Now that my good news has made your day, I think I'll get started on that shopping I told you about," Whitney announced.

Whitney hurried to the door and left the house, probably not even noticed since John and Hayley were so preoccupied by airing their feelings.

"Do you think for one minute that I can't see what's going on in your head?" Hayley cried.

John turned around and noticed Whitney was gone.

"Now see what you've done? You scared Whitney off! I wouldn't blame her if she never came back here again!"

"That *Bitch*! She's always made my life unbearable!"

With that, John said in a quiet, matter of fact tone, "You aren't good enough to kiss her dainty little feet."

There was a long awkward pause. Hayley studied John's eyes. She abandoned any further thought of inferring that Whitney wasn't reputable. Faced with a problem of such complexity and perplexed by these confusions, her defense mechanism was to lash out into tears of rage.

"You're an imbecile! You can't resist temptation!" Hayley cried out.

"How much longer must we live this farce?" John asked in a calmer tone.

Hayley thought to herself, *an executive can't be a crybaby!* She tried to face up to her dilemma. With an obvious effort to speak normally, she very cautiously said,

"I don't know." She would not delude herself; she was losing John and there didn't seem to be anything to do about it.

John stepped heavily through the hall toward the bedroom.

Hayley sniffed and asked,

"What are you doing?"

John said with no emotion at all,

"I'm packing."

Hayley vaguely remembered thinking that her knees were numb and her legs had become jell-o as she sank hopelessly into her chaise lounge. Sighing helplessly, the incident kept reverberating in her mind. All her battles with herself over her jealousy of Whitney had come to a head. John would not be persuaded to stay so she made no further attempt.

Hayley followed him to the front door. John smiled his disreputable smile. He felt tremendously happy and pleased with himself. An unairing sense of freedom, peace and relief overwhelmed him as he walked through the front door for the last time. He took a deep breath and breathed in a whole new sense of himself. He turned to Hayley, his face glowing with expectation of endless possibilities.

"Take care of yourself, Hayley!"

"Don't underestimate the power of a woman," Hayley replied in one last defiant attempt, she slammed the door shut behind him.

Hayley sat in the living room for hours in total bewilderment wondering if she'd ever become accustomed to this ensuing silence.

CHAPTER 9

▼

Whitney couldn't believe the size of the ship, she was thinking as she approached the landing. The excitement made her tremble as she greeted the cruise director.

"Whitney Blake reporting for her first cruise, Sir," she said as she saluted him.

"Yes! Whitney Blake, you're on Aloha deck, number two eighteen," the cruise director said.

"Thank you," Whitney said with great enthusiasm.

An unfamiliar voice addressing Whitney turned her head suddenly toward a tall, handsome, very well dressed man.

"Whitney Blake, I see no wedding ring. Am I to assume you're unattached?" he said.

Whitney shook her head.

"Unattached, I am!"

"I'm Josh Monroe. I passed you back there and had to come back for a closer look. You're a beautiful woman. You're so striking! I happened to overhear your conversation with the cruise director. I'm free too! Since we're both alone, would you mind having dinner with me tonight?"

Whitney was a little dubious but what could dinner in a dining room full of people hurt? After all, she *was* on this cruise for fun and relaxation and she was always open to the possibility of meeting her *Mr. Right.*

Whitney smiled and accepted his invitation graciously.

After making arrangements and deciding on the time, they went their separate ways to settle in and unpack.

Whitney found her cabin. She was amazed how lovely the room was decorated in spite of its size. She was open for what ever was in store for her. She was ready and eager to experience new things and new people and she would meet them head on. She managed to unpack in spite of her anxiety attack and tried to calm herself down by looking through the brochures that were left for her.

Whitney decided to wear her new black silk jumpsuit. Since there were rhinestones set in her three-inch wide belt, she decided to wear her favorite diamond earrings and necklace to set the outfit off. She wore her hair loosely around her face winged back around her tiny ears in order to show off her earrings.

Whitney looked stunning.

"Okay, Josh Monroe, I'm ready for you," she announced to herself in the full-length mirror, as she took a last minute check before gliding anxiously out the door.

Whitney made her *Grande Entrance* into the dining room, feeling like the Grand Duchess and turning every head she passed.

Whitney announced her name proudly to the Matre de. She was directed to a cozy little table for two where Josh had already been seated. He stood gallantly to greet her.

"You're quite the *vision*, Whitney!"

Whitney smiled sweetly.

"Thank you very much, Josh." She was promptly seated.

They chatted casually and pleasantly through a long leisurely dinner, taking inventory of each other, as any new acquaintances would do. They carefully answered well-guarded superficial questions about each other's lives, taking mental notes of mannerisms, gestures they may or may not be able to tolerate, judging each other and wondering what the other one was thinking of them.

Josh was smooth talking and very aware of his attractiveness. He didn't impress Whitney aesthetically because of the fact that he was a little too arrogant and too sure of himself, which clouded the picture for her. His easy grin was a little too practiced and his authoritative voice put her on the defensive. He was too quick to undermine the institution of marriage as if he wanted it quite understood up front that he was a confirmed bachelor and intended to stay that way. Whitney came to a quick conclusion, recognizing his possible neurosis; thanks to her professional training that she wanted nothing more to do with him.

It was unfortunate that Whitney had to have this bore interfere with her first glorious night and luscious meal on the cruise. But she excused the situation with the thought that she had to take chances or she might miss the chance for a good relationship to develop with the right person.

Josh offered to walk Whitney to her cabin, much to her dismay. Not having time to think of an appropriate excuse, she and Josh walked along the deck and back to her cabin.

Whitney opened her door and waited patiently for Josh to finish boring her with his infantile gestures to convince her to allow him into her cabin.

"Come on, Whitney, wouldn't you like to get this cruise off on the right foot? I guarantee you I'll give you a memory you won't soon forget."

"You mustn't flatter yourself, Josh!" Whitney said emphatically.

His untenable attitude was unnerving Whitney. Josh grabbed her and started kissing her in a cannibalistic manner, her face wet with saliva. She struggled to keep him from forcing himself into her cabin.

"What's going on here?" Whitney heard a welcome familiar voice.

"John!" she cried out in desperate relief.

Josh turned two shades redder in the face.

"Just showing the lady to her cabin," he said quickly.

Josh retreated and made quick steps down the hall.

Whitney launched herself at John and squeezed him with all her might.

"Thank God for you, John! I've never been exposed to such assault!" Whitney said still trembling. "Please come in here!" She insisted as she pulled him by the arm into her cabin.

"What are you doing here?"

John demanded with a firm tone of voice.

"First things first! What were you doing with a creep like that?"

Whitney tried to defend herself even though she felt she shouldn't have to.

"He invited me to dinner. I didn't see any harm in that. How did I know he was only out for *one thing*? He seemed nice at the time. You can't always judge a man right away."

John announced proudly,

"I guess I'll just have to keep an eye on you!"

"Which brings us back to my question, what are you doing here?"

John gave her his shifty eye.

"I'm here to keep an eye on you!" He changed the subject again.

"I'm sorry you had to witness my fight with Hayley. I also apologize for Hayley's treatment of you all these years and what's more my standing by and allowing it to happen."

"It's incredibly unfair and it's entirely my fault! I'm the one who should apologize," Whitney insisted.

John let out a sigh and shook his head in disbelief.

"That's so like you, to take the blame for something you had no control over."

"Hayley is suffering from a dreadful inferiority complex. She isn't really responsible for her actions," Whitney added.

"The devil made her do it, I suppose," John replied. "Responsible or not, I can't and won't tolerate it any longer. Hayley killed my love for her a long time ago."

Whitney tried to defend Hayley.

"Don't you see? This is why she acts the way she does. She's detected your feelings for a long time. This only makes her more irritable and hard to get along with. She's always on the defensive. You'd better think this out thoroughly. You've been married a long time."

John said emphatically,

"I have! It's over!"

Realizing that John's firm statement had closed off the subject, Whitney asked, "Where's your cabin?"

"Promenade Deck, one twelve," John answered with a smile, relieved that they were off the *Hayley* subject.

"Let's tour the ship tonight, do you mind? I'm still a little shaky from my ghastly close call and besides, I need the company of a dear friend," Whitney suggested.

John thought, *dear friend! How am I going to get through this without making a fool of myself?*

✳   ✳   ✳   ✳

John and Whitney walked arm in arm in the opaque moonlight setting their senses on fire with the possibility of dreams coming true.

John's such a good guy, Whitney thought. *He's nothing like that imitation of a man she'd encountered earlier.*

His friends knew John for his reliability, generosity, and loyalty. John was eight years older than Whitney. The men Whitney's age didn't appeal to her. They were so immature and irresponsible. There wasn't anything he couldn't do or hasn't tried. He had multidimensional talents and his intellectual endeavors proved his IQ must have been in the genius range. He exuded an aura of well-being and belief in himself. If only he wasn't Hayley's husband!

"Tomorrow's only an *I owe you* but today is *cash in hand.* Pretend you're happy and fulfilled. Visualize what you want; work at it, then act as if you already have it and before you know it, you'll be there," John was saying.

Whitney looked at John with admiration.

"John! You're so wise!"

"If you take yourself too seriously, you'll never get to the next level," John said.

"You know? Even though I preach these very same things in my profession, it's sometimes over-looked in my every day life. Are you sure you haven't studied psychology? But I don't think we're reading off the same page. All I need is to get my life settled and find the perfect person to share it with," Whitney said.

"How many guys are you willing to take a chance on? How about that reprobate tonight," John interrupted.

John's curtness startled her.

"It's dangerous for a woman to be alone on a cruise or anywhere, really," John continued.

Whitney squeezed John's arm with affection.

"I'm so glad you're here to protect me from all the wolves. To my Prince Charming, who will slay my dragons and protect me from all harm," Whitney teased him with an exaggerated *Noble* tone.

"I'm flattered but John, I'm tired. We've been walking for an hour and a half."

"Okay! I'll see you safely to your cabin," John said hating to give her up for a moment.

*   *   *   *

The days that followed were taut with anxiety.

Whitney suffered a restless night, confused by her assault and about the fact that John was on the cruise with her. She was excited one minute and depressed the next. Excited because she loved being with John, depressed because she couldn't reveal her feelings for John because he was Hayley's husband, separated or *not*. How frustrating! She had the man she loved all to herself on a cruise but her conscience gave her self-restraint that wouldn't allow her to indulge herself.

Dressing casually in white slacks and a multi-colored knit top, Whitney strolled to the breakfast buffet table. She was loading her plate with a hearty breakfast when she heard a male voice behind her.

"May I buy you breakfast?"

Whitney smiled mischievously.

"The food happens to be included in the price of the cruise."

She looked up at a nice, kind looking face grinning at her.

"Oh! Then, by all means, order as much as you like!"

They both giggled.

The nice man introduced himself.

"I'm Chad Brenner."

Whitney was determined not to allow the creep from the night before to spoil her view of all men.

"I'm glad to meet you, Chad. I'm Whitney Blake."

"Where have I heard that name before? Are you famous?" Chad asked.

Whitney rolled her eyes accustomed to this reaction. She answered with a sigh as if tired of explaining,

"I'll never forgive my mother for this! *No*, not at all. My mother loved the actress who played the role of Mrs. Baxter on the old television series, HAZEL. The actresses name was *Whitney Blake*. She thought it was cute since our last name was *Blake*! I've been paying for it all my life!"

"What a lovely name and how appropriate for such a beautiful woman!" Chad said.

Whitney blushed.

"Thank you, Chad!"

"Are you meeting anyone for breakfast?" Chad asked.

"No, I'm traveling alone," Whitney replied.

"May I sit with you?" Chad asked politely.

"You may only if you're not a wolf masquerading as an innocent sheep. I've met one of those already," Whitney responded.

Stunned, Chad said quickly, his face turning red,

"I assure you, I'm *not*!"

He seemed a little offended so to relieve him of his obvious discomfort, Whitney laughed.

"I'm sure you're not."

Whitney and Chad sat down with their breakfasts.

"Are you traveling alone?" Whitney asked.

Chad answered after a sip of his coffee,

"No, I'm traveling with two buddies. They decided to sleep in but I'm an early bird and I hate wasting a minute of my time on my first cruise."

Whitney agreed.

"I know what you mean. This is my first time too."

John walked up to them and pretended to be a jealous husband or lover.

"Well! This is what you do while I'm still asleep?"

Chad jumped out of his seat as if he'd just gotten an electrical charge.

"Oh! I beg your pardon!" he blurted, red-faced with embarrassment.

Without a *good-bye* or a *see you later*, he was off to another table.

"John! How could you do such a thing?" Whitney scolded quite indignantly.

John said nothing. He merely gave her a devious little self-satisfied grin.

"I mean it, John! He was a nice guy! You made me look cheap," Whitney continued to scold.

John still said nothing while Whitney carried on reprimanding him. He ate his breakfast with a great deal of pleasure. John loved to tease Whitney and watch her indignant reaction pretending to be completely innocent.

Later, Whitney and John decided to take advantage of the pool facility. Whitney approached John poolside. She took off her white lacey wrap to expose her beautiful, tanned body, clad in a matching white lacey bikini.

"When they say *women and children first*, they'll sure know who *you* are! Whew! I think I need a cold shower," John commented.

To emphasize his point John immediately turned and made a dramatic dive into the pool.

Whitney prepared her skin for the sun's rays with oil and placed her chair ever so carefully as close to the water as possible so that the sun's reflection would give her a double dose.

John, in his ever so typical mischievous way, where Whitney was concerned, quietly swam under water toward her. His arm and face emerged from the water beside her chair and suddenly, he grasped her arm and pulled her off her chair and into the water.

As she surfaced, sputtering, gasping for air and shaking her hair free, her facial expression was full of contempt.

"*Oh, you!*" she screamed at John as soon as she was able to talk. She swam over to him, grabbed him, slapped his shoulder playfully and pulled him under water as if trying to drown him. John laughed as they wrestled playfully in the water.

An older couple made a comment loud enough for Whitney and John to hear. They'd been watching them with wide-eyed envy, bringing back memories of their youth.

"Isn't love Grande?"

Whitney suddenly took hold of herself, trying to repossess her dignity; she climbed out of the pool. John climbed out after her wondering if the couple saw something that Whitney refused to admit. Maybe she *did* love him, he hoped.

Whitney thought to herself that she *had* to get control of herself. John is another woman's husband!

After the attack of uneasiness wore off, John and Whitney sunned themselves by the pool in verbal silence but their minds were on overload.

John was thinking how amazingly unspoiled and unpretentious Whitney was in spite of all her qualities. Just being with Whitney was sufficiently satisfying to John. He'd wanted her for so very long and the very sight of her excited him beyond depths of any experience he'd ever encountered. Just loving her was sufficient enough to sustain him. There was no heavenly experience comparable to the state that John was in at that moment, lying beside Whitney in the sun, on a cruise, just the two of them. Whitney had an innocent way of making John feel good about himself; he felt strong and protective. Even though she was so intelligent and self-sufficient, she still had a vulnerability about her that made John feel that she needed him. She seemed so small and fragile, that he wanted to slip her into his pocket and carry her with him always. John was serenely happy. ***Yes! Love WAS Grande!***

✳   ✳   ✳   ✳

Whitney visited the ship's hair salon before dinner. Her fun little mishap in the pool destroyed her hair. It wouldn't be at all suitable for the dining room.

✳   ✳   ✳   ✳

John and Whitney walked into the dining room together. The room was huge but the tables were arranged in a cozy, dimly lit manner to encourage romance in the dreamy flight of the imagination. Heavy red linen tablecloths and napkins, fine crystal, heavy ornate silverware, and a single red rose in a bud vase adorned each table.

Surely, Whitney would take much more pleasure in this dinner than the one she'd suffered through the evening before. She felt at ease with John. She was so happy and relieved that she didn't have to eat her meal worrying about trying to make idle chit chat talk with a complete stranger.

The food was exquisite. They shared their table with another couple, Dani and Mike Johnson, who enjoyed working as journalists. The cute couple obviously enjoyed each other's company, a refreshing view of the institution of marriage. Mike was tall and lean with quite an abundance of hair for a man. It was short in length but there was a lot of natural curl over his brows. His face was thin and sharply featured and very attractive.

Dani was tall and thin as well, with short, wispy, dark hair that curled toward her face. She reminded Whitney of Betty Boop with her huge, dark eyes, tiny nose and mouth.

John and Whitney listened intently with wide eyes and dropped jaws to a story the Johnson's were telling about their frightening visit to Cambodia. The picture they painted was so grim that Whitney succumbed to tears more than once during their story.

"Their pitiful, miserable huts were put together with anything they could find that someone else had discarded, even barbed wire," Mike was saying. "They were assembled haphazardly out of beat up oil drums and burlap. When Khmer Rouge took over, the Poor Cambodians fled to Thailand after Viet Nam invaded their country. They walked one hundred miles through the jungles. They were so sick. There was no education in Cambodia. We interviewed a refugee who made our hearts ache! Her clothes were rags, filthy, wet and smelly. Her poor little body was flesh stretched over her bones and she was pale and drawn. She witnessed her own father's dead, murdered body being thrown in her yard. She was only five years old when she was forced to work in the rice fields, digging ditches for irrigation. The soldiers nudged them with the butts of their rifles if they dared to slow down. They grabbed at anything to eat like wild animals. She was forced to watch them beat her friend to death for trying to escape. They couldn't have escaped alive, with the filthy water, no food and horrible disease."

"Oh, how inhumane!" Whitney exclaimed. "It's so hard to believe that human beings are capable of abusing a fellow human being like that and an innocent child, yet!"

Dani and Mike developed strong characters in the work they loved to do.

"Are you two married or lovers?" Dani asked.

"*Neither!* We're just good friends! I wasn't aware that John was even on this cruise until after we were sailing," Whitney blurted out in her obvious discomfort.

"Yes! We just ran into each other quite by accident," John added.

Dani seemed surprised. She commented without reservation.

"You two seem *so* close; *so* right for each other."

"Yes," John agreed. "That's what I keep trying to tell Whitney." His thick eyebrows raised in amusement, knowing full well that his comment would make her squirm in her chair.

"John's my friend's husband," Whitney quickly added defiantly. "We've known each other for years. Really! He's traveling on business and I'm on vacation."

Whitney's nervous rambling, without pause for a breath only succeeded in having the adverse affect on Dani and Mike, convincing them that indeed there was more to this story. Realizing this, Whitney bit her lower lip and glared at John with flashing eyes. She'd already done irreversible damage. Completely dismayed by this revolting circumstance, she trembled with a sudden loss of pride and peering at John through her lashes.

"You're incorrigible!" Whitney uttered. I'll get you for this!" She smiled at John through clenched teeth.

John only beamed back at her, quite pleased with himself. Teasing Whitney gave John such endless pleasure. He could never tease Hayley.

Whitney abandoned any further thought of trying to recover her pride. People will think what they want to think. Their misconception was annoying but there was nothing she could say to change their minds at this point if John wasn't going to help her.

The tension eased off after a while. The four of them enjoyed a few laughs and a few drinks finding that they genuinely found pleasure in each other's company.

Later, the girls excused themselves to powder their noses. While Whitney was waiting for Dani to come out of the powder room, she decided to buy some mints. While she was in line waiting to be helped, she exchanged a few casual words with a nice looking gentleman waiting in line behind her. The small talk led to the revealing fact that they were both on the cruise alone and the question popped up, "Would you care to go dancing with me tonight?"

Whitney saw Dani approaching hearing range. Still trying to avenge herself, she found the perfect opportunity.

"I'd love to!....You may meet me pool side at nine o'clock," Whitney announced a tone louder than needed just to make sure Dani didn't miss it.

Dani's mouth dropped open in disbelief.

"What have you done? Won't John be angry?"

"Why should he?" Whitney said with great satisfaction. "I told you that we were just friends."

The girls returned to their table and were greeted by their male companions.

"Mike and I were discussing the possibility of the four of us getting together tonight and going dancing in the Purple Room. What do you think, girls?" John announced.

Dani's eyes were round with apprehension as she made an obvious, deliberate turn toward Whitney and looked directly into her flustered eyes.

The girls exchanged questioning expressions with each other in the exceedingly long obviously uncomfortable awkward silence.

Whitney squirmed uncomfortably in her seat and stammered barely above a whisper.

"Well I….I just accepted a date for tonight." She squinted her eyes preparing herself for a possible reprimand.

John looked her in the eyes with complete astonishment!

"Haven't you learned yet? The single guys on this ship and probably half of them *aren't* single, are only out for *one thing*!"

Whitney tried to defend herself.

"Don't worry! I'm meeting him at the pool, *not* at my cabin."

"Well!" John said, "Maybe tomorrow night."

Conversation after that was a bit tense so the foursome decided to rest in their cabins to prepare for the late night exercise work-out they had planned.

John and Whitney's stroll on deck was strained, to say the least. Whitney thought to herself, *what a fool she'd been, accepting this date just to prove a point to Dani and Mike. She didn't want to go out with that guy. She wanted to be with John. She had to prove to Dani and Mike that she and John weren't lovers, didn't she? She had to get her revenge, didn't she? Oh! What a disaster! She wasn't usually prone to such vengeful tactics. She'd always thought herself to be so levelheaded and above such **silly** actions. What's gotten into her?*

✳   ✳   ✳   ✳

It was time. Whitney hadn't heard a word from John. She reluctantly donned one of her new slinky gowns. She'd rather *not* have worn anything so beautiful for this stranger she didn't even want to see. But *all* her clothes were new and beautiful. She had no choice.

Whitney looked gorgeous in spite of herself in her lovely red sequined gown. It was strapless and fitted to hug her body in all the right places.

"I wish John could see me in this masterpiece," Whitney said out loud into the mirror.

She grabbed her matching sequined purse, slipped on her matching sequined three-inch heels and slammed the door behind her.

Whitney paced nervously back and forth beside the pool waiting for her date, hoping he wouldn't show.

Suddenly, out of nowhere, a small yipping dog scampered past Whitney. Startled, she lost her footing. The last thing she saw as she fell into the pool was John's face.

Whitney surfaced with her hair plastered to her head *again* and a mortified expression on her face that no one could misconstrue.

Her date showed up just in time to witness John jumping in to save her.

Whitney saw John in the water next to her fully dressed and her date standing at the edge of the pool, horrified.

Out of relief and the absurdity of it all, and having lost her dignity once again, Whitney could no longer control her emotions. She laughed hysterically, so much so that tears came to her eyes and her stomach muscles ached. She was too tense to stay afloat so John grabbed her and laughed along with her.

Whitney's date seemed confused.

"I guess our date is off."

"I guess it is. I'm sorry," Whitney said, trying to calm herself down enough to be serious.

The poor bewildered guy walked away from the pool figuring she must be in good hands or she wouldn't have been exuding such elation.

Whitney's awe-inspiring amusement returned as soon as her ex-date was out of sight. She turned her attention back to John.

"Your gallantry leaves a bit to be desired, John," Whitney teased. "Splendid tactics! Where did you get the dog?"

"I have my ways," John said, smiling indulgently.

"I'll tell you, life can be a *real handful* with you around," Whitney admitted with a sigh. She felt a curiously warm swell of gratitude toward him.

Water to his chest, John put his arms lovingly around her shoulders, conveying such affection for her.

John wiped a wet curl from Whitney's eye.

"You didn't really want to go with that guy, anyway, did you?"

Whitney looked sheepish and shook her head, no. The pupils in her eyes narrowed in concentration.

They gazed into each others' eyes and for the first time, John saw in her eyes what'd been in his since the first year he'd known her. With this bit of encouragement, he was consumed with an uncontrollable urge. He brushed her lips lightly with his, hesitating a moment, not knowing what her reaction would be.

Allowing her mediocre existence turn into a fantasy for a moment, Whitney indulged herself. Their lips came together for the first time, ever so carefully, searching, surrendering, tasting, their senses on fire. This moment was their *Uto-*

pia. If only, maybe, if they didn't open their eyes, this moment would be their *Eternity.* There was nothing that could ever happen in their lives after this moment that could *ever* compare. They clung to each other with such desperation, such overwhelming need.

Whitney emerged from her trance. Her sense of reality had returned and with it disquiet belief that she was there, kissing her John….Who in reality wasn't *hers* at all! She fumbled for the right words. Hopeless tears filled her eyes.

"All of this goes very much against my grain," she said shyly but with an underlying sense of delight. "I need a mental readjustment!" She blushed from the nap of her neck to the top of her forehead and bit her lip to keep it from trembling in her extreme anxiety.

"I know I've been acting strange lately," John said.

"Strange! Strange doesn't nearly explain your actions lately," Whitney interrupted. She searched desperately to find words to cover her extreme discomfort and the impossibility of these latest developments. She decided that these last moments would be treasured in her memory forever and that she didn't need anything else, ever! These moments would fulfill her eternally. Such elation could not possibly be equaled. She needed nothing more.

"Whitney, I love you," John whispered hoarsely. "I've always loved you! I can't imagine myself with anyone else, *ever!* There's no room in my heart for anyone else."

Whitney put her finger over his lips to quiet him. She couldn't grasp what was happening. It was all happening too fast. Knowing in her heart that she *had* to protest, she forced herself to turn away from him and climb out of the pool. She couldn't allow this to happen. She'd avoided this so far all these years. She couldn't let her defenses down now. It wasn't ethical!

John climbed out of the pool after her. What John saw in her eyes and that kiss were all John needed to know. He would stop at nothing until he had Whitney, body, mind and soul for the rest of his life.

John and Whitney attracted disbelieving stares and chuckles as they made their way back to their cabins, leaving a trail of water behind them. They stirred many imaginations.

"Can't we discuss this rationally?" John asked.

"I just can't organize my thoughts right now, John," Whitney answered.

She had to plan a withdrawal from a non-productive situation.

Poor Baby! John thought. *She has such deep convictions but she loves me. I know she does! I'm sure of it!*

"I'll see you in the morning, Whitney. Okay?" John said softly.

She seemed so forlorn as she shook her head and entered her cabin.

The wondrous moment was over.

*   *   *   *

It was a long sleepless night for both of them.

John knocked on Whitney's door, half expecting her not to answer.

The door opened.

"John! You look awful!"

"You didn't sleep either, did you?" John said in return.

Whitney shook her head, no.

"Are you ready for breakfast? I know *I* am!" John asked enthusiastically and with high hopes.

Whitney wore a turquoise and black jumpsuit with a hand-splattered paint design.

Their stroll was a quiet one, no teasing, no small talk, just a simple pensive stroll to the breakfast bar.

Whitney decided it would be best if they sat with groups of people and Mingle to prevent further discussion on the sensitive subject utmost on both their minds.

When John walked into the room with Whitney on his arm, he overflowed with pride. He was trying not to worry about the fear that he may have over-stepped the bounds with her and pushed her beyond his reach. If he couldn't have Whitney, even just as a friend, life wouldn't be worth living. John was under Whitney's spell for good.

John and Whitney ate their breakfast slowly, wordlessly, concentrating on the other passenger's conversations. Whitney was nursing her second cup of coffee with cream.

Mike and Dani didn't notice John and Whitney right away. They'd found another journalist to discuss business with.

"A little diplomacy wouldn't hurt," Mike was saying.

The other guy was arguing.

"Under pressure of deadline we neglected to complete our observation so we improvised to balance out the story line. We made an instant confession and admitted our mistake. The error was corrected in the next edition."

"Yes," Mike said, a little agitated, "but the trouble with that is that the people who missed the next edition were walking around believing a lie!"

"Hey! There're John and Whitney," Dani announced.

Mike excused himself from this deep expose. Dani picked up both their plates and carried them over to join John and Whitney.

"Hi! How'd your date go last night, Whitney?"

"It didn't!" Whitney answered sharply.

Dani looked at John, then at Whitney, fully expecting some kind of explanation.

"Oh!"

"I had a little accident, one which made it impossible," Whitney continued.

John eased Dani's curiosity.

"She fell into the pool, gown, hair-do, and all!"

"What?" Dani exclaimed, incredulously.

"*I had a little* **help**!" Whitney proclaimed, indignantly.

Dani smiled understandingly at Mike without bothering to ask for the details.

"I'll have to spend another couple of hours in the hair salon again today, thanks to *John*!" Whitney continued.

"Is Whitney on the *Pity Potty* again?" John teased. John couldn't resist the temptation to tease Whitney in spite of their little *bone of contention*.

A friend of Mike and Dani's approached them.

"Hi! Mike! Dani!"

Dani acknowledged her.

"Hi, Yvonne! I'd like you to meet Whitney and John. Whitney, John, this is Yvonne Mantand. She's a dress designer."

Whitney perked up.

"Oh! How exciting! I used to design my doll clothes when I was little. I used to put on shows for my friends, and change my dolls into all the different clothes I designed and made. I can't imagine a more exciting career."

"Yes! I love it," Yvonne said. "It's tough to break into the field though because there are so many designers. I guess too many people feel the same way we do. It's every little girl's dream."

"How do you convince the women to change their style every season?" Whitney asked enthusiastically.

Yvonne obviously loved talking about her career and Whitney obviously loved listening.

Yvonne was a perky, bubbly girl with ingenious charm. Her long tapering legs, pretty face with shoulder-length black hair, feathered into a wild, tussled style all could have allowed her to be a perfect model as well. She could have a double career and model her own creations.

"If we didn't have subtle ways to change styles, we'd be out of business. We have to change them ever so slightly so as not to overwhelm them but to encourage them to buy a new wardrobe," Yvonne admitted honestly.

"Yes," Whitney said, "we women spend a fortune on clothes! Nobody *needs* all those clothes. We don't buy them because we need them. We buy them because we *look* good in them and they make us *feel good* about ourselves. How boring life would be without *change.* Take out all the curiosity and techniques for covering flaws and what would we have?"

"One big orgy?" John attempted *cute* answer.

They laughed.

"On the contrary, sex would become another every day chore instead of fun and games," Yvonne declared.

"That makes sense," Whitney said.

"Why is our country so preoccupied with looks?" John asked.

Mike finally found a road into the conversation.

"Because we're a rich nation with an abundance of money that we control. Other poor nations haven't the time or the money to worry about such frivolities. Their biggest worry is finding food to sustain their lives." Once Mike was on this subject, it was hard to pull him off. His anger and indignation on this subject was obvious.

"Yes!" John said. "We're a lucky nation, all right!"

"All these unfortunate nations that Mike and I have seen make us feel guilty for having such an extravagant lifestyle," Dani explained.

"Are you going to Acapulco?" Mike asked.

"Actually, we haven't discussed it yet," Whitney replied.

"Would you like to go with us?" Dani asked.

John looked at Whitney.

"Yes! We'd love to!"

"Bring your swimsuits in case we decide to hit the beach," Mike insisted.

"Sounds like fun! It's too bad you have to meet your friend in Acapulco, Yvonne. You could go along with us."

Yvonne peeked at her watch.

"Oh! Look at the time! I'd better run or I'll be late!" Yvonne rushed off!

"How about we meet at ten o'clock in the lobby?" Mike suggested.

"Sounds good to us," John said, looking at Whitney for approval.

*   *   *   *

The two couples walked off the ship happily.

Whitney decided to allow her excitement of her vacation to override her end-less puzzlement about John. After all, she was on vacation. She was supposed to be enjoying herself, not worrying about the *possibilities* concerning John. Should she *give in* and ignore her scruples?

"I'd like to come back to Mexico and really tour," Mike was saying. "I wish we had the time to go into Mexico City and get away from the commercial parts of Mexico. I'd love to see the cathedral of Mexico that was built on the ruins of the Aztec Temple of Teocall, Lake Xochinilco with its floating gardens and the ruins of Teotihuacan with its pyramids. I've been told that these are sights a picture could never do justice."

"I didn't know you were such an authority on Mexico," John said.

"I studied it in college and was fascinated by it," Mike said.

"Terrific!" Whitney said. "You may be our personal tour guide!"

"According to legend," Mike continued. "The image of the Virgin miracu-lously appeared on the mantle of the Indian Juan Diego which was enshrined in the Virgin of Guadalupe. I'd love to see the better artwork in person. Some of the murals painted by Diego Rivera and Jose Clemente Orozco are said to be master-pieces."

Whitney whispered to John.

"Mike has quite a capacity for retaining trivial facts. I'm impressed!"

"Don't be too impressed!" Dani said. "Mike brushed up before we left home."

They were all in awe of the spectacular flower gardens everywhere they turned.

"I'd like to see a bull fight! Do you think we could fit it in?" John suggested.

Whitney looked at Dani with a sour expression on her face as if she'd just tasted rancid milk.

"Oh! I don't know if I could handle that *and* all of this Mexican food all at once. I don't think my stomach is strong enough!"

"Maybe we can check out some of Mexico's shops while the guys are satisfying their thirst for bloodshed," Dani suggested, much to Whitney's relief.

*   *   *   *

The girls were analyzing and judging each object in each shop as if they were in one huge art gallery and they were the most discriminating of collectors.

They weren't surprised by the vast commercialism. The soaring skyscrapers lining the beach were magnificent and just beyond the skyscrapers the beautiful majestic mountains supplied such graceful depth to the view.

Whitney announced, "This isn't the way at all that I pictured Mexico!"

"You've seen too many old movies," Mike suggested. "That's the way it *used* to be. As I said, we need to get off the beaten tour path and check out the locals."

*   *   *   *

After a long adventurous day, the exhausted group managed to make it back to the ship loaded down with sombreros, ponchos, ceramics, and wicker for souvenirs and gifts.

After the two couples went their separate ways, John offered to help Whitney carry her souvenirs to her cabin. She was forced to accept his offer since his arms were loaded with *her* souvenirs and there was no way she could have carried everything herself.

After struggling to open her cabin door, they both rushed inside and released all of the bags onto the bed with a great sigh of relief. They both collapsed on the sofa and kicked off their shoes. They were sprawled out; their swollen half numb limbs seemed paralyzed in the position that they'd fallen.

John let out a huge, long, worn out sigh of relief.

"Whew! I'm exhausted!.... How about I spend the night right here?" Without waiting for an answer, he curled up in a fetal position on the mini-sofa and closed his eyes.

"John! Oh no you don't!"

A sudden burst of energy rushed through Whitney's body out of panic. She jumped up and hurriedly poured each of them a brandy from the bottle on their mini bar.

"Here! This should revive you enough to make it back to your cabin," Whitney scolded.

There was no reaction. She put the brandy down and tried to shake John awake.

Unexpectedly, John's arm reached up and grabbed her. Her caught off guard reaction and her sudden surprise momentarily permitted John to pull her down to him.

Once Whitney's wit was restored she protested wildly.

"John!" she screamed. "I'm not kidding! We have to behave honorably!"

She jumped up and straightened her clothes. John sat up abruptly and started sipping his brandy.

Flushed and out of breath, Whitney sat in the chair across the room from John to avoid further attack.

"Do you have any more of those chocolate cordials left?" John asked.

Refusing to get close to John again, her voice rose shrilly.

"They're in the top drawer beside you."

"You realize we have to talk!" John said seriously.

He walked to the end of the table, opened the drawer and took out the cordials. He sat down and before he took one bite, he looked straight into Whitney's tired eyes.

"We'll start with, *I love you!*" John said in all seriousness, in his easy, natural way.

"John, please don't put me in this position," Whitney said sadly, stiff and unbending.

"Double Jeopardy! I can't be tried twice for a crime I've already committed! I get the feeling you feel the same way about me," John spouted, trying to be clever.

Whitney didn't say anything in her defense. What could she possibly say? She'd be lying if she said he was wrong.

"I've always loved you," John continued. "Don't I deserve some kind of compensation or credit for abstinence all these years? Do you have any idea how difficult it's been to watch you with other men, hearing your problems, watching you get hurt and not being able to comfort you in the way you needed to be comforted? I've been content to merely share in your life as a friend. Just being with you in any capacity has given me joy beyond words. There will never be anyone else for me! You've never given me the slightest notion that you cared about me any more than you cared about any of your friends. Loving you *so* completely makes my life worthwhile. This feeling can't be matched ever. I would never have done anything to risk losing you in my life."

"What's important in life is to be happy and have joy in your life," John declared, hopefully, trying so hard to coax a confession out of her.

The gaze into each others' eyes was intense.

"I'm living the dream, being here with you, Whitney," John continued, in his soft, gentle tone of voice.

Whitney's long tapering fingers twirled her hair nervously. Obviously, she'd garnished similar praise in her past but coming from John…. Well, it was like the difference between a knock, knock joke and a dirty joke! The emotions John evoked in her were almost unbearable. She felt the heat travel through her body to her face, the longing stirred within her. She tried so hard to control her trembling body for fear it would certainly tip him off. The words were easier to disguise. She was so confused and her heart was crying out to him but her stubborn ethics didn't dare allow her the luxury. The whole trip had been fraught with awkward moments. Here she was with this burly, handsome man she'd loved for so long sitting only inches from her. She thought to herself to say something would be to confront herself.

John knew her so well. He knew that she was a very straight-up person, strong in her convictions, that even *if* she loved him she would never admit it.

"With self-restraint like yours, you could have been a nun!" John said, trying to make light of the situation.

Whitney smiled faintly but was still silent. After that heart-wrenching testimony, she poured herself another brandy, still confused. Her emotional state was in such distress! She asked herself despairingly, how could anyone be so euphoric and so miserable all at the same time? She was so excited on one hand by all that John was saying and able to relate to his confession completely. On the other hand, how could she interfere in someone else's life? Hayley would undoubtedly despise her. People would talk and her conscience would eat her alive. It was an emotional tug of war.

John had a tranquilizing effect on her and after her third brandy; she released her tension through hopeless tears.

John walked over to her and silently held her in his arms. He breathed in the clean, sweet, powdery fragrance of her so deeply that he felt dizzy. They stood together for a long time, not kissing, just pressing their bodies tightly together as two people would do who met after an absence too long to be spoiled by mere words. Comfortable in the silence between them, it was a moment in time that stood apart, as if time stood still as in a dream, to reveal mutual need. It only served to season Whitney's confusion. She found herself frustrated and heart-broken.

Finally, Whitney broke the lovely, touching moment.

"I'm so tired," she whispered in a drained voice.

John quickly emptied the bed of all the bags and packages, then turned around and scooped her up in his arms.

He pulled the covers back for her, guided her gently between the sheets and tucked her in. He leaned over her to kiss her forehead with great tenderness as her eyes closed.

So exhausted himself, John took the spare blanket out of the drawer and made himself as comfortable as he could on the much too short sofa.

This vacation had turned out to defeat its own purpose. This cruise was drain-ing both their energy and their emotions, but at least they were accomplishing something. They were searching for an end or a beginning after a long emotional battle.

✳   ✳   ✳   ✳

Whitney woke up the next morning rubbing her stiff neck and when she tried to stand she found that her legs were sore from all the walking she'd done the day before. She hobbled into the bathroom to take care of her morning chores.

Twenty minutes later, Whitney walked out of the bathroom. There was some-thing ethereal about her as she stood with the soft golden glow of the morning light coming in the porthole. She was fresh out of the shower and wrapped in a towel. She took her undies out of the drawer and slipped them on under her towel. The towel dropped to the floor as she put on her bra and reached behind her to fasten it. She walked over to the closet to choose her breakfast outfit. Despite her diminutive size, she was perfectly proportioned.

"Huh?" Whitney gasped out loud and held herself tense.

The sight of John lying on the sofa huddled under a blanket startled her. The sudden comprehension filled her expression with disbelief.

Obviously inordinately pleased with himself, John had a devilish grin on his face and only one eye open.

"I tried not to look," he said with a chuckle, "but one of my eyes wouldn't stay closed!"

"What are *you* doing in *my* cabin?" Whitney insisted with stubbornness in her well defined chin and horrified.

"You didn't seem to object last night," John said in his most reassuring voice. His grin gleamed with mischief.

Whitney quickly pulled an outfit out of the closet and rushed into the bath-room, her defiance fully in tact.

"It's too late for that, Whitney! You know? You're drop dead gorgeous, sheer perfection!" John interjected eagerly.

Through the bathroom door Whitney was still scolding.

"How could you spend the night in my cabin? What will people think?"

"Do you mind? It's been a long night. I need to use the bathroom," John interrupted.

Still distressed and alarmed, Whitney threw open the door.

"Help yourself! You've helped yourself to everything else!"

When John came out of the bathroom, Whitney continued to scold him.

"You'd better get out of here before someone sees you! Look at the time! It's ten o'clock! Everyone will be in the halls! This kind of thing is oxygen to scandal! My reputation will be unfairly tarnished!"

Thinking that a little humor may cut the tension, Whitney ended with, "and to think! I didn't even experience the pleasure to deserve such unrelenting criticism and demeaning accusations!"

John chuckled, relieved that she chose to vent her spleen in a humorous manner. She was openhearted and had a good-natured attitude. John admired her adventurous spirit.

"No one knows us and surely no one cares where I spent the night," John tried to assure her.

Just then there was a knock at the door.

"Oh! God!" Whitney whispered in a panic. "Who could that be?"

After a long stunned pause, Whitney tried to compose herself.

"Who is it?" she managed to utter.

"It's Mike and Dani," came a high-pitched, familiar voice from the other side of the door.

A sudden burst of paranoia surged through her. Whitney gaped at John with wild, frantic eyes.

"What are we going to do?" She was quaking in her shoes.

John's chest swelled with pride and a playful grin sped across his face.

John announced out loud, before Whitney could stop him.

"We'll be right there!"

Whitney smacked him on the shoulder to make sure he fully understood her disappointment in him.

John opened the door, smiling as if he'd just swiped the candy and had gotten away with it.

"Come in. We're not quite ready yet."

Dani looked at Whitney, confused at first. She gave her a cognizant smile.

They *could* have gotten away with it if John wasn't standing there grinning beyond *both* ears.

Noticing John was in the same rumpled clothes he was in the day before; Mike gave John a congratulatory slap on the shoulder.

"*Well!*" He deliberately cleared his throat with distinguished fervor. "How about if we give you two a little more time? We'll meet you at brunch in an hour."

Mike and Dani closed the door behind them.

Whitney heard them laughing all the way down the hall. She looked at John as a mother would look at her misbehaving child.

She fussed with fierce protestation.

"I hope you're satisfied! You're succeeding at playing havoc with my good reputation!"

John was still grinning.

"See you in an hour," he said quickly as he grabbed his belongings. He walked with great confidence and panache down the hall. Whitney watched him disappear around the corner.

✳   ✳   ✳   ✳

Whitney was lying across the bed, sipping the coffee she'd ordered from room service. Resting from the rigors of her late night hours, she couldn't help but think of her mind-boggling torment weighing one wrenching fact against the other.

She opened her eyes and looked at her watch.

"Oh! I've got to get going!"

Whitney quickly sat in front of her mirror, her neck extended, while skillfully applying her makeup.

Whitney was feeling serenely happy today in spite of Mike and Dani's dreadful misconception of her relationship with John. On the other hand, were they so far off base? All she'd have to do is turn off her defense mechanism and *Voila*! Her body quivered with the mere thought of the possibility. She *had* to avoid her impulses even though she was dancing with anticipation of being with him again. She'd become accustomed to controlling her desire for him but now it was becoming increasingly more difficult having John bare his soul to her and swearing his marriage was over. It was taking a lot of strenuous arguments to persuade her to let down her guard.

Whitney marched into the breakfast room with her curls bouncing on top of her head. She was conscious of eyes watching her as she overloaded her plate with eggs, hash browns, a muffin, bacon, sausage, cantaloupe, and strawberries.

John, Mike and Dani were already seated and smiling when Whitney joined them.

"My!" Mike commented. "That's a lot of food for such a little thing like you. What have you done to make you *so* hungry?"

Whitney refused to give him the satisfaction. She gave him a tight-lipped smile, realizing what he was aiming for. He wasn't getting a rise out of her today. She was feeling *too good*!

"You look downright exuberant today, Whitney," Dani said.

"Yes! I feel on top of the world today," Whitney replied happily, pausing to look at John, "and I'm not going to let anything or anyone spoil my mood. Is that understood, *John?*"

John saluted and obeyed.

"*Yes! Mam!*"

They introduced Whitney to a man who was sitting with them.

"Whitney, this is Tony Rosato," Mike said.

Tony stood up and shook her hand politely.

"He's a very popular painter in the area," Mike continued.

"How interesting," Whitney commented.

"I've been watching you," Tony said. "You'd make a perfect subject. You exude such vitality and character, not to mention your exceptional beauty."

John spoke up.

"Do you have plenty of red paint to paint that blush on her face?"

Tony was finishing his breakfast, looking at his watch. He took his last mouthful of food.

"I have to be going. It was a pleasure meeting you. Maybe we can get together again. Here's my card."

John shook Tony's hand.

"Yes! Maybe I'll commission you to paint Whitney's portrait for me."

"The pleasure would be all mine," Tony assured John. He winked at Whitney.

"My! He's quite the charmer," Whitney said.

"Whitney, look at that," Dani said.

They watched two women obviously ranking high on the social ladder. They were impeccably dressed and there was no doubt of their vastly superior attitudes.

"Delightfully thin, staggeringly wealthy, and enormously chic," Whitney said.

Everyone seemed to take great pains to please them and used a special intonation that seemed to be reserved for only the *Elite*.

"Let's take the logical approach. You don't dress for who you are, you dress for what you want to be," Whitney offered optimistically.

"In that case, I think I'll rush back to my cabin and do a complete overhaul!" Dani announced.

"I know an ambush when I see one. They're just out to trap some poor sucker," John said.

John had a genius for finding something humorous in every situation.

"*Oh*! Come on, John! They're probably *so* successful they couldn't care less about a man," Whitney said with a flattering smile.

John made a quick comeback.

"Money isn't everything. Without the love of a man, what does a woman really have?"

"Being wealthy only makes love suspicious," Whitney expounded. "How could they ever be sure the man's love is genuine? Frankly, I wouldn't care to be so loaded."

Dani agreed.

"I think too that it can be a detriment to have too much wealth."

"Being born rich can't be very satisfying," Whitney added. "How would you develop self-worth? If everything is handed to you, there are no goals, no achievement, and no self-satisfaction. I've worked hard to get where I am. I can't imagine what it must be like not to have that feeling of success and what would you do in life but play games and wander endlessly searching for that *something* for that something that is missing in your life. You *can* have too much time on your hands. Believe me! I get a lot of these wealthy people in my practice who are so confused about life. They wonder what their *purpose* on this earth is. I get a lot of women also suffering from the similar symptoms, lacking the same ingredient self-worth. So many women give up their careers for love and babies, falling for that old chauvinistic attitude that he'll take care of her for the rest of her life then they're totally bewildered when he gets tired of her and throws her over for a younger version. They're left holding the bag, fighting for child support, and no means of supporting the family. Cleaning up after other people isn't satisfying. She feels she's wasting her life away. A lot of these women are poor mothers because they're so unhappy and unfulfilled."

"Will you two put your attention in *park* for a while? What would you girls like to do this afternoon?" John interrupted.

*   *   *   *

After an action packed day of gambling for the gents and sunbathing for the ladies, the couples decided to wine and dine then dance into the wee hours. The girls devoted a couple of hours to the beauty salon endeavoring to transform themselves into another realm, another time, another status. They walked out humming the tune to, *SOME ENCHANTED EVENING.*

They succeeded. The sight of this impeccable vision of perfection mesmerized John as Whitney walked serenely and graciously toward him.

Although meticulously pinned to the top of her head, Whitney's curls appeared loose and soft. Soft, dangling curls graced her face and neck, which supplied just the right touch of sexiness that raised John's eyebrows. He tried to exercise self-control. Her turquoise, beaded strapless gown appeared to wrap and bound her curves in all the right places to reveal her perfect shape and rounded cleavage.

John, looking very gallant in his tux, was speechless. Thinking to himself, *how am I going to control myself tonight? She's the most beautiful thing I've ever seen.* Whitney's capacity for innocent sensuality was infinitely captivating. All John could do was make a growling sound deep in his throat as if he were ready to spring on his prey.

Whitney was hoping that she'd make an impression on John. The expression on his face was enough proof that she'd succeeded.

Both their hearts were thumping so hard, that they were sure the other heard.

John finally took her hand, raised it to his lips and kissed it gently and tenderly.

"Miss America, I presume," John said, his voice cracking from the overwhelming passion he was feeling.

Dani looked stunning in a black silk gown with spaghetti straps.

The two couples floated into the room filled with an air of opulence. The spirits of Oscar De Larenta, Bill Blass and Chistian Dior captivated the room with their unique creations. A pleasant blending of perfume pervaded the air. They'd never seen so many eloquent fashions in one place and not in person.

The music was slow and easy allowing the mind to slip into another time and to put aside any unpleasant thoughts.

The couples were seated at their reserved table where they studied the menu.

John couldn't take his eyes off Whitney. He felt supremely good all over, not forgetting the night before when he bared his soul to Whitney. What a relief it was saying the words out loud. He was convinced she loved him as well.

Having their food placed before them in grand style, they used their most gracious manners in consuming their gastronomic delights.

"Do you think there's any chance we could sneak into the kitchen and bribe somebody to give us these recipes?" Whitney asked Dani. "I've never eaten such delicious food! As a rule, I don't care that much for gourmet food but this is perfect."

"I hope all your meals have as much garlic in as mine does. Whew!" Dani said. "In close proximity, this stuff can be positively anti-social! How do you like it, guys?"

John and Mike agreed.

"We'd just as soon have fried chicken!"

"Good ole country boys, eh?" Dani snapped.

✳   ✳   ✳   ✳

The dishes were cleared; the lights dimmed and the music was luring people onto the dance floor.

"M'Lady, would you care to dance?" John asked Whitney, faking a thick British accent. He dropped to a low, exaggerated sweeping bow in front of her.

Whitney accepted graciously with a courtesy. She asked John as they were walking arm in arm to the dance floor, "When did elevate yourself to that lofty status?"

Mike and Dani chuckled.

"They'd make a cute comedy act."

Whitney's body quivered excitedly inside as she danced with John. He held her with such respect and affection.

In her heart, Whitney prayed, made the most profound wish to allow John and herself to find peace one way or another. She was afraid what would happen to them after the cruise was over. His friendship was so important to her. Would he hate her and refuse her friendship and avoid her if she couldn't allow herself to love him openly? And if she were to let down her defenses and allow herself the privilege of loving him and allow their love to come together, would their love last or fade away leaving nothing but indifference between them? What ever happens, their relationship will never be the same. It couldn't be. Loving him was easy but creating a relationship could be disastrous!

John carried a hint of nobility, an air of another time. His impeccable behavior and subtle charm, along with the magic of the evening placed Whitney under a spell. She wished that this protected soothing world could go on forever. John was witty, clever and wordlessly understanding, so much the *Ideal Man* that it frightened her that she was fortunate enough to have this man's heart. Whitney was overwhelmed by it all.

"I love you, Whitney," John whispered while he had Whitney trapped on the dance floor. "Words don't do justice to the way I feel about you. I need you in my life, preferably by my side every minute as my wife. But if you can't live with the guilt, I'll take you any way I can have you, even if it's only friendship. I don't want to cause you unhappiness in any way. Loving is caring for someone else more than yourself."

He gazed directly into Whitney's stubborn logical little face. He stopped, arrested by a fleeting expression of fear. He encouraged himself by thinking that something worth having is certainly worth waiting for and if it were time she needed, then time she would have. No one else would do. It *had* to be Whitney! His criterion was not to scare her away but to reach through her wall of ethics and convince her that their love was right in spite of anything or anybody else. John also realized, knowing her so well, that all the emotional damage she'd witnessed in her profession inoculated her against the idea that love could actually work. He was determined to exercise his infinite patience because Whitney was worth it. He wasn't living without Whitney.

The song ended so they made their way through the crowd back to their friends.

"Were you two trying to do a Fred and Ginger number out there?" Dani commented.

"Maybe more like Fred and Ethel," John said.

Everyone laughed.

John raised his glass.

"I'd like to propose a toast, *A Thing of Beauty is a Joy Forever,*" he said looking straight at Whitney.

John poured everyone another round.

"And to our new friends, beautiful Dani and a pretty fair chap Mike…and may Miss America cast her fears adrift!"

They clinked their glasses together and sipped their champagne.

In an effort to change the subject, Whitney turned to Dani.

"I wish I could take this maid service home with me. It's so nice to go back to my cabin to a freshly made bed with clean sheets, clothes folded, fresh towels and a new appetizing treat every day."

"Yes! I could get spoiled real fast," Dani said.

John ignored Whitney's attempt to change the subject.

"I wish I'd met Whitney before I married Hayley. Whitney's the best thing that's ever happened to me. If I hadn't married Hayley, I'd never have met Whitney so what is a person to do? Live with a mistake and be miserable forever or try to correct it? Love is as love does. Love isn't something you have control over. It just happens."

Whitney tried to make light of the embarrassing situation John was placing her in.

"Ah! You haven't seen me without makeup yet. You'll soon change your tune. I guarantee it," Whitney said nervously.

There was no stopping John.

"My wife, Whitney's long-time friend, and I have split up. She refuses to accept my pledge of love for her."

John smiled his winning smile.

"This has the connotation of an intoxicated man taking advantage of the current circumstance and making it his perfect opportunity," Whitney scolded.

"I'm far from intoxicated by alcohol," John pleaded. *You*, Whitney, only *You* intoxicate me! You meet someone extraordinarily perfect for you, like *Special Order* straight from GOD himself. Is it right to turn your back on it? What would God think?"

"I love this song. Let's dance, John," Whitney insisted.

Mike and Dani followed them to the dance floor.

Dani took hold of Whitney's arm to slow her a moment. She whispered in her ear, "I'd go for it, if I were you!"

Whitney continued to scold John on the dance floor.

"You embarrass me to no end! I feel so foolish I could jump overboard to avoid Mike and Dani!"

"I know," John said soothingly. "But if everyone jumped overboard every time they felt uncomfortable, there wouldn't be room for this ship! Don't you know how hard it is for me to repress my feelings after all these years and now finally being able to do something about it, I can hardly contain myself. You can't blame me for endeavoring to quench my desire when I know its right."

Whitney sighed.

"John, I'm sorry. I know how you feel," Whitney said, now feeling guilty *because* of *him*.

John's eyes widened with complete surprise.

"You do?" he blurted out without hesitation.

Whitney wanted to kick herself for giving him encouragement.

John thought that the ice must have been breaking up. He favored Whitney with a hopeful smile.

"That's the nicest thing you've ever said to me," John said with a quickening pulse.

The song ended. They started walking back to their table. John was so overwhelmed with the excitement from his newly acquired hope that he spun Whitney into his arms as a ballet dancer spins his partner. Trailing a finger down her cheek, his gaze tense and searching, John kissed her tenderly, sweetly in front of the world.

Dani and Mike spotted them and started clapping, encouraging the whole room to break into a cheering section.

Whitney was burning red inside and out with embarrassment.

The music started again so John and Whitney remained on the dance floor, trying not to break the spell. Their eyes connected and held for a brief moment fully understanding at that precise moment that an intimate wave of communication had been conveyed. Words weren't needed. Whitney's eyes reflected her innermost emotions. There wasn't a feeling in the world to compare with the bliss both John and Whitney were experiencing. John held her body tight against him but with gentle tenderness. Whitney's face nuzzled John's neck, her lips pressed against his bare skin. The excitement pulsating through his veins was almost too much to bear.

All the champagne Whitney consumed was causing her to be a little disoriented, or at least that's what she thought was causing it. The atmosphere, the collective moment and her overwhelming desire caused her knees to Buckle.

John sensed her condition, as the aura around them was ten degrees warmer than the rest of the room.

Suddenly, Whitney's knees gave way and in one glorious sweeping triumph, John whisked her up into his arms and carried her out of the room.

Since John and Whitney seemed to be the center of everybody's attention, the rest of the room full of people was aware of what was going on so this dramatic display induced another round of applause. John and Whitney were the envy of every man and woman in the room.

John carried his priceless treasure all the way to his cabin. They were both filled with a sense of the immediate future that was too ecstatic to be spoiled by mere words.

Standing outside John's cabin, he wrapped Whitney in his arms as she burrowed into them. They didn't speak for fear they'd spoil the magic. They held each other so tightly that they were aware of each other's heartbeats racing out of control. They held fast so as not to allow this moment to pass. This moment was more moving than a thousand words could ever express. This moment of surrender was as frightening as it was exciting. Saying only her name, he kissed her eyes gently, her nose, and then tasted one lip. His gentle, tender, loving kisses turned into a deep searching one as if all the years of their loneliness were experienced all at once. There was such a desperate need for each other. Urgent longing shot through him. Unable to restrain himself any longer, John's manhood pressed against Whitney's body whispering a hint of caution to her, but for once she chose to ignore her ethics and to go with her heart.

John finally opened the door. He maneuvered her gallantly through the door and closed it behind them.

With whatever compromise they'd made with normality, at least now they were together.

John and Whitney were consumed with an overpowering, long overdue passion that was well deserved. No ethics, no guilt, no barriers, no hesitancy, no more dreading when it would stop.

This moment was much more than Whitney'd known existed. All she cared about at that moment was that she was with the man she loved and yearned to be with for so long. All the suppressed desire, the pent-up emotions exploded. She was consumed with such desire that she couldn't get close enough to him. She felt as if she could actually bite into his skin and devour him, she wanted him so badly.

The rampant desire rushed through them and their bodies melded perfectly together.

"Love is the ultimate!" Whitney said impatiently and breathlessly, as John caught her mouth with his.

"I never knew my heart could be so full!" John said with a great deal of relief.

Luxuriating in the fact that they'd finally gotten together, nothing else mattered.

Whitney's head rested in the hollow of John's shoulder, as they snuggled, not wanting their skin to ever part. Her fingers fondled a piece of his hair as she giggled delightedly, joyously. Whitney could hardly contain herself. She wondered if she was going to wake up at any moment back to her dull, mediocre existence. This can't be happening! Heaven *couldn't* be better than this!

*   *   *   *

John and Whitney woke up in each other's arms, in total disbelief that their night wasn't one of their fantasy dreams.

Whitney woke first, pressing her body to his.

"Pinch me," she whispered.

John's eyes opened suddenly.

"What?" John asked.

"I said, pinch me," she repeated. "This isn't really happening, is it?"

Still not wanting their skin to part, they started all over again with Whitney crawling on top of John as their rapture continued.

"I have to go to the bathroom," Whitney pouted afterward. "I don't want to leave you for a minute. I love you so much! I'm afraid to let you out of my sight."

When Whitney came out of the bathroom, John had ordered juice and coffee to be sent to his room.

"Oh! No! I left my purse on the table last night! How will I get into my room to change clothes?" Whitney gasped.

"I'll call the steward," John suggested.

"No!" Whitney said abruptly. They'll know I spent the night!"

John laughed.

"After last night, I guarantee everyone on board knows about last night. I'll order two breakfasts sent to us. At least we'll be able to think better once we get some food into our stomachs."

When Whitney got out of the shower their breakfast was waiting.

John raised his glass.

"To fifteen years of suffering put to an end."

John held Whitney's loving gaze. Love illuminated her face and her eyes danced with excitement. To be able to give to someone who'd given him so much was a joy he had never known existed.

"I want to marry you as soon as possible. I want you with me every minute of the rest of my life," John said matter of factly.

Whitney peered into his handsome face and nodded, speechless, her whole being ascending to an idea she'd had for so long had not consciously entered her mind until that moment. She'd accepted long ago that she'd never have him.

"But Hayley," she started to say.

"Hayley knows it's over," John interrupted. "Having lived with Hayley all these years, I can tell you she's not good for either of us. We can't feel guilty on her account because her hate has no bounds. She has no respect for humanity. She's not capable of loving or being loved."

"She's not a happy person," Whitney said. "Even *you* didn't make her happy! We'll have to wait until the dust settles."

"I know that once it settles it'll be *gold* dust," John said.

Tears of pride welled in Whitney's eyes.

"I love you so much and now that we're together on this cruise raising my hopes, I couldn't bear it if I couldn't have you now!" Whitney cried.

"I'm glad you changed your mind. Finally, we can get down to some meaningful passion," John said, gazing into her eyes. He took her hand and squeezed it.

"Thank you for allowing me the luxury," Whitney returned the sentiment.

"Let's get down to some serious nuzzling," John said with a mischievous grin.

"I love you. Love really *is* the heart of life," Whitney admitted, settling into John's strong arms.

✴   ✴   ✴   ✴

"Well! We're stuck in your cabin with nothing to do," Whitney said after a lovely breakfast.

A devilish grin sped across John's face. Their eyes locked.

She dropped John's robe to the floor revealing her glorious, freshly showered body. She unbuttoned John's crisp, starched white shirt and unzipped his pants. John's clothes ended up in a heap on the floor as they tried to devour each other on the way to the bed.

John finally opened the channels for her to express herself freely. She felt that she was more herself here with John than she's ever been before.

Afterward, Whitney was lying in bed watching John comb his hair *again*.

"So, what do you think? Does Redford have to worry?" Whitney teased.

Just then, they heard a faint tap on the door.

Whitney made haste to the bathroom. John opened the door slightly as Whitney's purse was handed through the door.

It was Mike.

"Thought you might be needing this, eventually," he whispered with a chuckle. "See you later?"

John closed the door.

"Whitney!" John called out. "You'll be relieved to know that your purse has just arrived."

Whitney stepped out of the bathroom in a towel.

"Oh! What a relief! If you'll be kind enough to escort me to my cabin, Kind Sir? I'll change and we'll look for Dani and Mike. Maybe we can go to Puerto Vallarta together."

*   *   *   *

The days that followed were full of intense bliss for John and Whitney. They were like newlyweds, touching, squeezing and teasing.

They exchanged addresses and phone numbers with Mike and Dani before they were ready to leave the ship.

John and Whitney walked off the ship with high hopes for their wondrous future together. They were bubbling over with their much-deserved bliss.

While getting their luggage together teasing each other and giggling like teenagers enjoying their first case of puppy love, the police approached them.

"John Garber?"

"Yes?"

"You're under arrest for the murder of your wife, Hayley Garber." They read him his rights and handcuffed him.

John and Whitney's faces turned white with shocked disbelief.

"Murdered? Hayley's dead?" John managed to squeeze out in his horror.

"Where's my son?"

"He's in good hands with his grandparents," the officer answered.

Whitney couldn't hold back the tears.

"Oh, Hayley!" she uttered, adding a double dose of guilt.

Whitney had all of their luggage put into her car then she rushed to the police station.

*   *   *   *

"We have to check every angle. You have a motive and no good alibi. You had a fight with your wife and you left on a cruise with another woman. How does that sound to you? I'm afraid we'll have to hold you. I suggest you get in touch with your attorney." The investigator was saying to John.

When Whitney arrived, it was her turn to face interrogation. Whitney fought back the tears and tried to handle herself with grace and dignity.

"Would it be impertinent of me to say that this whole thing is ridiculous?" she began.

"Please calm yourself, Miss Blake! Did you and Mr. Garber plan to murder Hayley Garber?"

"Certainly *not*! Hayley was one of my longest friends. We've known each other since we were kids."

"How long were you and Mr. Garber having an affair?"

"We weren't having an affair! I didn't know he was going to be on the cruise! And anyway, John *did not kill Hayley*! He simply isn't capable of such a thing! He's kind and good and he's never so much as uttered an unkind word to anyone in my presence."

Whitney broke down into tears. She couldn't believe this was happening.

"Where were you on May twenty eighth between five and eight a.m.?"

"I'm sure I was home by myself preparing for my trip."

*   *   *   *

Stephanie was called into the station.

Stephanie waited in a tiny room behind one-way glass so that the suspect wouldn't see her.

She was horrified when Whitney was brought in wearing a dark wig and a lot of heavy makeup.

"No! No!" Stephanie insisted emphatically. "The height and eyes are all wrong! I'm absolutely sure she's *not* the woman I saw running out of Monica's house. What makes you think that Hayley's murder has a connection with Monica's?"

"We have a few leads and similarities that we can't risk revealing to the public yet," the officer replied.

Sadness crept into Steph's eyes. Poor John and Whitney. This was so humiliating and demeaning and *so* wrong. She was so sure that they had nothing to do with it!

CHAPTER 10

▼

Stephanie's days were plenty full enough without worrying about the murder business. With five children, she didn't have a lot of time to concentrate that much on it.

Breakfast was a big deal every morning. Trying to fry two packages of bacon and two dozen eggs while making sure the kids had their lunch money, homework assignments, shoes tied, teeth brushed, hair combed, beds made and rooms picked up.

Of course, Packy hated eggs so he had to have cereal or peanut butter and jelly sandwiches. Garret had to have baby cereal and Mandy would eat only soft-boiled eggs!

"Mommy! I need you to sign a paper for me," Zach mentioned at the last minute.

"Do you have all of your homework assignments in your notebook? How about library books? Packy, do you have your gym clothes? Today's gym class."

"Yes, Mom!" Packy answered impatiently.

"Hurry up, Kids! I'll run you to the bus stop," Stephanie said, a little out of breath.

It was a rainy morning, so that meant that *all* the kids had to be dressed and loaded in the van.

When Stephanie got back and managed to get three little tykes through the door, she let out a sigh of relief as she did every morning after the kids were off to school.

"It's so good to get the boys off to school and have a little less noise. Isn't it, Myra?"

Myra shook her little head in agreement and gave Mommy a big hug.

"Now to tackle these dishes," Steph said after turning on the coffee pot.

By the time the kitchen was clean, her coffee was ready for her. Steph saw to it that the wee ones had fresh diapers put on and that Myra's needs were taken care of so she could take a breather and sit down to enjoy her coffee and newspaper.

Steph missed Meg's regular visits but she realized that it was just as well. She had to sacrifice her close friendship with Meg in order to maintain a sane relationship with Ron.

Steph put her dishes on the counter after rinsing them and put on her favorite mood music, Barbara Streisand, Dean Martin, and the like. They eased her anxiety enough to get down to serious dusting. She put another load of clothes in the washer and took a load out of the dryer to fold. She had four or five loads *every* day. She needed to get the majority of her work done before naptime so she could spend that quiet time to work on projects that required concentration.

After only an hour of the afore said *quiet time*, her solitude was broken by Mandy's voice crying out to Mommy.

"I'm coming, Mandy."

Steph climbed the stairs quickly and peeked into Mandy's room.

"Ah, what's wrong, Sweetie? Did you have a bad dream? It's okay. Mommy's here."

Steph held Mandy in her arms and rocked her back and forth in a loving effort to comfort her. Mandy's crying woke the other children as Stephanie had anticipated.

It was time to start fixing dinner and prepare for the boys to return home from school. Steph fixed milk and cookies for them to hold them until dinner. They were always "starving" when they got home.

While browning pork chops and peeling potatoes and onions, Stephanie tried to listen to the boy's stories of their day's events. It was pretty difficult with all of these interruptions due to fights between the little ones and their countless demands.

"You'd better start your homework, boys. You know how your father feels about getting homework done early," Steph reminded them.

After Steph put the pork chops and potatoes in the oven, she started folding her last load of clothes for the day while she helped the boys with their homework.

"Myra! Please close the door! Mandy! Please put the pillows back on the sofa," Steph demanded between the boy's questions.

Little Garret's crying persuaded Steph to pick him up and rock him in her arms.

Zach finished his homework and closed his book loudly then ran into his room with anything *but* homework on his mind.

"Zach!" Steph called out sternly, "Back up! You forgot your books."

After dinner was over, Ron shut himself away in his office. Steph washed dishes while drilling Zach with his spelling words.

Afterward, Stephanie attacked her chores with renewed vigor, never hesitating for a moment; she continued to hang up coats, to pick up toys, shoes, socks, and other endless debris.

Before she knew it, it was time for baths. Youngest first, Garret was bathed and tucked lovingly into his crib. Mandy and Myra were bathed together, and then tucked into bed.

"Okay, Zach, your turn. Get your clothes off and into the tub. I have to wash your hair."

"No, Mom! Please. It's not time yet!" Zach whined.

"Don't you argue with me, young man!" Steph insisted.

"Packy, straighten your room, please, while Zach is in the tub."

Packy objected," But, Mom, I didn't make the mess!"

Stephanie was ready for the familiar retort. "I don't recall asking who did it! Get it done!" she demanded firmly.

Finally! Everyone was bathed and tucked in

"Mommy! I'm thirsty," Myra cried out.

"Myra! You know what happens when you drink before you go to bed."

"Just one sip? I'm so thirsty, Mommy! Please!"

Steph couldn't resist. "Okay, just *one* sip!"

"Mom!" Packy called out from bed, "I forgot I need you to sign some papers for school."

"I'll do it in the morning, Packy," Steph said a little impatiently. "*Please! Go to sleep*!"

Preparing for the morning routine before she finally gets to close her eyes at night, Steph would always lay out the children's clothes and set the table for breakfast. She placed their lunch money beside their plates along with their vitamins.

"*Ah! Peace!*" Steph said out loud as she undressed and drew her bath water. Just settling into her clouds of bubbles, she heard the usual whispering and scampering of little feet down the hall. Then she heard the refrigerator door open and shut. The children were pretty crafty and adept at choosing the most appropriate moments to take advantage of Steph's attention elsewhere to misbehave.

"Oh! Well!" she said out loud. "I'm too tired to fight any more tonight. This is my *only* time to myself."

By the time Steph got out of the tub, the kids were feigning sleep. She didn't have the energy or the heart to scold.

Knowing full well that there was yet another mess waiting for her in the kitchen, she trudged downstairs to meet it head on.

CHAPTER 11

▼

Bail was set and between John and Whitney they were able to raise the money to pay it.

When John walked out, Whitney launched herself into his arms and held him tightly in a desperate attempt to reassure them both that everything was going to be all right.

"Please, don't ever leave me again. I've never been so lonely," Whitney cried.

They walked out of the police station, silence between them and never letting go of each other's hands.

They were able to hire an attorney with an excellent reputation. He drilled John and Whitney endlessly trying to come up with something to clear him.

"Don't worry, Miss America! Together, we'll lick 'em all!" John said, trying to keep her spirits up.

They drove to John's house to unpack his clothes. As they drove up the drive, John's son, Mark ran out to meet them. Mark hugged them both, crying.

"You didn't do it! I know you didn't! Why do they think *you* did it, Dad?" Mark cried in desperation.

John looked at Whitney shaking his head unable to accept this preposterous indignation. He was angry. Wasn't it enough that Mark lost his mother? Now, he had to live with the fear that he may lose his father too.

Hayley's parents waited in the doorway, not knowing what to believe.

"I guess if you're home you won't be needing us any longer," Hayley's Mother said. They left without another word.

Whitney started to cry when she walked through the door.

"All of the memories in this house."

John didn't seem to be bereaved at all as he carried his bags straight back to the bedroom. He then took Mark by the hand and sat him down.

"I'm sorry that I wasn't able to be with you when you needed me most."

"It's okay, Dad," Mark said. "You couldn't help it and besides Grandma and Grandpa took good care of me. I think they needed me too."

"It might be a good idea if you stayed with them for a while until this mess is over with," John said.

"Why do they think *you* did it, Dad?" Mark asked, in tears.

"I guess because your mom and I had a fight before it happened," John answered honestly.

Mark went off to bed, leaving John and Whitney sitting solemnly reflecting in the living room. They couldn't be in each other's arms in front of Mark so they had to resort to exercising every ounce of self-control and will power. After he was sure Mark was asleep, John admitted that he wasn't sorry that Hayley was out of the picture. Of course, her death *was* extreme.

"She even manages to keep us apart after her death. She probably planned the whole thing and is laughing at us right now. Hmmmmm!"

John sat in silence for a moment, reflecting on the possibility that she may have been capable of callously determining her own fate *and* theirs.

John's long pensive expression momentarily threw Whitney off balance. She eyed him curiously.

John sat straight up in his chair, fixing a stern eye on Whitney's face.

"Is it feasible? Hayley *was* a calculating, schemer," John surveyed Whitney's expression.

Sadness crept into her eyes and her heart. This unanticipated thought shook her to her very core. That never occurred to her, not in a million years! What a daunting setback! Or *was* it a setback? Or *could* it be a solution? Poor Hayley! Could she have been that desperate? Could she have been capable of such ruthless revenge, to go to the extreme of ending her own life?

John beamed with almost a triumphant expression on his face.

Their eyes connected questioningly.

Whitney's guilt only intensified.

✳   ✳   ✳   ✳

Stephanie attended John's hearing fully intending to find a way or a clue to set him free.

The judge was seated and John was on the stand being questioned. He was asked all the same barrage of questions again, his whereabouts on the dates in question, about the argument with Hayley, why he went on the cruise, who Whitney was, how long had he known her, had they planned to murder Hayley?

John managed to enter in his suspicion of the possibility that Hayley could have planned and set this whole mess up because after the fight they'd had she was fully aware that he'd planned to divorce her.

John's suspicion gave his attorney another angle to search out.

Whitney was the next person on the stand. They grilled her with the same demeaning, humiliating, annoying questions again too. Fortunately for her, she had an alibi for one of the dates in question, but they still weren't ruling out conspiracy.

Stephanie was next in the *hot seat*. She was asked the identification questions over and over in different ways hoping to jog her memory. The only evidence they had was a necklace that Hayley had clutched in her hand. The necklace was presented to Stephanie as it was to John and Whitney.

"Have you ever seen this necklace before?"

Stephanie's breath caught in her throat. Panic rushed through her like a cold chill. She tried to hide her discomfort, her face turning white with shock. She was under oath! Reluctant to relinquish the truth, somehow her conscience forced her to say barely above a whisper, "It's mine!"

The room full of people suddenly sounded like a disrupted beehive with the buzzing of voices.

"This necklace is yours?"

She held it and checked it out thoroughly.

"Yes! I'm sure it's mine."

Her mind raced with erratic thoughts, possibilities, and questions. Her fear intensified, questioning her own mental stability. Could she be schizophrenic? Her momentary disillusionment made her a little dizzy.

"Did you kill Hayley Garber?" the attorney asked her.

Stephanie was in such a state of panic she wasn't entirely sure of the answer to that question.

"Not to my knowledge," Steph answered.

"Where were you the morning Hayley Garber was killed?"

"I was at home with my children."

A sudden attack of reprieve and confidence, she blurted out with relief, "I was at home with my five alibis!"

"Yes! I was at home with my children!" Steph repeated with great satisfaction.

Ron, she thought. Where was Ron when Monica was killed? She didn't know! Where was Ron when Hayley was killed? Thinking back she realized that he wasn't home that morning. He was working out of town. She sucked in her breath in panic. The sudden comprehension filled her with horror.

Stephanie couldn't get the necklace off her mind. She stared at Ron trying to recollect bits of conversation and comments Ron had made. She analyzed his every move with her keenly observing eyes.

The next day, Steph did some investigating of her own. She called one of Ron's employees on the pretense of needing his overtime that night. The books weren't clear on the time.

"Ron isn't here right now. Do you happen to know what your overtime was that night? Do you happen to know how long Ron worked that night?"

"Oh, he wasn't on the job that night," the guy on the phone said.

The words reverberated in her head as if they were trying to find a way out. Stephanie was devastated. She didn't know what to do. Should she tell someone? Should she report it? What's worse, should she be *afraid?*

Her inevitable guilt started in. Now she was thinking, *what kind of wife am I to suspect the father of my precious babies of such a horrific crime? Why am I always so inclined to believe the worst about Ron? I'm incredible!*

Her inquisitive nature wouldn't allow her to shake it out of her mind. Motivated by the facts that she'd just learned, Steph searched through Ron's closet and drawers for some kind of clue. Did he even know Monica? She knew he didn't care for Hayley, but enough to kill her? What about a motive? *Why* would he want her out of the way? Did she have something on him? She was always bringing Meg up to her, suggesting that she *Watch Out* for Ron and Meg. How many times did Hayley point out the possibility that the two of them were having an affair? How many times did she suggest what a fool she was to allow the teasing to go on? Maybe Hayley and Monica's murders weren't even related! But the police officer suggested that the two were linked somehow but he couldn't reveal it to the public.

Stephanie hated herself for thinking that her husband could even be capable of such an atrocity. He loved women, as most men do, or come to think of it, maybe he's punishing more women than just me. Whitney said he's really punishing his mother. Her mind was unstoppable. Oh! This was ludicrous! But then if she didn't check it out and if it was him and he murdered someone else, it would be her fault. He could be sick. Maybe he isn't aware of what he's doing. Whitney said he had a serious problem.

Stephanie cried as she searched through Ron's office. *"Oh! Ron!"* Please don't let it be you. The roses! In all cases Ron is the only one who could have done it.

She needed to search his truck, but when could she do it without getting caught? After he's asleep.

✳   ✳   ✳   ✳

Later, the kids were all tucked away in their beds and Stephanie was waiting for Ron to get home from his *night out with the boys,* which wouldn't be till the wee hours of the morning. Spurred by insomnia, *what a surprise,* she started mending, a job that was always last on her agenda. The station stopped broadcasting when Steph saw lights coming in her drive. She quickly put everything away and pretended she'd fallen asleep watching television.

Ron came in, took four aspirins, undressed quietly and dropped heavily on the bed.

It was no time at all before Ron's snoring clued Steph in that he was dead to the world. Ron was used to Steph jumping out of bed all night with the children so he never budged when she slipped out of bed and carried her robe and slippers downstairs. Not turning on the lights, she made her way to the front door as quietly as she could.

She opened the truck door and looked under and behind the seat. All she came up with was a Penthouse magazine. Her fear and anxiety turned quickly into red-hot rage. She ripped the magazine to shreds and threw them all over the inside of his truck.

"How dare he? Is nothing sacred in this life? It isn't right! It just isn't right! Love is supposed to be an outlet, making love to me, not thousands of other women. Why is *love* never enough? Why does a man need all of this variety?" Steph mumbled to herself.

Now she searched with a vengeance, almost hoping she'd find something incriminating. Maybe this would explain it. Maybe he really is *crazy!* She'd make him ache and suffer the way he'd always made her ache and suffer.

The tool panels were locked so she had to sneak back into the house to find the key.

Back in the house, Steph quietly searched through Ron's pants that he'd left on the floor. Nothing. Still in the dark, she groped running her hands blindly across the dresser and chest surface. Still nothing. She groped her way through the dark to the kitchen and checked out the counter where he'd taken the aspirin.

Her last hope was that he'd left them in the ignition.

She finally made her way back outside without disturbing a soul in the house.

There they were. In the ignition the whole time. Steph jiggled each key in the lock until she found the one that opened the toolbox.

Nothing but tools. Then she explored the remaining three panels. Not a thing. She carefully returned the key to the ignition and went back in the house.

Still angry about the magazine, when she crawled back into bed with Ron, she allowed her body to *fall* onto the bed with a bounce. Ron woke with a start then turned over and threw his arm over Stephanie. She grabbed that arm and threw it right back to him!

Needless to say Steph was wide-awake the rest of the night stewing over Ron, her life long career.

The next morning Ron was getting ready for work while Stephanie was already up and preparing coffee. Surveying him, her face filled with curiosity, she answered Ron's every question or remark with one word acknowledgments, *humph, no, yes, whatever,* nothing more!

He grabbed his lunch box and walked out the door to his truck without a kiss and mumbling to himself wondering what was eating Steph.

Ron opened his truck door. The sight of his magazine ripped to shreds all over his truck hit him in the face immediately.

"That's what's eating her!" Ron growled, as he slammed the door shut with a vengeance and walked heavily footed back into the house.

Always quick to flare, Ron bristled with anger.

"You green-eyed little whore!" he bellowed.

Steph's shoulders hunched guardedly, expecting exactly what she was getting.

"What's in my truck is *mine*! It's *my* business! *You* don't *control* me! I don't take orders from anybody! You got that?"

All her defenses going up, Stephanie countered indignantly in her coldest tone and in a tremendous voice.

"Have you ever heard the word respect? Respect for me, respect for women, respect for *decency.*"

In his fierce and angry display of temperament, Ron picked Steph up in an effort to show her who's boss and carried her over his shoulder. Her fists flailing, her face red and contorted, he threw her on the bedroom floor.

He screamed in his notoriously hateful manner.

"Don't you dare talk back to me! You just keep that fat mouth of yours *shut*!"

Stephanie was crying now. The boys ran into the room to see what the commotion was all about. Ron ran out of the room as usual leaving Steph to pick up the pieces and carry on in her *everything's okay* façade in front of the children.

Ron slammed the front door behind him, jumped into his truck and raced off to work.

Exerting newfound energy and a radical change in her disposition, Stephanie stood up and wiped away her tears. She explained nothing to the boys, only collected herself and calmly walked downstairs with a smile to prepare breakfast for the children.

Stephanie's unsettled mind was prevalent in everything she did and she somehow managed to work mechanically through her chores of the day.

Naptime finally rolled around. Stephanie kissed her wee ones lovingly and tucked them into bed. Falling into her chair in the bedroom, her exhaustion caught up to her. As hard as she was trying to concentrate, her sleepless nights overpowered her thoughts and allowed her troubles to be put aside, as she slept soundly for a luxurious two hours.

A gentle touch and a sweet little voice woke Stephanie.

"Hi, Myra! Did you have a nice nap?"

"Yes, Mommy." Then Myra started telling Steph about her funny dream.

It was time to start dinner but Steph was sure that Ron wouldn't be there. She had to carry on in spite of her problems. Her children needed her. She would not allow her problems to interfere in her children's lives. She knew what Ron's upbringing did to him and she wasn't about to allow it to happen to her children.

The boys came home from school. Dinner was eaten and the table was cleared without Ron's presence as Steph had predicted.

The evening had carried on as usual. The children didn't miss their father because it wasn't uncommon for him to work late. The homework and baths were completed and the children were tucked away and ready for the sandman's visit.

Steph hired her sitter to stay with the children. She was compelled to find out where Ron was. She drove out into the city nightlife to check out all of Ron's favorite spots. She figured he'd be Carousing the bars.

She spotted his truck parked in the parking lot of one of his favorite dives.

At least, she knew where he was. At least he wasn't out murdering some woman. She was wondering which of the two evils she preferred. At least, if he were the killer he'd be locked up for life. Stephanie cried out in pain. Five innocent little angels, who've done nothing wrong, didn't deserve to grow up without the balance of a loving family, which included their father. They didn't ask to be born. It isn't their fault that she may have chosen a killer to be their father. She's the one who should *pay, not them.*

*   *   *   *

Deep in her thoughts, Steph soaked in her bubbly bath water, thinking seriously about all the advice Whitney had given her.

Suddenly, without warning, Steph's bathroom door flew open and bounced off the wall.

Ron stood, his chest heaving, in the doorway after having savagely kicked the door open.

Their eyes met and held for a few moments.

"What's this?" Ron demanded with a scowl on his face. He held up a single red rose.

Steph shivered involuntarily.

"It looks like a rose."

"What's it doing on your pillow?" Ron continued.

"I don't know. I didn't notice it."

He walked over to her and pulled her soaking body from the tub of water.

"Who is he, you whore?"

"I don't know what you're talking about, Ron! When would I have time to have a boyfriend?" Steph protested. "It's your ego that's suffering. You don't really care if I have a boyfriend; it's just that you think I'd dare want someone other than you!"

Ron changed his tone.

"You really think I'd care if you had someone else?"

"Well, as the saying goes, *if the shoe fits….***Kick yourself with it***!*" Steph said calmly trying to maintain cool poise.

Whatever was going to happen or not going to happen was going to happen because of her.

"It comes with the territory; insecurity, you know," Steph stated bluntly as she dried herself and slipped into a mere wisp of a nightie.

Her tone of voice instantly infuriated him as he jumped nervously at her, his fists clenched and every muscle in his arms was tense with rage.

His unexpected appearance gave her chills but with a flash of desperate energy and courage, she forced herself to say in a tone of indifference, "Don't try to put me on the defensive! I'm finished with that!"

"Okay, *Your Ladyship*!" Ron said as he bowed his head.

Steph was a model of restraint.

He stopped in confusion and glared at her suspiciously.

Turning off a *know-it-all* isn't easy. The irony of that is that they're infinitely *dense*!

"How come you do all the barking but I'm always the one trying to get out of the dog house? Where were you tonight?" Steph asked distantly.

"What do you care? You wouldn't go with me anyway. You're nothing but an anti-social bitch!"

Startled, Steph stopped short and looked intensely into his eyes.

"I've grown accustomed to your inexhaustible vocabulary concerning my character, *My Darling*, but other people find your constant criticism of me appalling."

His eyebrows raised in surprise.

"No guilt, no remorse," Steph continued defiantly. She was adept at acting as if she knew nothing. She tightened her lips in annoyance.

"Ah, Steph, you're too emotionally oriented," Ron said alarmed and on the defensive.

"What a curious observation, considering I wasn't aware that a chauvinist knew that word existed."

"Suspicion is one of the most powerful aphrodisiacs in the world," Ron muttered trying to evade the question.

Ron cut off her words with a lengthy kiss. They created remarkable electricity together, even now.

Knowing that this threatening mood was supposed to end in sex, Steph uttered, "It's just raw animal attraction. Isn't that what you always say, Darling?" She felt a quiver of apprehension. She reached her limit of tolerance with him but refused to allow her wall to crumble. She vowed to remain strong. Whitney's words reverberated in her head, *talk to me with love and respect or don't talk to me at all!* She was determined to conquer the demon inside him. Ron was a creature of extremes. He was either hot or cold, whichever worked to his advantage.

"I've never seen a man who looks for so many ways out," Steph announced.

He studied her eyes as he received the full impact of her stand.

She maintained distance.

"If it gives you any perverse satisfaction, I was bar hopping," Ron admitted openly in an attempt to knock her resistance down a few notches. "You know how I enjoy the thrill of a woman's natural *form*? There are so many out there just waiting to be seen. All shapes and sizes, so many women and so little time."

Steph strode quickly in her characteristic pace determined to be indifferent.

"Whatever curdles your cream, Darling!" She thought she'd surely drown in her sea of pretension.

Steph switched on the light in her walk-in closet. The walls and clothes leaped into being.

The room was suddenly quiet and very tense.

"Is that a promise or a threat?" Ron exclaimed suddenly uneasy.

Steph felt an unexpected prick of tears but was determined to hide them. She continued to hang up her robe.

Steph took a long breath.

"You've made your point, Ron."

She turned and with minimal effort pulled off her nighty and panties.

"Indulge yourself!" she insisted as she danced around the room in every provocative manner she could think of.

"You're hyperventilating, Darling. Control yourself."

This was most unsettling to Ron. His brows stiffened with disapproval. He was profoundly shocked!

"What I've watched you become scares me to death! What ever happened to the sweet little girl I Married?" Ron demanded, voice rising.

"You're a man of many talents, Ron. You can even create a monster. You killed that little girl off years ago." Stephanie laughed with a self-satisfied expression on her face.

Ron grabbed her arm and pulled her down to him. He took her face into his hands tenderly and looked into her eyes with desire and admiration. She could have sworn she saw love illuminating his face.

Hayley's image entered Steph's mind, dispelling the feelings of love and desire.

Stroking her hair and pressing his body to hers ended in a flurry of misery. Ron tensed up and his face darkened with animosity.

Steph was no longer intimidated. This gave him an attack of uneasiness and was dubious of her actions.

Steph was merciless.

"What's the matter, Ron? Aren't cheap thrills motivation enough for your preoccupation with sex? It's all right for you to be a sleaze but not your wife, eh? Why is it alright for you?"

This deliberate provocation sent Ron into malfunction.

"You're the saint and I'm the sinner, is that it? I guess I misread the situation," Ron concluded lamely.

"What's this? I don't believe my ears!" Steph expounded.

"At least you accomplish what you set out to do," Ron admitted.

Feeling a sense of accomplishment, Steph walked into her closet and put on her robe.

"Ron," Steph said softly and sympathetically, "I care about you, it's plain and simple."

"Those words aren't plain and simple," Ron muttered.

"You're right about that. Nothing with you is plain and simple, Ron." She lowered her voice two octaves. "Don't let society dictate what your life is or isn't. Why rebel against me? All I've tried to do is love you. You try your damnedest to push me away. Why do you do everything possible to try to make me hate you? Sometimes, you succeed too! Sometimes I really hate you! There's a fine line between love and hate, so they say. I'm finding out that it's true. If you love me as much as you say you do then why do you seem to think I need to live my life in such pain? I can't bring myself to understand this kind of love. I was raised with love and respect. This is totally foreign to me."

Ron looked as though he was giving the matter infinite thought.

"There's a wall between us that goes beyond sex," Steph said, no longer distant.

"Sometimes I see the face of my enemy in the mirror," Ron said gravely.

Steph threw her arms around Ron and held him tightly. Tears flooded her eyes, feeling a spurt of triumph.

"The only people who can afford to be themselves are children and old people," Ron said.

Their bodies melted together.

Steph uttered a moan of pain as she thought of Monica and Hayley again.

"Ron, how do you feel about these murders, about Hayley?"

"Ah! Hayley was a barracuda! If someone had to be murdered, she was a good candidate. She was vicious. I won't waste my sympathy on her. You shouldn't either," Ron demanded.

Steph swallowed hard. *OH, Ron,* she thought; *Oh Ron,* with a faint whisper of caution.

CHAPTER 12

▼

After doing John and Mark's grocery shopping, Whitney backed into their drive ready to unload. Mark and John ran out to carry the groceries inside for her.

"What a gem you are, Whitney," John said, kissing her on the cheek.

After putting the groceries away Whitney started to prepare a meatloaf mixture. John walked up behind her and put his arms around her waist and kissed the back of her neck. Whitney shook John off.

"John!" she reprimanded. "What if Mark walked in?"

"I can't help it! I can't keep my hands off of you," John confessed.

Just then, across the room, the carton of eggs fell to the floor.

John and Whitney both turned with a start.

"How did that happen?" Whitney asked, with a touch of fear in her voice.

John was still staring at the eggs on the floor as if in a trance. Without turning his attention away from them, he admitted, "I don't know! But I'll clean it up. I wouldn't want to dirty those pretty little hands of yours."

Whitney finished peeling the potatoes and put them in the dutch oven along with the meatloaf.

John was helping Mark put a model together while Whitney started to pack up Hayley's clothes for John.

Whitney kneeled on the floor over Hayley's clothes.

"Oh, Hayley! I can't tell you how sorry I am about your passing so violently. I promise I'll take good care of John and Mark. I'd give John up if it would bring you back! Please forgive us," Whitney whispered.

The sound of glass breaking brought Whitney back to the present. She sprang to her feet with a snap and turned her head toward the sound. It was Hayley's picture. It had fallen off the dresser.

"John!" Whitney called out, her body trembling with alarm.

John rushed to her side.

"What is it? We heard glass breaking. Did you hurt yourself?"

She waved her hand airily toward Hayley's picture broken on the floor. She lifted her eyes to the ceiling with an expectant look in her eyes. She remained silent and reflective as she closed her eyes. The clear image of Hayley's face leapt before her mind's eye.

John's words snapped Whitney out of her trance.

"Don't worry, Honey. The glass didn't scratch the picture. I'll just buy another frame. It'll be fine!"

"John, I didn't knock it over. I was across the room when it fell," Whitney said very distinctly, exaggerating every syllable.

John paused for a moment, searching for a logical explanation.

"It was probably a sudden burst of wind, a strong breeze coming through the window, Whitney."

She gave him a silent apprehensive glare, obviously not believing a word.

Taking hold of Whitney's shoulders, John turned her to face him. He looked directly into her startling blue eyes, so perfectly set wide apart.

"Whitney! We can't allow our guilty feelings to rule our imaginations. Okay?"

"Sure," Whitney said simply.

John left to continue to help Mark. On his way out the door he turned and winked at Whitney.

A faint smile graced her perfectly lined glossy sienna lips, but her eyes were filled with concern. Whitney let out an inaudible sigh as if she were afraid to utter another sound.

In order to finish her job packing Hayley's clothes, she needed to walk out to her car to retrieve more empty boxes.

She carried as many as she could handle in one trip and dropped them on the floor in the bedroom. Whitney opened Hayley's closet and started packing up her shoes. She emptied her drawers, folding her clothes carefully as if Hayley were watching her every move. She saved her jewelry to store away for Mark as a memento of his mother. Whitney came across an old picture of John, Hayley, Meg, Dan, and herself. She studied it for a few minutes remembering the good times, and then she fastened it in John's family album.

These house hold chores some would consider a monotonous grind, Whitney found comforting and soothing. She wanted so desperately to help John and Mark. She needed them as much as they needed her.

Deciding she'd better check on dinner, Whitney walked out to the kitchen, opened the oven door and took out the meatloaf. She used tongs to turn the potatoes so they'd brown on all sides and then returned the meatloaf back to the oven to finish cooking. She took a pan out of the cabinet and opened a can of Italian beans. Allowing the beans to come to a boil, after adding salt, pepper, bits of cooked bacon, mushrooms and garlic powder, she turned the fire down low under the beans, then she returned to Hayley's room to finish her task.

After packing the last of Hayley's cosmetics and personal belongings, the timer went off in the kitchen.

Whitney and Mark entered the kitchen at the same time. Mark was always willing to help Whitney.

"Whitney, would you like me to set the table for you?"

Whitney smiled sweetly at Mark,

"Well, thank you! That would be a big help. Maybe you can help me find a big serving bowl for the potatoes and vegetables."

Mark loved Whitney for all of the attention and special kindnesses she'd given him his whole life. Her lovely inner warmth, sunny disposition and natural optimism reassured and comforted Mark.

Whitney had always loved Mark as if he were her own. After all, she was his Godmother and was always an important member of the family. She instinctively understood Mark's needs and never hesitated to fill them.

They worked well together setting the table.

"John, Mark and I have dinner on the table for you," Whitney called out.

John walked into the kitchen with a proud smile on his face. He sat down in front of his well-placed plate, feeling at peace, so right, as if this moment were meant to be.

They enjoyed their meal together, but most of all they enjoyed each other's company.

Afterward, Mark and John both helped Whitney with the dishes.

"Whitney, you're the greatest! I think we'll keep you! What do you think, Mark?" John announced.

Mark shook his head vehemently.

"Right, Dad!"

Later, Whitney carried the boxes to the front door so John and Mark could load them into her car.

Whitney walked through the bedroom on her way to the bathroom where she intended to pick up more boxes full of Hayley's memory.

Her step faltered then she stopped dead in her tracks. Whitney looked as stunned as if someone had thrown cold water in her face. Her eyes flew open wide and she gasped at the sight of the photo that she'd fastened in the photo album earlier. She immediately dropped everything and rushed to the family room in a panic to pull out the album. *Sure enough*! Just as she suspected, *it was gone*!

"John! Mark!" Whitney beckoned.

"What is it Whitney?" John asked, concerned about the frightened tone in her voice.

"Did either of you take this picture out of the album and put it on the dresser?" Whitney asked almost sure of what their answers would be.

John looked into Whitney's panicky eyes.

"No, I didn't. Did you, Mark?"

"Nope!"

Whitney sat down heavily in Hayley's chair.

"Thanks, Guys! I must have dropped it there myself."

"Whitney, are you all right?" John asked, worried about her peculiar actions. "Let's go to a movie. We're all tired and need time out. What do you say, Whitney?"

John turned to Mark, "How about it?"

"Great! Dad! I'm all for it!"

The guys left the room to look for the newspaper to check out the movie possibilities.

Whitney stayed behind.

"What is it, Hayley? What are you trying to tell me?" Whitney whispered to the picture in her hand.

The afternoon took its usual path. The boys came home from school; dinner was prepared and Ron managed to come home and eat it.

They sat through the meal much like any other; Packy complained that he didn't like anything; Zack had to potty half way through the meal and Myra had to sit long after everyone else was finished until she took three bites of her vegetables.

After dinner, Ron announced that he had to go back to work to finish a job and wouldn't be home till late.

"Would you mind dropping the boys off at Meg's? They're spending the night tonight," Steph asked.

"Okay, boys, pack your bags and hop in the truck on the double, if you're going with me," Ron commanded.

The boys hustled and got the job done in seven minutes.

"What job are you working on tonight?" Steph asked.

"Hadley's," Ron answered, not taking the time to comment further.

Steph intended to make sure he had an alibi in case another woman was killed. She fully intended to check out his story later.

Steph and her little helper cleared the table and washed the dishes.

"What a good little girl you are. Mommy's little darling. It sure is nice having another girl in the family to help me. I love you, you sweet little thing. What would I do without my little darlings?" Steph said to Myra, determined to give her encouragement.

Mandy had bronchitis and was feeling badly so Steph put her to bed early. Being that she was pretty drained herself, Steph decided to put Garret and Myra to bed early too. Steph needed to rejuvenate her body so she took a long peaceful bubble bath since it was so quiet for a change, without the boys and the other three sound asleep. There was no one to bang on her door or to cry for her or to ask questions through the door.

"I may never get out," Steph said to herself.

She kept her curls on top of her head after her bath because it was so much more comfortable than having her hair in her face and around her neck.

Planning to settle in early, she plumped up her three pillows and turned back the covers on her bed. Sitting up comfortably, with a diet sprite and freshly popped popcorn on her nightstand, she started to work a crossword puzzle. She'd prepared the house for the eventuality of falling asleep early, by turning off the lights, locking the doors and peeking at the children.

"Maybe I'll skip checking on Ron tonight. I'll just check with the men in the morning. It's worked before."

The house was unusually quiet. The only sound she was aware of was Mandy's heavy breathing due to her bronchitis.

Stephanie had just dozed off when suddenly; there was a break in the silence. She woke momentarily. Her eyes popped open and moved from one side to the other as if attempting to see what the noise was but her body was too weak from sleep to do more than that.

While asleep on her back, the sensation of lips on hers brought her slowly back to consciousness. Still in dreamy twilight, not fully conscious of whether it was a dream or Ron trying to arouse her, she felt two hands cup her breasts. Eyes still closed, Stephanie smiled, brought her arms up and dreamily wrapped them around her dream-lover's neck.

"Hunh?" Steph's breath drew inward in a sudden gasp. She bolted straight upright from her bed, her eyes round as silver dollars.

The sudden realization that Ron didn't have long hair brought her to an immediate state of panic. A hand covered her mouth to muffle her scream. Sweat beads broke out on her forehead and her face was blood red from trying to scream against a barrier.

It was the woman she saw at Monica's!

Steph managed to work herself out from under her and jumped off the bed as the woman caught her foot and sent Steph flying to the floor on her face. Seeing stars, her mouth bleeding, Steph was picked up and thrown on the bed. The woman was able to tie and gag a still dazed Stephanie. Her hands were tied to the headboard with extension chords. Finally regaining her senses, Steph became a wildcat thrashing her body from side to side and managed to kick her assailant in the head.

A wig flew to the floor. Steph gasped in total disbelief.

I should have recognized those eyes! Why didn't I see it before?

He took out a knife and lightly dragged the blade over her already bruised and swollen face, just enough to draw blood. His face was pale with makeup but his nostrils and ears seemed inflamed. His saliva spray hit her in the face as he whispered, "Shhh, Pretty Lady. What's the matter? Can't you stop me? Try! Oh! Come on! You can do better than that," he demanded, as he cut the straps to her nightgown.

"Stop me!" he ordered. He slapped her face with the back of his hand, as his rage seemed to heighten.

"Can't you stop me?" he screamed. He then sliced her nightgown and body along with it, all in one slow torturous sweeping motion.

Big tears streamed down her cheeks and her wet hair adhered to her face. Her whole body jerked with every sob. She cried out in helpless desperation against the gag in her mouth.

He said, "Come on, Mom! You can do better than that!"

Steph thought, *MOM!* He called me *MOM!*

Unfortunately for Steph, she also had a footboard to which he tied one of her legs. She was still kicking violently with the other leg and writhing her body, trying to get loose.

Steph's mind was racing. *Please Lord; don't let my babies find my body! Oh! God! This can't be happening! This is so undignified! Who's going to find my mutilated body? How did he get in here? Oh! I remember! I dropped my key in the grass. He must have found it. Why didn't I think to change the lock? Please God! If I have to go now, please don't let me feel pain! Are you listening, God? Please! Don't let my children wake up! At least do that for me! Don't let this maniac hurt my babies!*

Fresh tears started to trickle down her cheeks when she thought of her children being hurt. *If my children survive, what will they do without me? I wanted so badly to see them grow up! Please! GOD! Don't let my children find me!*

Stephanie's assailant continued tenaciously without pause. He ran the knife blade teasingly from one foot up to her groin very slowly as if he were tickling her instead of drawing blood. He couldn't leave her other leg bare so he repeated the same ritual on it.

Steph groaned. *How could any human being be so cruel, so brutal and someone who knew her personally yet? What have I ever done to him?*

The sound of Packy's voice brought a sudden halt to the vicious ritual.

"Mom, Mom!" Packy's voice came closer.

Stephanie really panicked then for fear of Packy's life!

The maniac jumped up from the bed and dashed out of the room.

He practically knocked Packy and Tyler off their feet trying to get out of the house.

"**Dad!**" Tyler screamed in horror. "Dad!"

These were the first words Tyler had spoken since he'd seen Monica's dead body. He witnessed his own Dad in a dress covered with Steph's blood.

"Tyler!" Packy screamed. Call an ambulance!

Dan Lane ran out of the house without a word to his son. He had big tears rolling off his cheeks.

Packy covered his Mom with a blanket and untied her. She slipped in and out of consciousness. Packy was crying tears of relief that his mom was still alive.

After Tyler called the ambulance, he went next door for help.

Ann and her husband rushed over with Tyler.

Ann stayed with the children so Packy could ride to the hospital with his Mom in the ambulance.

Thank goodness the pals, Packy and Tyler decided to walk over to Steph's house to retrieve a forgotten toy.

*   *   *   *

Ron walked into the emergency room in shock. He was directed to the room where Steph was being worked on.

"Ron!" Steph cried with relief.

"I could hardly wait till you got here! Did you hear? It was Dan! I'm kicking myself! Why couldn't I have seen that it was Dan? I knew those eyes were so familiar. I just didn't make the connection." Tears welled in her eyes again. "I didn't think I had any tears left."

"Oh! Ron! I'm so sorry!"

*   *   *   *

John and Whitney received word. Whitney announced suddenly as the thought hit her like a lightning bolt.

"That's it! Hayley was trying to tell me with the picture. *She* put the picture on the dresser after I put it in the album. It was a picture of Dan."

John gave her a strange look.

"Come here and kiss me," John commanded playfully.

Whitney's eyes twinkled as she peered into John's handsome face. Her eyes reflecting her innermost emotions, she hesitated then walked over to John.

He smiled reassuringly and took her gently, respectfully into his arms. He tilted her chin upward so his lips could reach hers.

They paused, waiting for something to happen. Nothing.

"She's gone," Whitney whispered. "She's resting in peace now. Her killer is caught and maybe she's forgiven us. That's how I choose to look at it."

"I love you, Miss America," John announced lovingly.

Whitney surprised him.

"Not as much as I love *You*, John," Whitney purred, tracing the outline of his lips with her finger.

John jumped up and announced in a loud, relieved voice, "Break out the happy brew! Let's celebrate!"

Mark celebrated too, with grape juice, of course. The three of them huddled together in a long group hug in the middle of the room, celebrating their special union and the fact that they could now resume their lives happily and forever.

*   *   *   *

Bianca and Ann took turns helping Steph take care of her children while she was recuperating. Ron treated her with kindness and respect and helped her take care of the household duties. Packy and Zach helped with laundry, vacuuming and dishes. Ron took time off to do family things together, such as taking long rides in the van over unexplored mountain roads, hiking and trips to the playground.

Whitney explained to Steph and Meg that Dan had such deep-rooted anger towards his mother because she'd chosen to turn a blind eye to his father's abuse. He was getting back at his mother with each murder he committed.

Ron and Steph's roller coaster marriage continued to take its toll from heights of ecstasy to the depths of despair.

*   *   *   *

Time was healing.

It was a beautiful, sunny morning. The weather was perfect; no humidity, not too cool, not too hot. Steph felt wonderful and joyous. The children wanted to do something fun and special so Steph consented to making an all day trip to visit her parents so they could all have that *Quality Time*.

"Okay, kiddies, get your things and jump into the van," Steph commanded happily.

Meanwhile…

Ron felt sorry for Meg as everyone did. His need to see her clouded his judgment. Knowing that Steph had planned to spend the day away from home he decided to spend time with Meg.

Ron drove into Meg's drive. Meg was outside with her children wearing her usual summer togs, the shortest white shorts and a black halter-top. On her it didn't look vulgar, just extremely sexy causing every man who saw her to salivate!

"How are you getting along, Meg?" Ron asked sympathetically.

"Not great!" Meg answered honestly. "I'm trying to find work but I have no skills and no one wants me. I'm getting welfare right now. I'll probably have to sell my house and move in with my parents. They'll really love *that*! I have no other choice. The children seem to be doing well. Better than I am."

"How are *you* getting along?" Ron asked.

Tears filled her eyes.

"I still can't believe this has happened! I lived with Dan all these years and never saw anything, only his horrible nightmares. In retrospect, I can see why it happened to him but..." Her voice trailed off. "How about a cold drink, Ron?"

"That would be great. Thank you."

They walked into the house together.

Meg's house was small scale but very charming. A fieldstone front and graceful porch columns gave it colonial charm. Meg obviously had a green thumb. There were lovely manicured flower gardens gracing the lawn front and back.

Meg's family room was warm and friendly as they walked through to the kitchen. It had a beamed ceiling and built-in bookshelves on top of wood paneled walls on either side of a raised hearth fireplace.

Ron sat down at the kitchen table while Meg fixed them both a cold iced tea.

"How did you manage to visit me today?" Meg asked, breaking the silence.

Ron took a sip of his tea and put it down on the table.

"Steph took the kids to visit her parents for the day. Steph's a stubborn woman."

"I miss the good ole days, the fun times we used to all have together," Meg said in despair. "I'd give just about anything to get those days back. If only we knew then what we know now, maybe all of this ugliness would never have happened. Maybe we could have helped Dan somehow. But no one knows what's in another person's mind. That's the only place we have that no one else can share."

"I miss them too. Those times were very special to me," Ron agreed.

Meg sat down across from Ron.

Ron looked into her desperate eyes.

"I miss being with you. I miss our talks."

Meg looked away, blushing and jumped up from the table nervously.

The subject was dropped.

The kids came inside to take care of their bathroom needs. Meg fixed a bowl of pretzels and some juice to take back outside so they could have a picnic.

Meg's hands trembled as she sat down with two pieces of cake.

"I haven't been in to see Dan," Meg admitted, feeling guilty. "I just can't force myself to go. I have nothing to say to him, but I *do* feel sorry for him. This person who is locked up isn't my husband. My husband is dead."

Ron tried to console her.

"That's perfectly understandable."

Meg put her hands up to her face to cover her tears.

"It's such an ugly situation and I'm so embarrassed. I'm afraid that everyone will associate me with it and won't feel comfortable with me any more."

Ron jumped up from the table and went over to her. He pulled her out of her chair and held her while she had a good cry.

Filled with a heart thumping desire for her, Ron took advantage of the moment, lifted her chin with his finger, and kissed her.

Meg pulled away, ran down the hall to her bedroom and slammed the door behind her.

Ron's emotional state wasn't about to allow him to leave so he sat quietly in the family room while Meg had a good cleansing cry in her bedroom.

He looked outside to check on the children. They were playing in their sandbox totally engrossed in their project.

Ron walked down the hall and knocked on the door.

"Meg, are you all right?" Ron paused for an answer. There wasn't one. "Meg, I'm sorry if I upset you."

A few minutes went by before her throaty voice came from the other side of the door.

"My emotions are on overload. I can't think straight."

She opened the door, then walked across her room and sat down heavily on the bed.

"I feel so lost and alone," Meg admitted.

Ron's pulse started to race as he walked into her bedroom and closed the door behind him. He sat on the bed beside her, neither of them speaking.

After a few moments of silence, Ron spoke first.

"I want you to know that Steph is right."

Ron looked down toward his lap as Meg gaped at him in amazement, as if she couldn't believe what she was hearing. He looked up and straight into her eyes.

"I *do* love you, God help me! And I *do* long for you." Ron admitted freely without the slightest hint of guilt.

They peered into each other's eyes for a minute then slowly they leaned toward each other. Their lips came together again only this time Meg didn't resist.

She *needed someone* to love her now. She *needed* reassurance that her life was going to be put back on the right track. Ron always seemed to be able to fix things and handle any situation that was thrown his way. She *needed* him to *fix it*.

They were both overwhelmed by the moment and neither of them hesitated as Ron untied her halter and unzipped those wonderful teeny-weeny shorts.

Ron waited so long for this moment he knew in his heart was bound to happen. *Yes!* Stephanie *was* right.

Ron impatiently, feverishly undressed himself without taking his eyes off of Meg's luscious body.

He kissed her soft sensuous lips. His mouth made a trail down her neck to her tasty shoulders. His lips continued their journey to her breasts and ran his hands down her perfect curves all the while lowering her to the bed.

Afterward

Ron held Meg in his arms, reminiscent of his favorite fantasy that he'd indulged in so many times before. Now, it was a *memory*. Reveling in the searing heat from this conquest of forbidden fruit, he kissed her forehead almost as in gratitude.

Lingering a moment, silent and reflective, Meg recognized with such clarity what a horrible mistake she'd just made. A shiver of repulsion snaked its way through her body. Flushed, appalled and so annoyed with herself for having permitted this atrocity to happen, she jumped up and dressed quickly.

Without a word she ran outside to be with her children, needing to shake this mistake from her memory and grab onto *her* reality.

Surmising that Meg was feeling her regrets, Ron dressed quickly and ran outside after her.

Meg was shaking all over. Her words caught in her throat.

"I feel sick! I think you'd better leave. I'm so sorry," she said trying very hard not to look into Ron's eyes.

Ron walked back in the house to get his shoes.

∗   ∗   ∗   ∗

Steph's parents thought it would be a nice idea if they watched the kids over night Ron and Steph could go out alone for a change. They asked the kids if they'd like to spend the night. Naturally, it was unanimous.

"Well! In that case, I'd better get home and fix my hair and make myself gorgeous," Steph said.

Stephanie drove home planning what she'd wear and where they might go if Ron consented to the idea. She missed her babies already but she knew they couldn't have been in better hands.

She passed Meg's house on her way home. She spotted Ron's truck in her drive. Instantly outraged, her foot slammed on the brake causing the tires to lock up and screech to a halt laying rubber for at least ten yards. Checking her rear view mirror that she was free of any cars behind her, she backed up and flew into Meg's drive with a vengeance.

Not bothering to knock, Steph threw open the door and rushed inside as if trying to catch them *in-the-act.*

Wide-eyed, lips tense over her teeth, she bellowed for all the neighbors to hear, "*You Son-Of-A-Bitch!*"

Meg rushed inside when she saw Steph jump out of her car and bolt in the house in a fury.

Steph's nostrils flared as she glared at Meg resentfully.

"I'm sorry, Meg, for your predicament concerning Dan but you seem committed to the total destruction of our lives!" Steph exploded.

Attacked by uneasiness but grateful Steph didn't blast her way in ten minutes before.

"I only came over to see how Meg was getting along after her ordeal," Ron muttered lamely, realizing her fury.

"Of course, you chose the day you thought that I'd be gone all day!" Steph snapped, infuriated by his nerve.

"You can't be mad, Steph. I haven't been over here in a long time," Ron continued in his defense.

"*Mad!*" Steph screamed. "If I calm down, I *might* be *mad*! **Let's call it over!**"

"Ah! Steph! We've been getting along so well lately. How can you say that?" Ron whimpered too disbelieving to be angry.

"A few sentimental words and a dash of remorse and you expect me to hop right back in the sack with you?" Steph spat at him.

Steph ran out the door dismissing any thought of reconciliation. She laid rubber all the way out Meg's drive. "There! Meg, *Darling!* Get out your scrub bucket!" Steph screamed.

Ron jumped in his truck and followed Steph home with his tail between his legs.

Steph ran in the house and locked the door behind her. A locked door always turned Ron into a maniac. With one swift kick, Ron was through the door and not so clumsily made his way up the stairs after Steph.

At first, he tried to humor her.

"Ah, Steph, you don't see the cows getting mad because the bull screws all the other cows in the field, do you?"

Steph snapped, "You're *so disgusting*!"

Ron grabbed her arm and stopped her in her tracks. She would no longer delude herself with his sweet façade. He was Dr. Jekyll and Mr. Hyde. That was clear. She reached up and slapped his face. Then in return, he slapped hers.

Ron wasn't about to take any abuse from a mere woman. That slap induced a totally different expression on his face. He was finished trying to be nice. There was a spontaneous explosion.

"You jealous *Bitch*! What makes you think you're the only cunt around?" Ron bellowed savagely.

"What makes me think that you're the only *type* of man around? Let's face it, *Baby*! *You're no bargain*!" Steph obliged.

"I'm the best thing that ever happened to you and you know it!" Ron retaliated. "What do you want, some little wimp to pull around by the nose?"

Steph looked daggers at him. "*Yes*! If a wimp is a kind, respectful, real, feeling human being! I want a man who isn't selfish or controlling, one who is capable of thinking well of someone other than *himself*."

"Miss Goodie Two-shoes! Hunh? Well, you're a little *too good* for me! Thank you," Ron said in his ever-condescending manner.

"You've got that right! I *am* too good for you!" Steph countered.

"Variety is the spice of life," Ron added with his usual get-even tactics. "Any man will tell you that! Men weren't meant to be tied down to only one body his whole life. A man gets *bored*!"

Ron grabbed her again only infuriating her to her limit. Steph grabbed a heavy ceramic vase and landed it across his back, shattering all over him and the floor.

He was astonished that she was capable of such rage. She was unrecognizable in her fury!

"That was for taking my friend *Meg* away from me!" Steph announced with great satisfaction.

She attacked him with her fists.

"This is for humiliating me in front of my friends!"

Ron grabbed her arms and threw her on the floor in an attempt to protect himself.

Steph came up with a suitcase in her hands and hit him as hard as she could over the head with it.

"And that was for the sleazy strip joints and magazines you deliberately flaunt in my face!"

She screamed and cried in her rage completely out of control. Ron fell to the floor with her last attempt to bring him down.

She fell to her knees, pounding his chest with her fists, crying.

"This is for robbing me of my self-esteem, making me feel worthless and insignificant!"

Ron jumped to his feet pulling Steph up with him by her collar. Then he backhanded her across the face sending her flying to the floor. She wiped the blood from her mouth, staying on the floor for a moment to try to get her bearings.

He was coming after her again. She picked up an iron lamp that had been knocked over in the scuffle. She managed to stand up in spite of her dizziness and hit him over the head one last time. It sent him to the floor with a thud, splattering blood all over.

Ron was out cold.

Still crying, Steph fell to her knees beside him and kissed his forehead.

"And that, My Darling, was for not loving me enough," she whispered.

As if in a trance, she stood up and walked into her bathroom, blood trickling from her mouth. Now seeming extremely serene and at peace, she took out a bottle of sleeping pills.

"And this is for my naiveté. Maybe now, My Darling, you can have your perfect love and you'll be happy." Steph took a handful of pills and swallowed them with tap water. She calmly changed into her most becoming negligee and repaired her face.

Steph left the bathroom, turned off the light and walked toward Ron. She dropped to the floor beside him, made herself comfortable and rested her head on his chest.

*   *   *   *

Hearing the fight from next door, the sudden silence scared Ann. She walked cautiously across Steph's lawn. The house was so quiet that it made Ann shudder. She stood in the doorway and called Steph's name. Knowing that they were both there, she continued to call their names as she walked through their house.

Ann took a deep breath and once again announced herself and called out, "Steph! Ron!" She entered their bedroom. Her heart almost stopped.

CHAPTER 13

▼

Ron had newfound respect for Stephanie. She had his reverent attention and she fully intended to keep it. He was dubious of their future together as he flashed back to the incredible bedroom scene. He didn't realize that she was capable of such uncontrolled rage, such fury! He'd never seen such savage behavior in a woman.

Whitney visited Steph in the hospital. This was an awkward embarrassing moment for Steph because she really regretted trying to take her own life. Her children needed her and she certainly needed them. She vowed that she would never do anything so selfish ever again. It would have been the worst thing that could ever happen to her children and to her parents.

"I'm setting up a series of appointments for you. You need to work this anger out of your system or you're going to destroy yourself and all the people who love you," Whitney said.

"Oh! I'm all right now. Really! It was a bad moment for me. All I could think about was stopping my pain. I just couldn't deal with any more pain," Steph pleaded.

Whitney interrupted.

"This was not a normal occurrence. I hope you never experience that rage and hopelessness again. You may not be fortunate enough to have a concerned neighbor next time. Thank goodness your children weren't there. If they'd been there, would you have been able to control your anger?"

"I've managed it many times before," Steph replied. "Everything is handled differently when the children are with me because I do everything *around* them and *for* them.

Just then Bianca rushed into Steph's room. "*Girl*! You spend most of your time in the hospital! What's with you? I hope you have good insurance coverage!"

"Hi, Bianca!" Whitney said.

"Hi, Whitney! I hope you can do something for this girl."

"I think we can work something out," Whitney said.

Bianca turned to Steph.

"At least this time you were smart enough to put Ron in here with you. This experience should do Ron some good. Maybe he won't be so apt to walk all over you after this."

CHAPTER 14

▼

FIFTEEN YEARS
LATER......

Stephanie rushed home from work so she could finish unpacking. She and Ron had just moved into their magnificent new home that looked very impressive sitting on a hill overlooking ten acres of beautifully manicured grounds of landscaped perfection. It was a picture of French Country elegance worthy of any Home and Garden magazine.

A grown up Packy and his wife were expected later to help unpack. Zach was already home from his classes and unpacking his room. He was attending a local college so he could live at home. Myra was attending the same college majoring in journalism. Mandy was graduating from high school and Garret was a sophomore.

Steph was thankful that she was able to keep all her children close to her. All her influence seemed to have paid off. She had beautiful, healthy girls and handsome, strong and responsible boys. They were all intelligent, good, kind, and caring young adults who were fortunate enough to have missed out on the need to rebel, raise hell and fall victim to peer pressure.

Steph's children supplied her with an enormous amount of pride and her lifestyle had turned out pretty much like she'd visualized in her youth. She had unabashed pride in her possessions and enjoyed extravagance immensely. Her exquisite taste was prevalent throughout her house and everything she did. She had a natural knack for adding a touch of class to everything she did.

Zach came downstairs to meet his mother.

"Hi, Mom! Did you have a hard day? You look beat."

"No, from a lack of sleep over all of this excitement of moving," Steph replied.

"My friends and I are kicking around the idea of going to Ocean City this weekend," Zach announced. "Do you mind if we go?"

Steph smiled.

"Sounds like fun. Sure. You deserve it. You work so hard."

"When are Packy and Jen coming?" Zach asked.

"After dinner," Steph said, bending over to move a box out of her way.

"Are they bringing Amanda?" Zach asked hopefully.

"They'd better! I don't get to see her nearly often enough," Steph complained.

Amanda was all of six months old and was the spitting image of Steph's daughter, Mandy.

"Did Marie make lasagna?" Steph asked.

"She sure did!" Zach answered.

Steph was fortunate enough to have a housekeeper three days a week to help her keep up with the housework, laundry and meals. She put long, hard hours into her career. It was impossible to keep up with all the household chores in order to maintain a huge house full of young adults with lots of friends.

Steph put the lasagna in the oven. Marie had set the table all ready and prepared the salad. The French bread was ready to warm in the oven.

Mandy and Garret came downstairs.

"Hi, Mom! We're finished our homework. What's for dinner?" Mandy asked.

"Lasagna, and it'll be ready in forty five minutes. How's the unpacking coming?" Steph asked, anxious to get her new house in immaculate order.

"Mine is almost finished," Mandy said with pride. "I'll help Garret with his when I'm finished mine. He's not quite as excited as we are about it."

Steph sighed with relief.

"You're a blessing, Mandy! Thanks. Where's Myra?"

"She and Mark went to the library," Mandy answered. Myra had been dating John and Whitney's Mark for a year. They seemed to be very compatible and shared quite a few common interests.

"How does Myra's room look?" Steph asked.

Mandy defended her sister.

"She's been working so hard on her term paper, Mom. She hasn't had much time to unpack."

"Well, maybe we can all pitch in and help her," Steph said.

Ron came home for dinner.

"Hi, Hon!" He said as he kissed her. "What's for dinner? Don't tell me! He raised his nose to the air and sniffed. "Lasagna."

"You got it," Steph said.

"Have you found anyone to do our lawn work yet?" Ron asked.

"Not yet," Steph admitted. "I was thinking about hiring the maintenance man at work. He does good work and he looks like he could use the extra money. Besides, he's single. Maybe he and Marie could get together. They both seem to lead such empty lives."

"Always the romantic," Ron said.

Steph gave Ron a playful slap across the rear.

The old cliché, *you're not getting older, you're getting better* certainly applied to Ron. His rugged, careless, dangerous looks mellowed into eloquent, charming, beautifully dressed sophistication. A touch of gray added a certain distinction to his appealing look of dignity. His eyes transmitted an intelligence that only years of experience could supply and the sexy cleft in his chin seemed more pronounced. He had a warm, open friendly quality and was quite unpretentious in spite of his looks. Ron and Stephanie hadn't had a fight over another woman in fifteen years. He'd finally grown up and taken responsibility for his actions and Steph was self-disciplined, refined and no longer vulnerable.

Myra walked in just as the family was sitting down to dinner. Ron and Steph tried to keep their family close by having their children attend local colleges and having their evening meals together where they kept in touch by sharing their thoughts and activities.

✳   ✳   ✳   ✳

That evening, in spite of all the unpacking that needed to be done, Steph visited her brother in a VA hospital where he now lived. She visited him on a regular basis. She was the only one left he hadn't alienated. Bianca and their daughter were no longer in his life thanks only to himself.

Rick had developed an infection and needed constant care. When Steph walked into his room, she was overcome by her emotions. The sight of her brother broke her heart. She tried to control her tears in front of him.

Rick was totally motionless with his hands crossed over his chest. There was a ghastly looking tube through a hole straight into his stomach to supply him sustenance because he could no longer swallow. He was so pale and there was nothing left of his body that had once meant so much to him. There was no fatty tissue at all. The muscles had wasted away long ago. His facial expression appeared retarded because he could no longer control his facial muscles. He could no longer speak and he saw very little. The only thing he could move was his eyes.

Stephanie stood motionless at the door a few moments, trying to get hold of herself before she allowed him to see her.

Finally, she walked in attempting a smile to lift his spirits, and provide some sort of diversion for him to help pass the endless lonely hours.

"Rick," Steph said, putting her hand over his to supply a little human contact other than nurses handling him. It was difficult carrying on a one-sided conversation.

"We moved into our new house and we're in the process of unpacking as fast as we can," Steph said, trying to be cheerful.

She never knew whether to act happy, for fear of seeming to brag or solemn because he must get plenty of solemn. She usually decided to live *for* him to provide some sort of entertainment. He got plenty of *solemn* every day of his pitiful life.

"I'm so proud of my kids! They're all doing well in their studies and my little granddaughter is a doll. Zach studies so hard. I've never seen anyone so determined and so serious to succeed at his goal. He should take some time out for fun once in a while. He's going to Ocean City this weekend with friends. But, I guess that's the stuff doctors are made of. Dedication is one of the most important attributes in being a physician. My baby's growing up much too fast."

Steph was thankful Rick couldn't see that well at that moment because sudden uncontrollable tears streamed down her cheeks as she watched the nurse check the tube in his stomach. She could see how painful it was to him because tears welled in his eyes. Steph continued to ramble on about her family, trying to take his mind off the pain.

Steph had news for him that she felt an obligation to reveal.

"I hate to give you bad news, but Tammy's been dragging her legs and having numbness in her hands just like your MS symptoms started."

Just as Bianca dreaded, their daughter, Tammy, was diagnosed with Multiple Sclerosis.

Fresh tears came to his eyes.

"Can't you reconcile with her?" Steph continued. "You really should leave your house to her. It's designed for a wheel chair and she's going to need it sooner or later."

Rick blinked his eyes twice, which meant *no*.

Steph raised her voice slightly.

"Rick! You're the most stubborn human being I have ever met!"

Steph tried to change the mood, knowing full well that nothing she said would change that stubborn mind of his.

"I bet the nurses wouldn't believe what a devil you used to be! Do you think I should tell them?"

Rick blinked once for, *yes*.

"I think you've paid dearly for your discrepancies. Nobody deserves a fate like this!"

Stephanie hugged her brother gently so as not to cause him further pain.

"I'll be back next week, Rick. I love you!"

CHAPTER 15

▼

Zach had grown into a solid, dependable and trustworthy young man, quite uncharacteristic of his years. Along with depth and compassion, his brilliant blue eyes transmitted intelligence, all essential gear embarking on securing a medical destiny. He inherited his father's distinguished cleft and warm, friendly quality. Tall, dark and handsome, charm personified; one look took a girl's breath away.

Zach and his friends were enjoying a friendly game of volleyball on the beach in Ocean City. Running backwards, arms outstretched to the sky, in an effort to catch the ball, Zach fell backwards over a sunbather.

He jumped up immediately, completely apologetic. He pulled the girl to her feet attempting to wipe the sand from her oiled body but retrieved his hand, red-faced, because it didn't seem to be the gentlemanly thing to do with so much skin exposed.

Zach was stunned speechless at the sight of this gorgeous creature standing before him. She had exquisite icicle blue eyes. Her nose was arrogantly tipped upward just slightly and she had a sensuous, full mouth. Her angelic face was framed by soft blonde curls that had fallen from her blonde ponytail. She had a perfect, *Ann Margaret* body that was capable of bringing any man to his knees, seductive but not indecent or vulgar. She had a look that men lust after and women would sell their mothers for.

After resuming a normal breathing pattern, Zach managed to say, "Oh! I hope I didn't hurt you! I'm sorry!"

"I'm fine. Really," The girl replied with a giggle.

Zach picked up the ball and continued playing with his friends. Preoccupied by the girl's unsurpassable looks, Zach found himself fumbling and clumsy because he couldn't keep his mind on the game.

One of his friends grabbed the ball under his arm, walked over to Zach and rested his arm on his shoulder.

"Hey, Buddy, what do you say we take a break while you introduce us to that little *Fox* over there?"

"Now you know I can't afford to get involved with a girl right now! I have too many years of studying ahead of me," Zach insisted.

They sat down on their blanket and opened the soft drinks.

"Talk about a magnetic personality! Zach can't seem to control his eyes," Zach's friends teased.

Zach watched her sunbathing, tummy down, her bikini top untied to give her back an unbroken tan. Her cheek was pillowed on a folded towel and her breasts showed white when she lifted one elbow to make a point to her friends. Zach's eyes were seized by hers frequently throughout their break.

"I'm starving!" Zach's friend, David announced. "Let's take a walk on the boardwalk and check out some food prospects. Zach! Did you hear me? *Zach!* If you want that girl, I suggest you introduce yourself to her before your mind turns to mush!"

"No! I'm hungry too," Zach said.

They packed up their gear and started back to their hotel room. Zach took a last look catching the girl's gaze.

An hour later, the guys returned with their bags of food and drink. Using his peripheral vision, trying not to be too obvious, Zach discovered that his stunning discovery was no longer sunbathing. His emotions were torn between relief and disappointment. At least, his temptation was removed and he no longer had to exercise his phenomenal will power.

"Looks like the evil apple of temptation was removed for you, Zach," Dave remarked.

"Yep!" Zach said in a gruff, self-deprecating manner.

He *had* to refrain! There was no room in his life right now to get emotionally tangled with a girl. He was determined to become a doctor. He knew he had many years of total devotion and concentration ahead of him and couldn't allow himself to falter like so many of his peers had done. On the other hand, he couldn't seem to push the sight of her out of his mind.

"Zach! *Zach!*" Dave was trying to reach through his trance. "*Zach!* You're becoming a drag over this little beach bunny," Dave scolded.

"Hi!" A sweet feminine voice turned the guy's heads abruptly, squinting from the bright sunlight in their eyes.

The two pretty fresh-faced young women seemed to shimmer like a mirage in the distance with the bright sunlight behind them.

His feelings soared, as a charismatic smile crossed Zach's face in spite of himself. He recognized the little temptress to be the curvaceous little doll he'd tripped over earlier.

With a flirty, breezy eagerness, the girl introduced herself and her friend.

"I'm Blythe and this is my friend, Jackie. We were wondering if you guys would care to get up another game of Volleyball."

Appearing shy and circumspect, Zach replied.

"It's nice to meet you. This is Dave, John, Pete and I'm Zach."

After a lengthy, uncomfortable pause, Dave rescued them.

"In answer to your question, *sure*! We'll play!" Dave announced flashing Zach a cunning smile.

Blythe's anxious, great eyes held Zach captive as he joined the crowd in another game. Watching Blythe stretch her glorious body to reach for the ball, her young, firm breasts bouncing with every jump only added more anxiety.

The game was over. Zach offered the girls some soft drinks from their ice chest. The rambunctious group settled into casual chatter. The girl's effervescent chattiness fell silent as the guys absorbed their attention.

"Some of our friends equate intersession with only one thing: absolute and total inertia," Zach said, as he looked out over the beach at all the sunbathers burning the mid-day oil, tanning oil, that is.

Dave broke in trying to impress the girls.

"The key to good surfing is consistence. The waves have to break in a measurable pattern."

"Dave used to live in Hawaii," Zach interrupted to explain.

"Yes," Dave continued. "I used to be pretty good on the surfboard! I took pictures with a sixteen-millimeter lens while inside a wave; a tube, a wave that doubles over the surfer. I also used a six hundred millimeter and a thousand millimeter lens from the beach."

"I just read that in some cases it's possible to determine the murderer of a murder victim by his eyes. If the eyes of a murdered person be photographed within a certain time of death, on the retina will be found depicted the last thing that appeared before them, the murderer," Zach offered.

Blythe was astonished.

"That's Wild!"

"A physiology professor in Rome discovered that the external layer of the retina is a purple color. This purple surface whitened on exposure light but regained its original color in the dark. At first he thought this color left in death but he changed his opinion when experts showed that the retina stayed sensitive under certain conditions for up to twenty four hours after death," Zach continued.

Blythe's blue eyes flickered with the attempted vision.

In this maddening opacity, the girls felt that these guys were way over their heads.

Sharing an elusive quality of reluctance, Blythe jumped up.

"Look at the time! We have to be going. See you guys later."

A silence fell between the guys. They were dumbfounded.

"What did we say?" Dave asked with a puzzled expression on his face.

*   *   *   *

Much later, in the oblique moonlight, Zach sat on the boardwalk, too keyed up to sleep. He wouldn't let the inevitable disappointments and mistakes shake his view of what mattered and what didn't.

A sweet voice came out of the darkness.

"Would it be presumptuous of me to ask if I may share your moonlight with you?"

Startled, Zach looked up suddenly to see Blythe's sweet smile. He jumped up gallantly offering her a hand.

"Not at all! Please, sit down."

"We enjoyed playing volleyball with you this afternoon," Blythe said.

"And we enjoyed it too," Zach added in turn. "Where are you from?"

"Altoona, and you?" Blythe responded.

Zach replied, getting more interested by the minute.

"Washington Suburbs."

"I understand that you're studying to be a doctor," Blythe said.

"Yes! I have quite a long haul ahead of me," Zach said, trying to get things off on the right foot, reaching an understanding up front.

There was an air of innocence about Blythe that appealed to Zach. He asked her, "And what are you studying?"

"I'm majoring in computer science, but I'm really having a hard time keeping up. I may have to change my major."

"The computer field is always a smart move," Zach said. "No one can be without knowledge of the computer any more. My mom's a programmer and she's done real well over the year. She loves it. Making a successful career is a knack. Mom reached this eminence on her own with few to thank for it. She was laden down with five children most of the time we were growing up, feeling we needed her more than she needed the work."

"Marriage is only good for men," Blythe added, much to Zach's surprise. "Most families are tragedies for ambitious women. It's wonderful how young women today have a choice. They get their careers started put the money away, then postpone their careers to raise their children themselves."

Zach sat astounded at her willingness to share this with him as if she could read his mind. He looked at her quizzically.

She smiled indulgently as if she realized she'd scored a point with him.

Zach let out an audible sigh of relief. An involuntary smile crossed his face revealing to her that he was unquestionably pleased. Shaken by the intensity of the moment and finding himself in a state of confusion he suddenly suggested, "Would you care to walk along the beach?"

"I'd love to," Blythe answered airily.

Zach had built a fortress around himself but with this girl, his fortress was crumbling. He was aware of an uneasy feeling that made his body ache.

"Are you being pretentious, trying to impress me?" Blythe asked, after Zach finished describing his new house.

"What makes you think that?" Zach asked, a little surprised.

"Do you really live in a house that big?"

"Well, I have two brothers and two sisters and we're all living at home, except my oldest brother and he's married."

"Well! I'm impressed," Blythe exclaimed. "You're so different from anyone I've ever met. You're so mature and sensible and you know where you're headed, accepting no nonsense on the way. Not to mention, you're just about the handsomest guy I've ever seen!"

"I'm flattered," Zach said, red-faced.

"Most guys are only out for the fun of the moment, instant gratification, too precarious for my taste. Most people seem to drift through life in a trance, not knowing or caring how they end up, a comme ci, comme ca attitude," Blythe continued.

Taking obvious pleasure in her company, he was already subconsciously incorporating her into his plans. Walking and talking to her was like dancing to a slow, comfortable waltz, everything falling into place. They seemed unified by their uncanny common opinions and interests. They both seemed obsessed by the idea of having their career goals met before attempting to settle down. They both loved tennis, photography and swimming. They enjoyed tranquility, thinking time alone. They shared an animosity toward people who think they're above everyone else. They were both baffled by people with the lazy brain syndrome. They shared a sense of adventure and tried not to take people too seriously because, "people are too complex to really know anything about!" If it wouldn't be defeating their purpose, they may have discussed the possibility of sharing a harmonious life together.

He showed her extraordinary consideration and admiration but was puzzled by the way she managed to evade his questions concerning her life. It was an intoxicatingly delightful experience for both of them.

"Look at the time! Jackie will be worried about me," Blythe said looking at her watch.

"Would you like to meet me for breakfast?" Zach asked.

"Sure," Blythe said without pause.

"Where? When?"

"Where are you staying?"

"The Sahara."

"Okay, I'll meet you there at nine thirty."

"How about the Pancake House?"

"Great! I love pancakes."

"Something told me you might," Zach said with a smile.

CHAPTER 16

▼

Stephanie and Marie were busy preparing for the Multiple Sclerosis Fund Raiser party that Stephanie was having at her house.

Stephanie's new house was a dream come true. The enormous entry hall was floored in ceramic tile where the magnificent oak staircase demanded everyone's attention. One could almost visualize Scarlett sashaying down the stairs to greet Rhett. If Stephanie had nothing else she *had* to have Scarlett's glorious staircase. To the left of the entrance hall was a study where they kept all their books displayed in a built in library filling one whole wall. This was Ron's sanctuary where he spent most of his time. Just inside the entrance hall were two cavernous closets and a powder room.

There was a knock at the service entrance. Marie answered the door. It was Raymond, the grounds keeper Steph hired from work to take care of grounds work part time.

Raymond's teeth were brilliant white against his tanned skin and salt and pepper, mostly pepper, neatly trimmed beard. His glasses blended perfectly with his hair and beard which lended a well-kempt professor appeal.

Stephanie thought that Marie might have a crush on Raymond, just as she was hoping for.

"Hello, Raymond. I'll get Mrs. Adams for you," Marie said.

Marie called for Steph over the intercom.

"I'll be down in a minute. Both of you, please take a break and have a cold drink and a snack," Steph answered.

A half hour later, Steph made her appearance in the kitchen, hoping that she'd given them enough time to get better acquainted.

"I'd like you two to come to the party as guests. We'll donate your tickets to the MS Foundation," Steph said.

Marie looked at Raymond quizzically. He was strangely dubious looking.

"I know neither of you is committed to anyone," Steph continued, rather brazenly, "Would you mind escorting Marie to the party, Raymond?"

Marie averted her blushing face. She projected a certain virtuousness and giggled nervously with the anticipation of going to a fancy party with Raymond.

Displaying his charismatic smile, he looked encouragingly at Marie and asked, "Would you care to go with me?"

Marie nodded eagerly, delighted to oblige.

Steph flashed Marie a congratulatory smile.

Marie stood abruptly and swept back and forth carrying the glasses and plates to the sink.

Stephanie took Marie to her bedroom after instructing Raymond what she wanted him to do.

"Marie, you're welcome to try on my gowns and choose one you like, except this one that I'm wearing. I'll have it altered for you.

Marie beamed. She couldn't remember ever being so excited!

*   *   *   *

It was after eight o'clock and Steph and Ron's guests were arriving, donned in formal attire. The men were polished, sophisticated and elegantly dressed in black tie.

Stephanie wore a shimmering strapless in a luscious shade of crimson.

John and Whitney arrived, such a dignified, elegant couple, time seemingly to have stood still as their *Perfect Couple* image was the envy of everyone who knew them. Their union was obviously made in heaven and their happiness lifted spirits wherever they were. Whitney, as beautiful as ever, looked like a Grecian Goddess in a lovely yellow wrapped floor length gown draped over one shoulder.

Mandy and Garrett were visiting friends but Packy and his wife, Jenny, and Myra and Mark attended the party. Zach was expected later with his new love interest, Blythe.

John and Whitney's friends from the cruise, Mike and Dani, Bianca, and a date and twenty-five other couples attended Steph's very worthwhile function.

A band was playing from the lower terrace and a lovely buffet was set up in the dining room. The fare included a choice of ham, turkey, prime rib, or crab imperial, potage a la reine, quiche Lorraine, salads and a dry Chablis, chardonnay, merlot, along with a multitude of interesting and beautiful hors d'oeuvres and deserts.

Stephanie had become an accomplished hostess and had developed quite a social expertise.

"What should the aesthetics of modern housing be?" John asked, "Should there be any beyond utility and cost?"

Mike chimed in.

"Did the peasants who lived on dirt floors and in thatched huts worry about aesthetics? We're so spoiled! We have an instinctive sense of beauty and greed. We're more apt to spend our money on something aesthetically beautiful as opposed to something that was actually practical," Mike said, still after all these years fighting for the underdog's rights.

"As long as I keep making money and can make a living, I'll build anything people want, whether it be aesthetics or primarily functional," Ron said.

Whitney was on the terrace in a deep conversation with several people in her community.

"Dreams are a way of letting out our frustrations and suppressions, which usually have to do with sex or our parents. It's not a question of natural or unnatural or right or wrong. It's understanding why we do things so we can stop doing them. Jessica doesn't make herself happy. I don't think she enjoys life very much."

"She has everything, seemingly to us but obviously, something's missing," Dani added.

"It's just those types of people who are the unhappiest," Whitney said. "The ones who seem to have everything are the ones who panic, where the rest of us are too busy scrambling to make a living to notice if we are one way or the other."

"We're all outside looking in. We can't read people's minds. Don't compromise your professional integrity," Dani said, putting her hand on Whitney's shoulder.

"Something happens to a woman when she doesn't feel wanted or needed," Whitney continued.

A neighbor interrupted.

"What an archaic idea! Women aren't supposed to need anybody or anything any more."

"The mind goes in different directions as a refuge from reality," Whitney said. "Few people have the imagination for reality. We all have our own reality. We all can *make* our own reality. No one can make us happy. That's our responsibility. We make ourselves happy and any *special* person in our lives is icing on the cake. The word *happy* is a misconceived idea, I think. One day at a time, each with different things that make us happy. *Notice! See! Feel! Experience!* On purpose! All those little things, from driving the car you love, listening to the music you love, from the fabulous sound system that you love, enjoying that beautiful, warm day (or the rain, or the snow, or the fog), enjoying the company of the people you love, all these little things make you happy! Enjoy the moment; then the next moment; throw away that next *bad one*; on the way to the next moment. Yah! That one was *spectacular* and *there you are!* You were happy and you didn't even notice!"

Whitney was so unpretentious that she didn't intimidate her friends. Her friends smiled remote aristocratic smiles when speaking to a lot of women who attended these parties, seemingly gazing disinterested into space. Her friends felt that they could say anything to her. Whitney was interesting, intelligent and dignified as well as beautiful and young looking where most of her friends in her age bracket were either fat or on the verge of. The flesh on their upper arms was loose and their hips were of girdled hardness. These seasoned women, after losing their youthful appearance hid behind their expressions of serene superiority and their monetary success. Where their beauty faded there was expensive jewelry to make up for it hoping that the jewelry would be an ample substitute.

"You're the most sublimated woman I know, Whitney," Steph said as she joined Whitney and her little group.

One of the husbands had to have his say.

"We get what we unconsciously want."

"Rubbish!" Steph protested, "Only a *man* would say that!"

"They're starved. Their marriages have gone stale," the man said.

The statement conjured up a malicious devilish spirit in Stephanie so in order to maintain her cool as the *Perfect Hostess*, she'd always been revered as, she excused herself and moved on.

Their contemporaries considered Ron and Stephanie charming and intellectual.

"You don't put things very gracefully," the man's wife said.

"I don't feel graceful," he retorted. Steph heard while walking away. Steph found the man presumptuous and offensive. *Oh! Well! As long as he makes a nice contribution to the MS Foundation!* Stephanie thought.

Bianca's date's tall muscular frame was enviably trim, his voice rich, and his face handsome. He was wealthy, had impeccable breeding, a stately home and all the right friends. His ability to laugh at himself was one of his better-known virtues. He worked hard all his life, had principles of always fulfilling a promise and was a very honorable person, much to Bianca's liking, quite the contrast to poor Rick.

They walked through the fragrant gardens to greet Marie and Raymond who obviously felt out of place.

"I hope you're enjoying yourselves," Bianca said.

"I'd like you to meet my friend, Philip Leighton."

"Phil, this is Marie, Steph's housekeeper and Raymond, her grounds keeper."

Phil extended his hand with great ease. Marie was a tightly wound, nervous woman who had to have things placed clearly in front of her. She was attractive; small featured and had been divorced for five years. Her husband had brutally beaten her, making her leery of men. Winning her trust was quite a task. The only people she trusted were Ron and Steph and only then after a few years of their kindness and generosity was she able to let down her defenses and relax with them. Ron and Steph welcomed her into their home as a member of the family. Having no family of her own, her whole world revolved around the Adams household.

"An adult has to accept limited objectives in life," Whitney was saying. "We all have dreams of greatness when we're young but if we keep this up after a point, it's not realistic and it inevitably ends in disappointment which can lead to low self-esteem then to self-hatred, even to self-destruction."

Ron spoke up.

"I don't think that's necessarily true. I still dream of taking a new road, stumbling onto a new vein of talent that somehow I overlooked and *astounding everyone.*"

"You already astound everyone, Ron," Stephanie interrupted.

Everyone laughed.

Another neighbor entered the conversation.

"The most unbelievable human downfall is the capacity for self-deception. We all strive to get better. We all strive to better ourselves. The fact is we don't get better. From the minute we're born, we're losing ground; we're dying."

"But we all gain wisdom," Ron suggested.

The negative guy came back.

"What for? Life is downhill. Man is essentially predatory. I don't believe in any of that non-violence crap. The only way history has been made so far is from bloodshed, sweat and suffering or some kind of sacrifice. In Jesus' time, Christians were thrown into the lion's den for entertainment. To settle any dispute or political argument we resort to bloodshed…"

He was putting reverse English on the conversation trying to shock his audience and he was succeeding.

The guy ended with, "Do you really want a *Black Man* to run our country?"

"*If he's the right man for the job*, Yes," Ron answered with great pride.

Ron deliberately and blatantly leaned over the table and asked Whitney if she had a business card.

Whitney answered right away.

"*Always!* Here you are, Ron!"

"Thank you, Whitney!"

Ron took it from her and handed it directly to the man in one continuous motion.

"Here's Whitney's card! I think she might be able to help you."

Ron took hold of Whitney's arm and led her away from the man, as he stood dumbfounded looking at Whitney's card.

"Don't mind him. He just likes to psych people out," Ron whispered to Whitney.

"He's so prejudiced and bigoted. He must be a miserable soul. Unfortunately, some people just love to be miserable," Whitney said.

Ron moved on to the next group where John was talking.

"I didn't have much bliss in my first marriage just periods of mutual apathy."

Someone else made a comment.

"Success should provide some kind of protection against divorce. They're so costly! If you're with someone for twenty years, there's something of value there."

"Yeah! Monetary value," one of the neighbors chimed in. "We get used to the sweet life. You get bored *at home*. You go out and have an affair, the next thing you know you're stripped of your home, and half, if not *more* of your money and possessions." The guy was drinking like it was prohibition eve. "Well, I couldn't help it! My wife lost her appeal. I wanted someone with young tight skin again."

The canons of morality were aimed and ready to fire. One of the wives responded hostily revealing that she was militantly against straying husbands.

"How dare you glamorize infidelity! What? You're *so perfect*? You don't have any sagging skin? No receding hairline? No thickness around the middle?"

The guy continued in spite of her.

"One of the most deluding notions people have is that they can only go to bed with one woman at a time."

"Gee! I hate to put sugar in your tank but I consider you barbaric and inhumane!"

He remained calm under all the provocation.

"Women are always quick to criticize the better known failings of man."

The women moved in like predators around a wounded animal.

"I'd like to see you turned into cat litter and we'll all be more than happy to shove you under the family cat!"

"Ah, the awesome sanctity of marriage. If it makes you feel any better, I'd never doubted my point of view until I lost my family for good. My pride suddenly was no longer important. The girl left me after I was stupid enough to admit to her that we had nothing in common but *sex*. I guess I told her once too often that she was acting like a baby."

He was subject to ostracism and insult until he started his pitiful repentance. His attempted humor and charm hadn't worked and they were showing signs of wear. A muscle in his jaw clenched tightly.

Unintended sympathy lit up Whitney's face.

"Evolutionary melancholia. It's a stage in a man's life when he questions his worth and happiness," Whitney was saying to one of the women.

"Look! Isn't that April Kerens, the journalist?" Whitney said in an attempt to change the subject.

"It sure is!" Ron said. "I'm sure she finds this a good opportunity to dig up some dirt for her magazine. She has quite a reputation!"

"Who is she?" one of the neighbors asked.

"She makes friends with her subject or victim as it sometimes turns out. She wins his confidence so he reveals all to her then she writes her piece. Later, the victim reads the article in complete horror, things were written out of context to make him look foolish or disreputable. After it's published, nothing can be done. Freedom of the press, you know! Literature should celebrate people's humanity; commemorate the good and people's experiences. She'll write anything for the almighty buck!"

"I feel like Cinderella at the Ball," Blythe sighed, as she and Zach entered the grand entrance hall.

"You mean I'll only have you until midnight?" Zach said, trying to be witty.

"I really thought you were putting me on about your house! I'm *so impressed*," Blythe gushed.

Her skin was tingling all over as if she were being tickled all over with a feather.

"This is a *Palace*, Zach!" Blythe remarked excitedly. "I'm so nervous!"

"Oh! You'll be fine! They'll love you," Zach assured her.

Zach gave her a long hug to reassure her.

Packy walked up to them.

"I know we have a happy ship here, but this isn't the *Love Boat*," Packy said with a teasing smile. "Who's this gorgeous creature?"

"Packy, this is Blythe Lane," Zach said. "We met in Ocean City. Blythe, this is my *married* brother; may I repeat, **married***?*"

"It's so nice to meet you, Blythe," Packy said. "It's times like these that I wish Zach and I were still competing."

Blythe giggled nervously, taking hold of Zach's arm.

"Please excuse Packy. Subtlety isn't one of his virtues!"

Stephanie was sitting on the terrace with friends. She caught sight of Zach and his new love interest approaching them. Numbness stung her tongue.

Silence fell between Steph and her friends. They were all very aware of Zach and his new friend.

Steph downed her gin and tonic, her heart churning. Her face suddenly looked very fragile, guarded in repose, her chin set and the corners of her mouth down drawn with studied sadness. She received full impact of this curvaceous, very lovely girl with the smile of an angel.

Ron's eyebrows rose in surprise and he was sure his heart skipped a couple of beats. He stood in obvious discomfort as he watched Zach and this new girl approach Steph from across the terrace.

Ron started toward them, pipe smoke trailing behind him.

Trying not to concentrate on her rotating inner discomfort, Steph stood with complete dignity to greet her son and his new friend. Steph was appalled by her discomfort. She imagined herself shaking it off as a dog would shake the water off of himself coming in from the rain. She was over her immature insecurity. She was a model of restraint.

Steph said magnanimously as she held out her hand to welcome Blythe,

"You must be Blythe. We've heard so much about you, all good, of course!"

Steph turned to her son and hugged him.

"She's as lovely as you described."

The buzzing of voices in the room suddenly grew quieter as Ron joined them.

"Dad, this is Blythe Lane," Zach said.

Ron smiled.

"I'm glad to meet you, Blythe. Where are you from?"

"Altoona, Pennsylvania," Blythe answered.

Ron and Steph exchanged a quizzical look.

"Have you lived there long?"

"All my life," Blythe answered, shy and circumspect.

"Double, double, toil and trouble," John whispered to Whitney.

The room started buzzing.

"Why can't grief take a holiday?" "Hasn't Steph had enough?" "Not wealth nor beauty nor homage shelters her."

The rumored infidelities and snide remarks struck Whitney as pathetic.

Gaily rattling ice cubes, Ron was mixing a drink for Steph.

"May I fix you something, Blythe?"

"No thank you, Mr. Adams. I don't drink."

"To think! I once scrubbed their diapers, made their formula and fed them. Their dependency on me made me feel proud and needed. Now, my biggest function is to safeguard their privacy," Steph was saying.

Stephanie was being gracious and dignified. She laughed a cultivated laugh.

"We've never danced together. How about it," Zach asked Blythe.

"I'd love to!"

Ron and Steph continued to sit pensively while watching Zach and Blythe dance.

"I haven't the slightest doubt that Blythe is Meg's daughter!" Steph sighed.

A grin that hinted of a beautiful secret tasted was still on Ron's face when Steph looked at him.

"You stole those exact words right out of my head," Ron said.

Steph not so discretely picked up a knife from the table and held it in her hand. "Here, allow me to perform a lobotomy and I'll stick them right back in there," Steph retorted.

Ron hadn't expected such a curt response, as he looked at her face in surprise.

She refused him an easy victory.

"I'm sure you have an absurdly idealized picture of her in your mind! Maybe she's grown fat over the years. Did you ever think of that?"

"Not once!" Ron said angrily, still trying to talk through a smile for appearance sake. "What's your private name for me, Beelzebub?"

Steph's eyes slitted in a malevolent expression.

"Why is everyone so shocked if a man gets the hots for his wife's friend? After all she's the one she gets closest to," Ron persisted.

"Spare me your vulgar fantasies," Steph insisted.

Ron's head sat heavier on his shoulders as the notion sank in, his lips tense.

It seemed that Meg was determined to screw up Steph's life even from Pennsylvania.

Ron sat in secretive and contented silence.

Steph gave Ron one of those; *you're going to get poison in your coffee one of these days,* looks. Her blood was boiling. She wanted to empty both barrels of a shotgun into his smug face! She hadn't felt so ominous in fifteen years. What is it about Meg that throws her into such a tizzy after all these years?

"We'd better get back to our guests," Steph said forcing herself to smile graciously.

Stephanie joined Bianca and some other acquaintances trying to take her mind off the ugly, painful feelings welling up in her soul. She was determined to remain strong. She was now the person she needed to be and she couldn't allow this familiar pain to threaten her peace and joy of living.

"She sure has a terrific nuisance value, doesn't she?" Bianca whispered.

Steph was surprised.

"Does everyone see it?"

"I'm afraid so," Bianca said.

"Oh! I'm so embarrassed!" Steph admitted.

"No need to be," Bianca said.

They looked around the dance floor.

"Hunh! Ron's with Blythe!"

Steph sashayed calmly, still trying not to lose her dignity, toward her husband and Blythe. She smiled sweetly, tapping Blythe on the shoulder.

"You're much too sexy, Blythe! You'll give this old man a heart attack!"

Switching places with Blythe, Steph assumed the dance position in Ron's arms.

"Back in your own back yard, Ron," Steph whispered in his ear.

Blythe stood alone on the dance floor confused and embarrassed, but only for a short time. Zach rescued his *Damsel in Distress.*

"Put your eyes back in your sockets!" Steph said to Ron through clenched teeth when she noticed Ron's eyes following Zach and Blythe on the dance floor.

Later, Zach gave Blythe a tour of the house.

"I shouldn't have come," Blythe uttered. "They don't like me!"

"That's not so," Zach insisted, even though he noticed the tension not only between his parents but in some of the guests as well.

"I'm fundamentally stupid! That's it, isn't it? Everyone here is of substance and I'm not," Blythe rambled on in despair.

"That's absurd!" Zach protested. He wanted to kiss her and make it up to her but a kiss may have seemed condescending to her at that point.

"You're the prettiest girl here! And you have more substance than all these people put together!"

"You're kidding, of course," Blythe smiled shyly.

"Would I kid you?"

"Maybe!"

Blythe refused to be comforted by his words but at least for his sake she smiled and pretended to be lifted by his attempt.

They walked into Myra's room. "Oh! This is lovely!" Blythe gushed.

The single bed was built sideways under white shuddered windows with built in storage shelves and cabinets on each side of the bed with a decorator stepladder leading to her bed. A hanging fern hung in front of the windows, one on each side of the bed. Matching throw pillows and a wall lamp made the bed look like a huge cozy window seat. The whole room was done in dramatic contrast of baby blue and white.

Blythe bounced on Myra's bed.

"Ahhhh! I feel so at home in this room. I love it! Your Mom is so talented."

"I told you, Mom is a remarkable woman."

"My mom's whole life revolves around complete subservience to my Dad," Blythe said sadly. "She never seemed to have any goals. Her house, fixing meals and pleasing my Dad seems to be all she thinks about! I don't want to waste my life away like that! Not that I don't want love, children, *family*, and the like, but I need something else too! Something that keeps me excited about life, a challenge of some sort, a purpose, and a reason for *being*, I need that kind of fulfillment too. A lot of my friends are even considering never having children. They say they don't want to bring children into a mess of a world that we're living in now."

"Have you ever heard of a mess being cleaned up by unborn children?" Zach said in his endless wisdom.

Blythe laughed.

"Oh, Zach! That was so profound! That's one of the many things I love about you! You keep me thinking and always in a positive way."

"Well, on my friend's behalf, their arguments are that a baby is kind of an impulse purchase, a lot of times, maybe more often than not they're *a* product of *oops,*" Blythe continued. "Of course we all know that that little mistake alters your whole life. Everyone knows that you don't need one. Now that so many women are business and career oriented they're finding that babies would be too much of a burden and that they'd stand in her way. I can think that way at times but then when I'm face to face with a baby, holding it in my arms, something so warm comes over me. I picture what my own baby might look like and I'm hooked. I definitely want a baby some day! Only *one* though," Blythe continued getting no response from Zach. "My girlfriend argues that the freshness and innocence lasts only a short time. She's not about to make such a lifetime invest-ment." She paused and looked down at her feet. "I hope you're not offended but all of this extravagance is a bit overwhelming and just a little intimidating."

Zach found Blythe fascinating. She was unpretentious, sensitive, sensible and altogether quite unique.

Zach walked over to the bed and sat down. He lifted Blythe's chin and gazed into her lovely bedroom eyes.

"I'm glad you could make it tonight, Blythe." He kissed her sensuous lips with great gentleness and tenderness as if he thought her so fragile she might break with the slightest disturbance.

"I'm sorry! This is what I've been trying to avoid!"

Blythe's eyes were dancing with excitement and her pleased smile followed right behind them. She grabbed him roughly and urgently.

"Oh! Let's avoid some more!" Her kiss was quite the opposite of Zach's, full of passion and need.

Zach jumped up, trying not to lose his head.

"You know, we're driving a little too fast here! I think I'll run downstairs and fix us some appetizers, and then we'll talk. I'll be right back. Enjoy Myra's room."

"That's okay! I think I can struggle along without you for a while," Blythe said.

Zach searched out his Mom in the crowd.

Finally spotting her, he waved to get her attention and motioned for her to meet him outside.

Steph politely excused herself and walked toward the terrace to talk to Zach, fearing what he wanted to talk to her about.

"Mom, what's going on? Blythe is hurt and senses you don't like her! It was obvious that when we walked into the room we caused quite a bit of tension. What is it?"

Steph paused to collect her thoughts before she spoke.

"Do you remember Tyler Lane?"

"Of course! Why?"

"Blythe looks...well, she bears a striking resemblance to Tyler's Mom and her last name is Lane. The last we heard Mrs. Lane married Dan's brother and that's why her last name is Lane and they moved to Pennsylvania. It seems like *too* much of a coincidence. If she *is* Meg's daughter, are you aware that she can't be older than fifteen?"

Zach let out a nervous sigh.

"Fifteen? GOD! She's jailbait! To involve myself with a woman now and a fifteen year old *kid* yet! It's ludicrous!"

Steph looked at him sympathetically.

"I'm sorry, Honey. Ask her."

Zach was confused. *She seemed so much older! She seemed so mature!* He was thinking. He thought back to their conversations. *She **can't** be only fifteen! She did always manage to avoid discussing herself. She appeared to be extremely interested in him.*

Zach filled a plate with finger food and fixed himself a Dubonnet frappe on shaved ice and a soft drink *for the kid!*

He carried the refreshments on a tray, climbing the stairs slowly and carefully and trying to find the words, a tactful way to handle this situation.

Zach walked through the bedroom door without a word and placed the tray of food on the small table. He carried the food, table and all to the bed.

"Is something wrong?" Blythe asked.

Trying to side step a direct decisive confrontation, he handed her a soft drink.

"You said you don't drink so I fixed you a soft drink. Is that all right?"

"Sure! Thank you!"

There wasn't a part of her that wasn't perfect, *except her **age**!*

She perceived that there was *definitely* something wrong.

"Okay, it's cards on the table time," Zach said, foiling all tactics of evasion. His neck muscles were taut.

"Is your mother's name Meg Lane?"

Blythe's eyes opened wide, puzzled by the question. She sighed and answered reluctantly in a barely audible tone.

"Yes. How did you know?" She seemed confused as to how or why this question even was conceived.

"She used to live near us a long time ago, before you were born," he said simply.

Blythe looked worried.

Zach paused a moment to collect his thoughts, not wanting to ask the next question knowing that the answer would change everything. He was a patient, even-tempered young man.

"How old are you?"

Tears filled her eyes but she didn't allow them to go any farther. She knew that he already knew the answer. She took a deep breath as if she were going to answer then she didn't. She knew the magic would be over the minute she opened her mouth.

"You never asked my age before. I didn't think it mattered. I guess you must know now that I'm fifteen," Blythe offered, not exactly as an excuse finally.

Zach stood abruptly and gulped down the rest of his drink. He put the glass on the table and cleared his throat.

Blythe didn't move a muscle. She was afraid to move, even breathe.

"Why didn't you tell me?"

She shrugged her shoulders.

"As I said, I didn't think it was a big deal! You're sure a pillar of virtue for a man, Zach!"

"In mathematics you can never lose yourself, but just let your emotions control you…." Zach said. He shook his head hopelessly. "You were forbidden candy from the beginning. I can't take unfair advantage…I mean, you're too young and I'm too busy!"

His words evaporated again.

"I'm too old to cry but it hurts too much to laugh," Zach said, finally.

He scratched his head nervously.

"I could use another drink! Excuse me!"

Zach walked out of the room feeling confused and heartbroken. He needed time to think without her beautiful face in front of him.

Ron saw Zach leave the room. He felt compelled to peek in the door to see what was going on, if anything.

Silent tears were streaming down Blythe's cheeks.

"I was in the vicinity; may I help?" Ron offered.

Startled, Blythe looked up and wiped her tears away. She shook her head, no.

Ron made in an attempt to soothe her a little.

"Zach is a very dedicated and practical young man. He knows what he wants and he's determined to get it."

"And I'm in his way," Blythe sobbed.

Ron held her in his arms and tried to comfort her.

Steph walked in the room at that very moment.

"Well! My Mother always told me not to knock that I'd meet more interesting people that way! Look out, Blythe! My husband is a stud in old man clothing!" Steph sharpened her appetite for revenge. She looked as if she were ready to spring, teeth bared and eyes frantic. Her face was distorted in an effort not to cry. It was like gazing into a mirror of the past.

"The obvious is often misleading," Ron uttered. His mouth tightened and his face livid.

Steph turned abruptly and left the room.

"I want to go home," Blythe sniffed, befuddled by the whole evening. The resulting turmoil of her visit was too much for her to handle.

Zach walked in.

"What's going on?"

"Now that you've succeeded in reducing Blythe to hysterics, I think you'd better see to it that she gets home safely," Ron suggested.

"Blythe," Zach said sympathetically, "I'm sorry!"

Ron left.

Zach sat on the bed beside her and held her hand.

"Your Mother hates me! I want to go home!"

"My Mother doesn't *hate* anybody! I'm sure you misunderstood," Zach said. "Now, go into the bathroom and freshen your face and stop crying. I'll take you back to your girlfriend's house.

Back downstairs; Ron joined a group where Stephanie was sitting on the arm of the chair with an arm draped around a friend of his. He exchanged a quizzical look with Ron over Steph's uncharacteristic display of flirtatious energy. She was boiling under a smokescreen of indifference.

"Contrary to what seems to be the popular impression, the constitution tries to guarantee quality of opportunity not equality of status," a guest was saying.

"Quality and status go hand in hand," Steph chimed in. After a moment's pause, she said, "Excuse me, please." She stood and walked casually to another group of people.

Poor Whitney was cornered by someone else with problems Steph observed. Another distraught man was dumping on her.

"I made my sacrifices to society and to my family. I've spent too much of my life serving others. When is it my turn? Why can't someone take care of *me* for a change? I could sustain myself just fine in the sanctity of *selfishness!* Relieved of all those endless responsibilities, I feel free, invincible!" He was saying looking for applause.

"It takes great courage to break out of habit, or what is expected of you. Everybody is afraid to live," Whitney offered in her usual kind and dignified way.

Steph thought that everyone was so analytical all of a sudden. Her jaw ached from a suppressed yawn.

This guy's wife, in his opinion was a tennis enthusiast without aptitude. She lived like a queen on *his* money and he was sick of it! He *needed* an uncomplicated life! Wine, women and he'd surely break into song, as the saying goes.

Steph thought he seemed maladjusted and lonely in spite of what he was saying. But he kept going through the motions.

"I grew to realize that the world was mine if I wanted it...."

Feeling that this guy should make an appointment with Whitney instead of getting a freebie, Steph interrupted.

"Excuse me. May I steal you a moment, Whitney?"

"Of course, Steph! Excuse me, Don, won't you?"

Walking away from Don, Whitney whispered in Steph's ear.

"Thanks for the rescue, Steph! That's one of the hazards of my profession, I'm afraid."

Steph walked Whitney over to her loving husband where they were discussing intracranial hemorrhaging, contusions and lacerations and someone was saying that they were wrapped in a cocoon of bandages.

Steph smiled as she left the group to check on Zach and Blythe. She figured that they must have left after her much-regretted infantile scene. She thought that she was above and way beyond that sort of behavior. But apparently the old wounds hadn't healed as well as she'd thought.

"Thank you so much for your generous contribution," Stephanie was saying to one of Zach's professors, as he and his wife were about to leave. They were the last couple to leave. She closed the door, and leaned her back against the closed door, letting out a weary sigh.

She walked straight up to their bedroom. Ron followed.

From the hall on, Steph started dropping her clothes on the floor as she took them off, her shoes, pantyhose, dress, and lastly her underwear just outside the bathroom door.

She soaked in a long relaxing bath trying to unwind and face up to the various dilemmas the evening had brought. The pain of the past hit her smack in the face without warning. Ron had become the ideal husband since Meg moved out of their lives. She couldn't allow this ultimately frustrating situation to start again. She worried that seeing beautiful, completely flawless Blythe would revive Ron's old feelings for Meg. What would Whitney say to her? *I'm no sack of potatoes. My figure is better than ever. Why should I be insecure? It's **his** problem, not mine! If he wants to pine over **her**, let him! I don't need him. I'm not ground chuck. I'm Prime rib!*

Steph walked out of the bathroom.

"You have a genius for saying the wrong thing at the wrong time, Steph! How could you have been so unkind to the poor girl?" Ron asked.

"A good time was not had by all tonight," Steph said. "Still Mr. Smooth, aren't you? Every time I turned around tonight you had Blythe in your arms! How American of you to always want something better! You were behaving like an egocentric jackass! You should be horsewhipped, putting yourself into competition with your own son!"

"Stephanie! Listen to yourself! You're acting like a schoolgirl! Everything has been copasetic up until now. Why are you trying to ruin it?"

Steph couldn't stop.

"Did Blythe waken your *Tomcat* instincts?"

Ron squinted blindly into space.

"Women smell so intoxicating; maybe if you *cut off my nose*!"

"I'd be aiming too high! Don't patronize me, Ron," Steph interrupted.

"I guess I always thought there was something wonderful out there for me and I just didn't want to miss it," Ron continued.

"I find the unvarnished truth too dull to endure," Steph said calmly, putting up her smokescreen.

"Stop being so melodramatic! Don't glare at me like that," Ron said crossly.

"How can you be so blasé? Do you really feel like a caged animal and I'm your cage?" Steph asked.

"Truthfully? Not any more," Ron said

Ron reached up from bed and grabbed Steph's arm.

"Come on to bed, Honey!"

He'd never suffered; merely dodged the bullet and Steph resented it!

"I've been telling you for years, you're too emotionally oriented," Ron said.

Steph looked at him intensely.

"Ron! If you only knew how much I hate you when you show me such disrespect or when I picture you and Meg together, you wouldn't treat this so lightly."

Ron decided the only way to get out from under this moment of desperation was to try to ignore it.

"The Lady doth protest too much!" With that, he pulled Steph down to him on the bed.

"Doesn't anything dampen your ardor?" Steph asked.

CHAPTER 17

▼

The next morning, Steph's mood was much better after relieving her tension by facing Ron with her feelings.

Ron handled himself well and was able to turn Stephanie around without causing any more anxiety.

They hadn't had a good argument like that in years. Ron rather enjoyed it.

Steph and Ron invited Marie and Raymond to join them for brunch before cleaning up after the party.

Steph prepared fresh fruit and crepes suzettes and had everything on the table ready for them when they arrived.

"It was a wonderful party, Mrs. Adams," Raymond said, as he looked over at Marie and put his hand over hers, with a smile.

Marie blushed and smiled sheepishly.

"Yes, we enjoyed the party very much!"

Zach and Myra came downstairs sleepy-eyed and famished.

"We met quite a few interesting characters last night," Raymond said.

"Characters. You've got that right!" Ron commented. He looked over at Zach and Myra. "Zach! Myra! Are you two awake?"

"Only half, Dad," Zach replied. He was remote and aloof and seemed troubled.

"Good crepes, Mom!" Myra commented.

"Let's face it, life's a soap opera," Steph said.

No one mentioned Blythe until Raymond made a comment.

"Zach, your girlfriend is quite a knock out! I've never seen her before!"

Zach forced a polite smile.

"She's from Pennsylvania. I met her in Ocean City."

"Yes! Mark couldn't take his eyes off of her all *night*! I had to jab him in the ribs a few times to get his attention," Myra added.

"I noticed quite a few people had that problem last night," Steph admitted.

"Would you care for some fruit?" Steph asked Raymond, in an effort to change the subject.

"No, thank you. I've had plenty."

After a pleasant brunch, Marie cleaned the kitchen before she tackled the party mess. Raymond stayed to help, out of appreciation of being invited to the party and besides, he enjoyed being with Marie. They grinned at each other frequently while they collected glasses and plates.

Steph was happy that Marie and Raymond hit it off so well. She tried to work in another part of the house to give them privacy. They obviously had an accelerating affection for each other and were doing a little emotional exploration.

✳   ✳   ✳   ✳

Four days had gone by when Zach received a letter in the mail.

It read: *To my RELUCTANT GOD, Help! I need a Doctor! There's something wrong with my heart!* Signed, *your* FORBIDDEN FRUIT!

Zach didn't call Blythe. He had to stick to his decision for both their sakes.

"It's better to be cold and safe than hot and *sorry!*" Zach said, out loud.

The next day, Zach received another letter in the mail.

It read: TO THE PARTY OF THE FIRST PART, I LOVE YOU! From: THE PARTY OF THE SECOND PART.

Zach's heart was churning.

"What's this girl trying to do to me?"

Instead of discarding it, he put it in his drawer along with the other letter.

With a surrendering sigh he thought, *she does make my whole world come alive! And I can't get her off my mind! What is it? I've never had any trouble like this before! After all, I'm only six years older than she is! In the scheme of things, once she's out of her teens the age difference won't mean a thing! If we keep our relationship platonic until I graduate.... That's a* **tall Order**! *We bring out the best in each other! Who says we have to follow a blueprint to happiness?*

Zach suddenly jumped up, glad for the reprieve. He called the long distance operator to find her number. Meg answered the phone.

"Hello?"

"Hello! My name is Zach Adams. May I please speak to Blythe?"

"Yes, of course. Hold on, please."

Blythe came to the phone.

"Zach! Hi!"

"Blythe," Zach said, then paused not sure what to say next. "I'm sorry about last week. You're *heartbreak* material, you know, Blythe! You're giving me mental fatigue and you know I can't afford that. I've grown sourer and sourer every day since the party." His voice was warm and soothing.

"I'm not a clinging vine," Blythe said softly.

Zach's voice deepened with emotion.

"I'm sure you're not! Love turns people into fools." He paused realizing what he'd just said, *Love*! He sighed heavily.

"I've been a good candidate for a straight jacket since the party and every day seems to get worse instead of better. Time doesn't always heal," Blythe said.

"Do you think you could go out with me this weekend so we can talk?" Zach asked.

Blythe hesitated, and then whispered.

"I'm really not allowed to date yet. I only double date once in a while!"

"Then how did you come to our party?" Zach asked confused.

"I fibbed! I'll talk to you about it later. Maybe I'll write and explain it to you. I have to go," Blythe whispered.

They hung up.

The next day, the phone rang.

"Hello?" Stephanie answered.

The voice on the other end of the phone was very familiar. Stephanie felt her heart lurch.

"Stephanie? This is Meg."

The shock of her voice left it impossible for any audible reaction at first.

"Yes! Hello! How are you?"

"I'm sure you know that your son is seeing my daughter," Meg said.

"Yes. Why?" Steph asked.

"I think Zach is too old for Blythe, too mature. She's not allowed to date in the first place. Please don't take offense, but considering our past problems I don't think it's wise."

"Well, what do you want me to do?" Steph asked.

"Please try to discourage Zach and I'll do the same on this end. I've already spoken to Blythe."

"Okay, I'll see what I can do," Steph said.

"Thanks, Steph!"

＊   ＊   ＊   ＊

To solve their problem, Zach, Blythe, Myra and Mark conspired together to form a plan of attack. Mark started picking Blythe up on the pretense that he was seeing her. They'd have another couple in the back seat since Blythe was only allowed to double date. Mark always brought Blythe straight to Zach and most often they'd see a movie or go to a dance together.

"What a perfect day," Blythe said.

"Yes! Any critic would surely give it four stars," Zach said. "You know what I thought when I first saw you, Blythe?"

"Do tell," Blythe said.

"I thought, now that's the kind of smile I'd like to see over breakfast every morning for the rest of my life and I'm sure I'd never tire of it."

"Sounds like an overture to a wedding march to me," Myra chimed in from the back seat.

Blythe was his total field of vision and he no longer cared who knew it.

"I brought my camera gear. Let's go to the park and shoot some cheesecake of the girls," Zach suggested.

"Sounds like fun! Let's go!"

The girls giggled looking at each other with excitement and enthusiasm written all over their faces.

They stopped at the Falls where they jumped out of the car and started hiking.

"I'd love to be another Skrebnesti," Zach said.

"Isn't being a doctor enough for you, Zach?" Blythe asked. "And besides, who is Skrebnesti?"

"He's the photographer who did Vanessa Redgrave's nude, way back in nineteen sixty seven. You'd never believe it was her to see her now."

"Isn't he the one who shot Orson Wells in a black turtleneck?" Mark asked.

"Yes. He teamed the black turtleneck with the black background. That way only Wells' face was noticed instead of the distraction of color, which would have made his girth the subject matter instead of the man. He shoots Estee Lauder layouts for magazines, you know, where the world looks perfect like the models appear perfect?"

"Oh to live the life of a model!" Blythe gushed.

"Dream on," Myra said.

"You're beautiful enough to be a model, Blythe," Mark admitted, "and so are you, Myra!"

"Thanks a lot, Mark!" Myra said in a snit, "I've always wanted to be second billing! Especially in my boyfriend's eyes!"

Zach commanded quickly to avoid an argument.

"Girls! Climb up on that rock. Myra, stand up and prop your foot on the higher part of the rock. Blythe, sit on the rock with one knee up and rest your elbow on it, please."

Zach looked through the lens, adjusted the shudder to suit the brightness and focused.

"Ah! What a shot!" He snapped the picture. "Beautiful! I think that was a prize winner!"

They played with the camera till dusk then decided to go back to Zach's house for snacks since his parents weren't home.

They saw a strange car parked in the driveway as they approached the house. A young man emerged from the darkness to greet them.

"Tyler! How the heck are you?" Zach asked in a pleasantly surprised tone of voice.

"Myra, this is an old playmate of ours. Remember Tyler Lane?"

"Not really! But I wish I did now! Wow!"

"Control yourself, Myra," Mark intervened quickly.

"Paybacks are hell, aren't they?" Myra teased.

"What's wrong, Tyler?" Blythe asked.

"I hate to break this to you but, Mom's on the war path. She found out that you're sneaking around with Zach," Tyler warned.

Everyone's heads pivoted to gape at Blythe in concern. Her skin was flawless, looking like a porcelain doll ready to crack. She sat down heavily on the car seat with her feet still on the driveway.

"She's fighting mad! I've never seen her like this," Tyler continued.

"Would you care to elope, Zach?" Blythe asked in a panic.

"You're using school girl tactics again. You have to grow up first," Zach teased. Zach had never experienced insecurity, fear or a moment's doubt. He flashed his dazzling smile at her.

"Don't worry. It will pass. You'll be punished; then it will be over."

Blythe accelerated into a feeling of despair. Panic and confusion crowded her thoughts.

"Think of something!" Blythe said in a pleading voice.

Mark and Myra stood in tactful silence. Tyler shifted his weight in discomfort and Blythe rested her chin on her fist resembling *Rodin's THE THINKER,* trying to come up with a solution.

"We all have the inevitable personal crisis sooner or later," Zach offered in his matter of fact, sensible, unflustered tone of voice.

"Yes, but why does it have to be so soon?" Blythe asked, in a moment of despair and fear of never being permitted to see Zach again. This only amplified his scrumptious looks to her.

Zach expertly hoisted Blythe up from the car seat.

"Don't worry! I'll face the firing squad with you."

Blythe nodded solemnly.

"Maybe if we pretend we had an accident and you guys wrapped me up in bandages, she'll feel sorry for me," Blythe suggested anxiously.

"I'll be glad to help with the wrapping," Mark offered.

Myra frowned at Mark with a vengeance.

"That attitude of yours is getting a tad bit *old*, Mark, Love!" Myra said sternly with a scowl to beat all scowls.

"One thing for sure," Zach said unequivocally, "*We* **have** to face the music! This is only a minor disaster in the scheme of all things relative."

"It may be minor to *you*. But to me, it's the end of the world!" Blythe blurted unimpressed.

"Can't you guys think of some diversionary tactics?" Blythe pleaded. She felt a prickle of tears begin.

They piled into the car and headed to Altoona.

✳   ✳   ✳   ✳

The next morning Steph received another frantic call from Altoona. It seemed that Steph was to receive a visit from the ever-popular Meg.

The doorbell rang. Stephanie sat with a drink in her hand and a book on her lap. Marie led Meg into the living room to greet Stephanie.

"Marie, will you bring us a couple of drinks?" Steph looked at Meg and asked, "Still a pina colada?"

"That will be fine, thank you," Meg replied.

"Two Pina Coladas, please, Marie," Steph said.

Steph waited for Meg to make the first move. She motioned for Meg to sit down.

"Your house is incredible," Meg said, trying to break the ice a bit.

"Thank you, Meg," Steph said with an aristocratic smile.

Steph thought Meg looked tired and worn but still beautiful and well sculpted.

"It seems we weren't able to tear Zach away from Blythe," Meg began. "They've been sneaking around together in spite of our warnings!"

Steph looked at her disbelieving and sat in silence for a few moments.

"My! It seems that history *does* repeat itself! What is it about you Lane women that you have this uncanny ability to hypnotize men?"

Meg looked Steph directly in the face with those huge sad eyes of hers.

"Steph, I can't begin to express how terribly sorry I am for that! Believe me when I tell you that so-called power isn't always a plus! Sometimes it's a curse!"

Marie walked in and served them their drinks.

Trying to be cordial, they lifted their drinks to their lips. The coolness was refreshing after a heated busy day and the heat of the moment as well.

"I feel uncomfortable on a high moral plane, Steph," Meg confessed.

"Well, you should," Steph said discreetly below the level of audibility.

"What's so urgent that you needed to make this trip to see me in person?" Steph asked.

"Oh! Don't be so pretentious, Steph; You and your superiority!" Meg said, angered by Steph's attitude.

Meg only served to heighten Steph's vastly superior attitude, even if it was the only defense mechanism she could live with! Steph looked at Meg appraisingly and determined that she was under considerable strain.

"Well, what does the reigning *Mother Hen* want me to do?" Steph asked.

Fear surmounted patience in her voice.

"As you wish, Steph!" Meg took an aggressive stance and presented herself to Steph, her secret churned to a rage that burst forth uncontrollably, "Blythe is Ron's daughter!"

Meg seemed quite serious and definite, no room to doubt.

Steph refused to cry. She stood abruptly; with all the dignity she could muster, marveling at herself that she'd found the energy to control herself. Why didn't this astounding truth surprise her? Imagine! A child, a binding of their chemistries and their union! Her hands went numb and a moan caught in her throat. She refused to compromise her acquired dignity.

"Well, Meg! No one can say that you've lost your capacity to astonish me. Do you eat nails for lunch?"

Feeling sincere guilt and misery for Steph, knowing that this *had* to destroy her, and probably even end in their divorce, Meg continued, sympathetically.

"It was only one time! I was so vulnerable and needed comfort after that whole ugly mess with Dan! I hated what we did! Honestly! I can't tell you how sorry I am that you and I even met in the first place! If we hadn't met all of these horrible things wouldn't have happened to you," Meg's eyes welled with tears.

In spite of this overwhelming catastrophe, compassion warmed Steph's heart. Meg's life certainly hadn't been easy either! God knows Steph loved Meg under the pretentious façade and would have given just about anything if they could resume their special friendship. After all, Meg really was a good person under all that sex appeal!

"Meg," Steph said, as she walked over and held her in her arms to comfort her. "I'm sorry too!"

"Does Ron know?" Steph asked softly, rasping against taut nerves.

Meg sniffed and blew her nose before answering.

"No and I prefer he didn't know and if it gives you some perverse satisfaction, I'm begging you not to allow Blythe or my husband know!"

"What do you suggest we do?" Steph asked after a long pensive silence.

"Tell only Zach the truth. That's the only way to keep him away from Blythe!"

Steph responded, trying to protect her own family.

"How can you expect me to do that to Zach? It'll destroy his faith in his father! Why are we so vulnerable to the sex that nature dangles before us, to tempt us? Men are such irresponsible fools! Why can't you tell Blythe instead of destroying *my* family?"

Steph was overcome with the injustice of this whole situation. Her fists clenched and every muscle in her body was tense.

Meg flinched and aloofly waited. They both sat in dumbstruck silence.

"Meg, I need time to think," Steph said tensely. My brain is operating on overload at the moment. It's a lot to digest all at once. May I call you?"

"Sure," Meg said.

"Marie! Please show Mrs. Lane out," Steph beckoned, giving Meg one more hug for the road.

Steph climbed the stairs as if her legs were filled with lead, to her sanctuary where she descended into total malfunction the rest of the evening.

*   *   *   *

Much later, Steph was exhilarated by the revelation that she was able to maintain her cool and dignity under this devastating circumstance. Draped in a burgundy silk jumpsuit, she walked into the kitchen to prepare dinner. Marie had already started the steak and peppers cooking so all Steph had to do was cook the linguine.

Marie was a blessing. She'd already cooked the chicken and red potatoes and cleaned and cut the broccoli for her to finish the chicken, potato, and broccoli toss. She was mixing mayonnaise, milk, tarragon vinegar and tarragon together for her cold salad when Ron walked into the kitchen.

"Hi, Honey! How was your day?" Steph asked as she did every day. She calmly proceeded to greet him with a kiss.

"Somehow that kiss seemed patronizing and maternal," Ron said. "The heat was sweltering today and we were nailing cedar shakes over insulating foil yet. The sun reflected in our faces and made it almost unbearable."

"You don't have to work like that. You're the boss," Steph said.

"Yeah! But you know how I like to get my hands dirty," Ron replied.

"Yes! I certainly do," Steph said with a hint of sarcasm.

"Honey, what's wrong?" Ron asked concerned. "Your lips are smiling, but your teeth and eyes aren't"

"You're imagining things, Ron," Steph said.

She was clever enough to hide her pretension.

Steph continued working virtually non-stop as Ron rambled on about the job. She walked like a lioness, a superior being, needing no sympathy and asking nothing of anyone.

She seemed vague and distracted to Ron. He knew something was on her mind, but he knew better than to press her. He also knew he'd surely find out sooner or later on her terms.

Steph was thinking that she had to keep him worried. She wanted him to suffer so she played with him as a cat wrestles and paws at his mouse before he *kills it*!

"By the way, I had a visitor today," Steph announced intentionally casually.

"Oh, who?"

"Meg Lane."

Ron's face reddened.

"Oh? What did she want?"

"She's determined to keep Zach and Blythe away from each other, for some reason. She seemed rather frantic about it."

She paused and dropped it to allow him to stew in his own juice. Steph walked with a jauntiness that was perfectly calculated to make Ron uncomfortable. She was demure, poised and perfectly composed, much out of character with Meg being the subject matter.

Steph intercomed the family to dinner and said nothing more on the subject.

Steph so enjoyed watching Ron squirm. She knew his curiosity was gnawing at his ego.

Steph and Ron were seated at the dinner table enjoying a nonchalant conversation.

"Oh, by the way, I need you to sign some insurance papers. I've decided to raise our life insurance premiums," Steph mentioned.

An eyebrow arched questioningly as Ron nodded.

Steph was unscrupulously polite where she was usually irascible on a subject concerning Meg.

Ron stewed, *this can't be good!*

Zach and Myra were unusually quiet after facing the firing squad the day before.

"What's wrong, kids?" Steph asked.

Zach opened up to his Mom like he'd always done.

"Blythe's Mom told me that she would have me arrested if I came near Blythe again!" Zach admitted, his expression revealing his pain and loss.

Steph could see clearly that her son's heart was broken.

"Honey, I'm so sorry! After the kitchen is cleaned up, I'll come upstairs and we'll talk, just like when you were little."

Dinner was over and Myra started clearing the table.

Ron retired to his office. Steph followed him. She calmly poured champagne for the two of them from a frosty magnum. Ron sat in his over-sized leather chair that faced his desk. Steph perched herself on Ron's desk while sipping her champagne.

"All surface, no substance. How typical of poor ole Meg to choose a sleazebag to comfort her in her hour of need," Steph announced casually.

Steph demonstrated her power so effectively.

Ron's brows stiffened with disapproval. His heart was pounding with anticipation of what was coming next. Her invulnerable manner puzzled him. In fact it frightened him!

"By the way, here. Sign this! If you kick the bucket the kids and I'll never have to work again!"

She extended the magnum to refill his glass. She looked into his eyes.

"Such two-timing carelessness," Steph said eerily.

Ron was starting to sweat and his breathing became deeper and more labored as if it were hard for him to draw a breath.

"A relationship without mental accord is sterile. Sexual stimulation doesn't last." Steph continued mercilessly knowing Ron wished she'd get to the point and get it over with.

"It's your responsibility, your decision and you're entitled to it, Ron."

Ron felt lightness in his limbs, a strange uncomfortable sensation.

Ron couldn't take it any longer.

"What decision? What responsibility? And I'm entitled to *what?*" he blurted impatiently.

"The decision and responsibility of telling Zach that Blythe is his **sister!**" Steph stated bluntly.

Allowing the shock to sink in and take root, Steph grabbed the magnum again.

Ron bolted upright and out of his chair. He was stupefied with an apprehensive look of dismay on his face.

Steph focused on his luminous eyes.

"Congratulations! You're a father again," she said as she poured his drink in order to raise his glass in a toast.

"My hospitality has its limits, ya know. How's my BS artist going to get out of this one?" Steph said with just a hint of sarcasm, but still remarkably calm.

Steph sat seemingly indifferent, staring at him.

"I don't understand," Ron responded with difficulty, alarmed and defensive.

"What's to understand?" Steph asked. "That's what happens when you get caught with your hand *up the wrong skirt!*

Steph jumped off his desk and walked to his love seat. Her stride didn't falter. She was poised, dignified and gracious.

"It was nothing but a glandular thing," Ron said in his defense.

Steph's upper lip lifted, her teeth a glint, she said, in an authoritative manner, "That's the way it usually happens!"

Ron was suddenly annoyed, feeling backed into a corner that he couldn't get out of.

"You're so *fantastically* above it all," Ron bellowed.

He was trying to antagonize Steph into a rage or *some reaction*. She was making him nervous by her casual attitude.

Steph had learned from Whitney that this was his usual goal as a child demanding attention.

Sighing, their eyes locked. Ron was uncomfortable with the way Steph seemed peculiarly oblivious to this devastating news.

"When you're carrying the ball you don't like to fumble it and lose it," Ron said.

"Thank GOD!" Steph exalted.

Why no animosity? Why no, no tears? Ron was totally ambiguous to the whole situation.

"Are you filled with paternal pride?" Steph asked in a soft voice.

"You're exacerbating!" Ron exploded. Ron was thinking that if one were judging a person on the way they behave under stress, Steph was brimming with mental health!

Steph walked across the room and opened the window. She sniffed the floral fragrance in the air, then turned and looked at Ron as he sat in dumbstruck silence, bombarded with multiple dilemmas. She walked to the door. I'll leave you to figure out what you're going to say to Zach."

✳   ✳   ✳   ✳

It was after eleven when Ron entered the bedroom reluctantly not knowing what to expect next.

Steph put her book down and smiled.

"Do you *have* to look like that? It's so depressing!"

"No one said you had to look," Ron said sarcastically. He paused then said in a softer voice, "Am I ill? Or am I dying?"

Steph laughed.

"Not that I know of. Why?"

He shrugged then went into the bathroom to take a shower. He was so bewildered by Steph's strange attitude. She seemed to have scant interest in a problem of such complexity. Instead of being outraged, she seemed almost delighted. During his shower, he never took his eyes off the door, half expecting Steph to come at him with a knife. He couldn't seem to shake the shower scene from the movie, *PSYCHO*, out of his head. He turned off the water and wrapped himself up in a bath towel. He brushed his teeth after opening a fresh new tube of toothpaste, *just to be safe*. He couldn't be too careful!

Steph was still reading her book when Ron walked out of the bathroom. As he drew nearer, Steph put her book away and watched Ron drop his towel. He sat on the edge of the bed, twisted around and took Steph's hands into his.

"You know, I love you even more today than I ever have. I've grown to *need* my existence to be stable and orderly. I'm content in my life and that's the way I *need* it to stay. This whole situation is preposterous," Ron said hoarsely and sighed heavily.

He looked up suddenly finding the warmth of her lips on his. His eyebrows arched in surprise. With a flash of desperate energy and courage, he buried his face in her hair and held onto her for dear life. He longed for her voice to descend from this bizarre indifference to forgive him. He nuzzled her neck and fondled her body. Ron slipped her shoulder straps down to her waist while nibbling at her skin and her lips. He was surprised that she was responding. Why wasn't she furious? He found her nonchalant attitude distressful.

He pulled away, his face dark and brooding. His heart pounded with suspicion.

Steph's hand reached tentatively to touch his.

"That's all right, Darling. You have a lot on your mind. It's not the end of the world."

Steph had never known Ron to be impotent, only that once when he'd kicked her bathroom door in when she was in the tub. Of course, she was playing with his head. *Hmmmmm, something like she's doing now!*

Defeat and fatigue among them suddenly, the room went silent and they drifted off to sleep.

*   *   *   *

After a long, well thought out discussion between Ron and Zach, Zach made a phone call to Pennsylvania.

Luckily, Blythe answered the phone.

"Hello, Blythe! How are you?"

Her voice cracked when she realized that it was Zach.

"I miss you, "she sniffed.

"Blythe, I had a long talk with my parents." Tears blurred the numbers on the phone as Zach continued, "They made me realize what a mistake we were making." He was compliant to their wishes. "If our parents are so adamantly against our dating then we must obey their wishes. I want you to date other guys because I intend to date other girls."

There was silence on the other end.

Finally, "All right, Zach, if that's the way you want it. If that's the way you really feel!"

There was a lull.

"Good-bye, Zach," Blythe said in a tiny, barely audible voice.

Zach hung up with a tear stinging his eye. He threw the phone across the room in a fit of temper, very uncharacteristic of Zach.

CHAPTER 18

▼

Marie and Raymond were a twosome. They enjoyed being with each other so much that they often helped each other with their work.

Steph asked Marie and Raymond to stay for dinner since they were kind enough to have picked the mushrooms for their Deviled Swiss Steak.

All the kids had other plans for the evening so the four of them were able to enjoy a little *Senior* conversation for a change.

"Do you think you could plant some of those beautiful exotic plants in our garden like the ones you planted at work?" Steph asked Raymond.

"Those plants require less sunlight and their roots rot easily so they have to be wrapped with moss and inserted into some kind of cypress root or driftwood. I think I can manage it for you, Mrs. Adams," Raymond explained.

"Marie, the meal is delicious," Ron commented.

"Thank you, Mr. Adams! Raymond helped!"

Ron turned to Raymond.

"Thank *you too*, Raymond!"

Raymond smiled in acknowledgement.

"Are you two going out, tonight?" Steph asked.

"We haven't made definite plans yet," Raymond replied earnestly.

He turned to Marie.

"Have you decided on a movie yet?"

"I haven't had time to give it much thought!"

"The paper's in Ron's office if you'd care to check out the movies. I'm finished eating. I'll check it for you," Steph announced.

Marie and Raymond were giggling in the kitchen when Steph entered with the paper.

"Thank you, Mrs. Adams."

"Ron, you don't look well. What's wrong?" Steph asked.

"I don't know. I have terrible cramps in my stomach," Ron answered.

Steph had never seen Ron look so sick. He's always been as healthy as a horse.

"I'm calling the Doctor. In fact, I'm calling Whitney first."

"Whitney, this is Steph. . Oh! My GOD! Ron's just collapsed! His skin's blue! And he had cramps in his stomach!" Steph cried hysterically. Whitney said, "Hang up! I'll take care of it!"

"Raymond! Marie!" Steph screamed.

Crying uncontrollably, Steph dropped on the floor next to Ron.

Marie and Raymond rushed in to see what the screaming was all about.

Zach walked in about that time.

"Mom! What's wrong?"

"I don't know! Daddy said he had terrible cramps, then he collapsed," Steph explained in a high-pitched panic voice.

"What did you have for dinner?" Zach asked.

"Deviled Swiss Steak."

"With mushrooms?"

"Yes! Fresh mushrooms!"

They heard the siren of the ambulance. Zach ran outside.

"I need a stomach pump!" Zach yelled. "Get me a stomach pump! Atropine!"

"Thank GOD for Whitney and Zach!" Steph was saying to the kids beside Ron's bed. She jumped up and hugged Zach.

"My son the *Doctor*!" Steph said proudly.

"Thank God the ambulance had Atropine! Dad would have died without it," Zach said.

Ron's eyes strayed back to Steph suspiciously. *She seemed genuinely concerned, as if she cared. Could it be just a coincidence? Ron wondered uncomfortably*

*   *   *   *

A week later, Steph was entertaining Bianca on her day off, sitting over a cup of coffee after lunch.

Steph was telling Bianca.

"You think you're being a kind and generous parent by buying them a complex stereo system, a Kenwood receiver with Boston acoustics and Dolby Digital surround sound, anyway, all the technology I know nothing about. Garrett had his friends over and all of a sudden, we thought we had ghosts in the house the way all the glass was vibrating and our insides actually almost ached from the bass. Ron came to me complaining that his desk equipment had come to life with rhythmic thumping. We both looked up at the ceiling and rushed upstairs to make him tone it down a bit. We all know they're going to be wearing hearing aids by the time they're our age."

"I read that these ear phones that the kids wear all the time are causing hearing loss, not to mention the dances. The music is so loud," Bianca said.

"Garrett's my baby and already he's fast approaching his teens," Steph said. "It breaks my heart! I remember when he was just a little tot asking me if I'd please leave the bathroom while he bathed. That was my first rejection! My beloved sources of pick up, clean up, wash up, wipe up and never ending bickering and battles to break up are soon to be over. I've had them in my life so long; I'm going to be lost without them. OH! I miss them already just thinking about it," Stephanie sighed and stared off into space a pensive moment.

Ron came in the front door carrying the mail.

"Here's the mail, Honey. What's for lunch?"

"Hi, Bianca! How's it going?"

"My life is going great! Thank you for asking."

"I'm glad. If anybody deserves a great life, it's *you!*"

"Vegetable soup, Ron?" Steph asked.

"Love some!"

Steph rejoined Bianca after ladling some soup into a bowl for Ron.

She opened the mail casually, still discussing the trials and tribulations of child rearing.

She opened a blue envelope addressed to her. Steph stood abruptly still looking at the contents of the letter.

"Ron," Steph beckoned. She looked frightened.

Ron walked into the dining room.

"What is it?"

Steph handed Ron the letter.

It read: YOU'RE UNFINISHED BUSINESS!

That was all and it was stamped at their post office.

"What is it?" Bianca insisted.

They handed her the note.

"Oh! My! You'd better show this to the police!"

Ron didn't want to leave Steph alone so he called the police station and asked if a police officer could come to the house.

"We'll have someone with you at all times."

"We'll hire Marie and Raymond to keep you company when I'm not here."

"I'll stay with Steph until you get home from work, Ron," Bianca offered.

"I may not go back to work."

"Ron, finish your soup before the police get here," Steph suggested.

Too late! The doorbell rang.

Ron answered the door.

"Come in. Please sit down. This is my wife, Stephanie."

Ron handed him the note that Steph had received.

"Steph was assaulted sixteen years ago. She's had enough!"

The officer asked the details of the assault.

"The man was arrested and committed for psychiatric rehabilitation."

"What was his name?" the officer asked.

"Dan Lane."

"Have you had any run-ins with anyone lately?"

Ron and Steph gaped at each other reluctantly.

"Well, it's a ridiculous story," Ron began.

Steph frowned and rested her forehead in her hand, hiding her eyes.

"We just found out that I have an illegitimate daughter by Dan's wife. She's fifteen years old."

Ron looked at Steph questioningly as if asking her if he should go any further.

"Our son had to be told because he became romantically involved. I don't think anyone on that situation would be mad at me. Mad at Ron, maybe, but not *me!*" Steph added.

"We have to check out every possibility," the officer said.

Bianca was stunned by this news flash. Steph didn't want the news to get around so she hadn't mentioned it to a soul.

*   *   *   *

That night in bed, Ron held on to Steph as if he were trying to protect a precious gem.

"The greatest thing about love is that you know it's there but there aren't words in our language to express the feeling," Ron announced, as if having made a discovery in some cavity hiding in the bottom of that callous heart of his. "I can't imagine my life without you, Steph! No one else could ever take your place in my heart or my life. You're a part of me. You and I have so much history that to lose you now..." His voice trailed off. He was actually choked up fighting back tears.

Steph had always known that Ron had a real aptitude for delivering surface schmaltz. She eyed him curiously, momentarily thrown off balance. This unanticipated thought never occurred to her before, this radical change in his disposition; could he possibly have developed *heart*?

Ron continued to bare his soul.

"Whether we're in bed, making love or whether we're doing something with the kids, I feel I'm making love to you. I admire you and respect you for the truly good person you are, for the special woman you are. No other woman would have ever shown me the pure devotion, faithfulness and dedication to our union as a family. You've always put your children first! Sometimes that made me jealous but at the same time that was something I've always admired you for! A true *Mother* always puts her children before herself. If anything would ever happen to you; well, the most important part of me would be dead!" Ron's eyes reflected his innermost emotions.

Was it feasible? What was this unexpected lovely warmth she was feeling? Steph had waited her whole marriage to hear those words.

Their eyes met and held for a few moments, both touched so deeply by those words, mostly those feelings behind the words that were so hard to articulate. A sudden mutual burst of joy surged through them, wanting so badly to prolong this intimate moment of mutual need, understanding, acceptance, and *oneness*!

Steph didn't bother to suppress her tears.

"Ron, *I Love You*! My life is complete! I've never been happier in my life than I am at this very moment. I could die tomorrow and it would be all right. I accomplished my ultimate goal! I raised my children to the best of my ability and whether it was due to my input or me or not, they all turned out to be good, decent, wonderful human beings. I'm *so proud of them*! And now to feel this *oneness* with you truly is the unexpected wish come true. This is the hardest goal to have accomplished."

The next morning Steph left for work with her head in a cloud of fulfillment and joy. She'd actually taught Ron how to love. Her work was done and she no longer had fear of the threatening note.

*   *   *   *

Ron was on his way home from work early in order to be there when Steph arrived home. He knew that this wasn't Marie's workday and Steph needed protection.

Ron's foot hit the brake at the stop sign but nothing happened. He rolled right through the intersection and just missed an on-coming car. His chest was pounding heavily. He turned off the ignition, downshifted and rolled to a stop without collision.

He was in a residential section and not traveling at high speed. He realized how easily he could have been killed and tried to push the suspicion out of his mind that this was the second close call since Steph found out about Blythe. *Surely after baring my soul to her last night, she wouldn't,* **couldn't** *want me dead?* Ron contemplated while sitting in his car trying to collect himself.

Ron walked to the nearest house and called a tow truck. Needing to know that Stephanie was all right, he called home.

"Hi, Honey! I just walked through the door. Yes! I'm fine! Don't worry! Raymond told me at work today that he was going to come over and plant my exotic flowers for me. So you don't have to worry. He'll be here soon. I'm sure. Yes! I promise. I'll lock all the doors and windows."

The phone rang again after Ron hung up. It was the police station.

"We just found out that Dan Lane has been released from custody over eight months ago. We're going to pick him up for questioning."

"Thank you very much," Steph said. She hung up. A lump was growing in her throat causing her a shortness of breath.

Ron had forgotten to give her the number where he could be reached.

Now suspicious and jumpy over every sound, noise in the back yard made her race to the window and peak out the curtain.

"Whew! Thank God! It's just Raymond." Steph said out loud.

She opened the door to greet him.

"Hi Raymond. Would you mind sticking around the house and please keep an eye open for anything or anybody that is the least bit out of the ordinary? Then, let me know immediately. Ron won't be home for a while. Would you mind staying until he gets home?'

"I'll be glad to stay as long as you need me," Raymond said kindly.

"Thank you, Raymond."

She closed the door and locked it. After turning on soft music to calm her nerves, she sat down to sort her mail, positioning herself so she could see Raymond at all times. He was busy planting her flowers and would frequently look up at the house and around the yard obeying Steph's request.

Steph gasped and bolted upright out of her chair. There was another blue envelope addressed to her. She swallowed hard, her heart thumping so hard she could actually hear it in her ears. She forced herself to open it. There was a crudely drawn pornographic caricature of her and the words *ARE YOU READY? WHY DO YOU KEEP LETTING HIM DO IT?*

Steph rushed to the door in tears.

"Raymond! **Raymond!**" She beckoned in a nervous, raspy voice. "Would you please come inside?"

He dropped his shovel immediately and rushed to the door.

"Mrs. Adams, what is it?"

She handed him the picture.

"Would you please keep me company until Ron gets home?"

Raymond wiped his feet, and then politely took off his shoes.

"Of course!" He came inside and locked the door behind him. "Have you locked the windows too?"

"I think so," Steph said in a slightly skeptical tone of voice.

"Would you like me to go through the house and check to make sure, just in case one may have been overlooked?" Raymond offered.

"Thank you, Raymond; that's probably a good idea."

Steph sighed nervously.

"So how are you and Marie getting along, if you don't mind my asking?"

Raymond started chattering away about their dates, movies they'd seen and the laughs they'd had.

After checking the house Raymond rejoined her in the kitchen and helped her cut up the vegetables for the salad.

"I propped chairs under the latches of the French doors. They're pretty easy to break into," Raymond.

"Thank you. I never would have thought of it," Steph admitted.

They sat down to eat. Steph looked at her plate of food and sighed. She tried to swallow a bite but her throat was so tight from nerves that the food wouldn't pass.

"I'll wash the dishes for you Mrs. Adams," Raymond offered.

"Thank you but I need to keep busy. You wash and I'll dry," Steph said.

After the kitchen was clean again, Steph announced that she was going upstairs to read.

"You're welcome to watch television or whatever you would like to do. I'll be glad to pay you double time for babysitting me."

"That's all right, Mrs. Adams, Marie and I didn't have plans tonight anyway. I'd just be watching TV, unwinding at home anyway!"

The phone rang.

"Steph! Is everything okay?" Ron asked frantically.

"Yes! Raymond is here and watching TV. He agreed to stay until you get home. I have another newsflash for you. The police called. It seems that Dan is free."

Ron's voice bellowed through the receiver.

"What? How could they let him out? There's something wrong with this justice system! ***There's no justice!*** How can they be sure he's rehabilitated?"

"Calm down," Steph said.

"Well, to add to your stress, it appears that my hydraulic brake line was deliberately cut!" Ron added.

"*Oh, fine,*" Steph said.

"Here's the number to reach me, if you need me, 774-8018. I have to go. The station attendant needs to talk to me," Ron said.

"Sure! Hurry home, Honey! I need you!"

Steph walked to the top of the stairs.

"Still there, Raymond?"

"Still here, Mrs. Adams. All is well."

Not more than fifteen minutes later, Steph heard noises coming from Zach's bedroom. She stood up and called Raymond's name. There was no answer. Hoping he'd gone into the kitchen or the bathroom, she peaked out her door into the hall. The house was quiet except the noise of the television set.

Steph walked down the hall to Zach's room.

"Raymond? Zach?"

Still there was no response. She heard water running in the bathroom so she opened the door.

"Raymond! Why didn't you answer me? I was ready to jump out of my skin! Why are you shaving?"

The sudden comprehension filled her expression with panic, that he hadn't answered any of her questions and, *why **was** he shaving?*

Steph started shivering all over in terror. She turned to leave the bathroom but he grasped her arm and pulled her back into the bathroom with him.

"Sit down! Make yourself comfortable," he ordered.

Steph didn't say another word. She obeyed him and sat on the side of the tub and watched him shave.

"You're woven into the memory of my past," he said.

Steph sat under a mask of compliance out of momentary shock. She listened and watched.

He finished shaving, took off his glasses and flashed Steph that famous grin. He gazed directly into her eyes.

"You were always unattainable. You thought you were better than the rest of us. You've changed."

Steph breathed, "I hope *you* have!"

"We have some unfinished business to attend to, don't we?"

He moved relentlessly toward her, took her hands and pulled her to her feet. He leaned over and kissed her nose gently then pulled back and peered into her eyes.

Still shivering, knowing what he was capable of, she didn't resist.

He studied her eyes, finding her pleasantly obedient. He kissed her lips, and then tasted her neck. She stood as rigid as a statue.

"There was a time you were quite a wildcat," he said. He was unusually kind as if this were a mere liaison.

He reached behind her and turned on the shower, then unbuttoned her blouse and pulled it off; next, her skirt, pantyhose and bra.

He checked the temperature of the spray and then disrobed. He made a motion with his finger so she reluctantly rotated for him.

They stepped into the shower together. He sudsed up her whole body. He propped her foot on the tub wall then dropped to his knees, to inspect and wash the lower extremity of her body. He then positioned her in a bent over stance in order to rinse her thoroughly, as he tasted her vital wares with great pleasure.

He stood upright and put the soap in her hand, then directed her hand over his body. He leaned over to kiss her again, then held her body tightly against his, reaching behind her to turn off the water.

They stepped out of the shower together.

He slowly toweled her dry, then placed the towel in her hands and directed her to towel him dry in return.

He scooped her up in his arms and carried her down the hall, into the master bedroom. Depositing her on Ron's bed, he towered over her.

"This is the least Ron can do for me since he had nerve enough to take *my wife* to bed! Don't you want revenge, Steph?"

Stephanie didn't speak nor did she move.

He slowly bent over her and lowered his body on top of hers. He kissed her deeply as if he really loved her.

Hanging on to her, he rolled her over on top of him.

Ever so slowly, Stephanie reached under the mattress until her fingers touched cold metal. Cautiously, she pulled a gun onto the bed beside her. Still pretending to respond passionately, her left arm and body weight aided in pulling his body to expose half of his back as if attempting to roll him over on top of her. Her right hand managed to blindly aim the gun at his back. She grabbed the butt of the gun with four fingers and worked her thumb to find the trigger. Stephanie's thumb squeezed the trigger.

THE END

About the Author

Linda came from humble beginnings growing up close enough to Camp David to have actually swum in President Kennedy's pool, thanks to the prestigious position of her girlfriend's father.

Always the duck out of water, as far back as she can remember her father asked her, "Why do you dress like you're from New York?" In his ever respectful approach, scolding with the utmost tact, "Why do you need to wear make-up? Your mother doesn't wear make-up!" Still the eternal misfit, she claims she doesn't even seem to fit right in her beloved family of thirty-five years. She loves beautiful things around her, wonderful art, beautifully designed rooms, hot cars, dance and all of the arts. She's not one who enjoys idle chit-chat. She'd rather be writing, doing research for her current project, or creating in some manner. Her husband's fondest dream is to live on top of a mountain like a mountain man, on a dirt floor with no running water. Her children are more into trucks, technology, and going to a museum wouldn't even be last place on their agendas.

She needs a lot of "Alone, Thinking Time." Her family would rather "Party". She's searched her whole life for a gateway to acceptance.

Having been brought up in a stable, "Leave It to Beaver" family of four, she was encouraged and taught by her parents and second parents, her aunt and uncle, "Save your money!" "Save your money!" So she did. She always felt that she could have anything as long as she saved her money long enough.

Married in 1971, thanks to all of her "saved money" multiplying, her marriage got a wonderful start. Having come into the marriage with a brand new four-on-the-floor Javelin with a 343 cubic inch engine, which she paid cash for, she put more of her savings to good use. She bought every pot, pan, dish, piece of furniture, carpet, and window treatments to decorate their one bedroom apartment. They had a cozy little "love nest."

Still saving that money and watching it grow after three years, Linda quit her paying job to become her husband's unpaid secretary. Her business-educated sister-in-law gave her a crash course in double-entry bookkeeping because Linda had graduated with an academic diploma, intending to continue her education to become a French interpreter. She had no background for secretarial skills. Four thousand dollars out of her savings started her husband's contracting business.

Thanks to her husband's income Linda was fortunate enough to have been able to raise her three wonderful children herself, without the assistance of a babysitter. She believes that children should always be top priority. Her husband, an expert carpenter and contractor, built their home on eight superbly wooded acres in Howard County, Maryland. They chose to bring three children into the world so she felt that parents owed their time to them.

Always gifted with a restless mind and the innate need to make money, Linda babysat nine children at one time to make extra money, sold Avon, got into Transdesigns, then started writing her manuscript while the children were in school and their baby Shannon was napping. Over the years, between family needs, she managed to write the rough draft via long hand, and later typed it on a borrowed portable typewriter after her other teacher sister-in-law told her that she couldn't send this into a publisher hand-written. Linda ended up editing, rewriting, adding chapters and retyping it yet two more times. She used an electric typewriter this time. For the final time and through many revisions she used an old computer; one that had been given to her by her daughter, who forced her to learn how to use it, whether she liked it or not. Linda whipped her lengthy narrative into manuscript format constantly referring to her WRITER'S DIGEST and bothering her poor, busy sister-in-law with endless questions. Even if it never got published, it fulfilled that spot in her restless need to accomplish SOMETHING to be valued!

Coincidental to all her writing and typing, Linda started her portrait studio business, Focus on Elegance by Linda, from her home as soon as her baby started kindergarten....Then there was her doll art business, Galerie des Enfants, again managed from home, around family.....Babysitting her precious grandangels 12 to 14 hours a day, 3 to 5 days a week happily consumed Linda for six years..... But her greatest entrepreneurial adventure ensued when Linda used some inheritance funds to invest in a villa/studio and personal retreat which she decorated to the nines in European classic splendor.

It is in this forty seven hundred square foot villa where Linda finally feels in her element. She has designed her personal utopia, a specialized, peaceful atmosphere and sanctuary for her multi-faceted creativity. She researches, shops, and chooses fabrics, rugs, fabulous art, and accessories to pull her clients' home décor dreams together. As a photographer she has the power to turn a perfect treasured moment into timeless masterpieces worthy of painting. Linda loves graphite. Her photo quality pencil art has been printed and sold in limited editions.

Somewhat shy she has always preferred *writing* her intensely passionate feelings and literary dreams over all forms of oral communication. And thus her book….. Begun so many years ago, revised endlessly, her spiraling mind wants to add/change, delete, and reinvent elements of her story into eternity. Like most dedicated writers she has never felt that her work was actually complete, but her book has once again become exciting to her in light of some internet publishers having invited her to submit the manuscript for a reading. And there is little doubt that Linda Masemore Pirrung, the writer, prays for affirmation in this her most personal creative adventure to date…

Update: "I'm excited about having just finished my second book that only took me three months this time, having had the time and a computer."

"I guess you'd say I'm the true entrepreneurial spirit. As I always say, if you have to go to school to learn it then it really isn't yours!"

978-0-595-40732-3
0-595-40732-3

CPSIA information can be obtained at www.ICGtesting.com
Printed in the USA
235702LV00001B/220/A

9 780595 407323